I0715038

THE RESCUE SISTERS

THE RESCUE SISTERS

ELAINE WHITEFORD

First published by Sterlini Publishing 2024
www.sterlinipublishing.com
ISBN 978-1-7384981-1-6

Copyright © Elaine Whiteford 2024

The right of Elaine Whiteford to be identified as the Author of this Work has been asserted in accordance with the Copyright Designs and Patents Act 1988.

All rights reserved. No part of this book may be reproduced or utilised in any form or by any means electronic or mechanical, including photocopying, recording or by any information storage and retrieval system, without permission from Sterlini Publishing, except for the use of brief quotations in a book review.

This novel is a work of fiction. The characters and incidents portrayed in it are the work of the author's imagination. Any resemblance to actual persons, living or dead is entirely coincidental. The opinions expressed are those of the characters and should not be confused with the author's.

Author photo © Jackie McKenzie

*For the Andersons, McPhersons and
Whitefords who have led me to this place*

CHAPTER 1

July–August 1893

"So ended my hour or two at Gowanlea Children's Home, where Miss Frew, of gentle presence and affectionate heart, reigns – Queen and mother in one."

It was hardly believable. This wasn't the front page of the *Stirling Sentinel* or the *Stirling Observer*, it was the front page of the *Dundee Advertiser*, no less. Eliza looked away and prayed that the good Lord would forgive her for indulging in the sin of pride. Then she admired the article again. What a splendid front page it was.

The door to her study burst open as Rona, the cairn terrier, came sliding in, followed more sedately by the collie, Jackie, who at least managed to keep his footing on the tiled floor. Eliza cocked her head towards the window, listening for footsteps on the driveway. She couldn't hear anything yet, but there would be someone. The dogs were never wrong and Eliza very much valued their regular alerts, which allowed her a few moments before visitors arrived to smooth down her black dress and push back any stray hairs which might have escaped the filigree barrette that held her chignon in place.

She'd noticed an increasing number of grey hairs of late, so it was gratifying that in her sketched portrait in the *Dundee Advertiser* her hair looked as dark as it had been in her youth.

Three thuds shook the front door. Eliza rose from her swivel chair – a donation from Graham & Morton Furnishers, who had delivered it as soon as she'd made known there was a need. She paused in the hall and pushed the bridge of her round spectacles further up her nose. It was still quiet outside and she was certain now that the visitor was a man, one in desperate straits. That was what a single series of thuds made by the side of a closed fist signified. Anger brought a barrage of thumps that quickened the longer the trouble-maker was kept waiting; anguished women used their knuckles, the force of the third knock offering a clue as to the urgency of their plight.

She opened the door in a smooth, slow sweep, and immediately looked down to see two children, heads bowed, dressed in rags that were leaping with vermin. They stood either side of a man who, although probably not yet thirty, looked older. All those who came to Gowanlea's door did. Not even young faces could hide hardship.

He removed his cap and put it in the pocket of his faded black jacket. "Miss Frew?"

Eliza smiled and spoke softly. "Yes."

The man put an arm around each of the children. "We've just come from burying their mother. The baby's away to my mother's in the Hillfoots and my sister's taken the two-year-old. But there's nobody for them." He pushed the children forward and Eliza reared slightly – standing at a graveside in the fresh air had done little to blow away the stench of their poverty. "I want to keep them but I can't keep them and work. It's no' that I don't care for them but I ... I don't want them to be neglected. You ken?"

"Yes, I do know. Mr ... ?"

"McKellar. James McKellar. You ken, I would if I could. But I don't have enough for a housekeeper and ..."

"Mr McKellar, you don't have to explain."

"You see, Miss Frew, I don't want them ending up on the streets like some o' them. It's criminal what happens to these bairns. You'll ken that more than most. You'll have seen enough o' them in your time I've no doubt."

"Yes, I'm afraid I've seen some sorry sights over the years. But never anything we couldn't work with. There are many we've lifted from the gutter, then cleaned, trained and polished and sent out to the world as new creatures in Jesus Christ."

"Aye. And I couldn't put them to the poorhouse. That's why I've come to you. So you'll do for them what I could never do."

Mr McKellar sniffed. The children looked up at him. The girl's cheekbones were raw with tears, the boy's smeared black from trying to wipe them away.

"I understand. As a widower you cannot mother them and be the breadwinner too. Much as you may want to, and much as you may try to do a father's part, children miss their mothers. We've rescued many in similar circumstances." Eliza glanced at the children then smiled at Mr McKellar. "And also kept their fathers from sinking under great burdens and heavy losses."

He wiped his nose with the back of his hand. "Aye, that's exactly it, Miss Frew. You understand what it's like."

"I do. And I also understand that although I can't replace their mother – no one can do that – I can try and do the next best thing for the little lambs who grace our doorstep by exercising Christian influence on them so that they become good citizens able to support themselves."

"Aye, that's what folk say about you."

"Well, that's certainly good to hear, Mr McKellar. Usually what I hear them say is that they'll see me in court!"

The hint of a smile appeared on his face. "Aye. I might have heard something like that too, mind."

"But God's work isn't done in a hurry. It's done little by little, step by step."

"I'm no' sure about that, Miss Frew, all I ken is that they'll be better off wi' you than wi' me for the moment. If I've faith in nothing else, I've faith in that."

The girl started to quiver. A tear fell plumb from her eye, splashing onto the step. The boy clasped his hands tighter in front of him, his knuckles white. Going by height and weight, he looked about seven, and his sister, six. But then again the children of the poor were often stunted.

"What are their ages?"

"Hugh's eight and Winnie's seven." Mr McKellar tugged at their shabby jackets. Some lice fell to the ground. "Stand up straight and let Miss Frew look at you. They're good bairns, Miss Frew, they'll no' give you any trouble."

"I'm sure they wouldn't, Mr McKellar. However—"

"So can you take them, Miss Frew?" He pushed the children forward.

"Well, the girl, we may be able to accommodate, if you're absolutely sure this is the course you wish to follow. Just last week we had two leavers who obtained very good placements in service with very respectable families."

Mr McKellar gave his daughter a little shake on the arm. "You hear that? You see what can happen to you if you bide wi' Miss Frew? Would that no' be good?"

The girl's eyes welled up and her face crumpled.

"But we don't generally take boys of his age," Eliza said. "When they're getting bigger, they need a different sort of discipline to prepare them for the world. We can't keep them here with the little ones so we send them to our branch in Fife. However—"

"Could he no' go there, then?"

"I'm afraid not. Only those boys who've been prepared here at Gowanlea can go."

"Please, Miss Frew." Mr McKellar reached out to her, then pulled back. He had filth under his fingernails and grime engrained in the lines of his hand. "I can't have him go to the ..." His voice started to break. "... poorhouse. I'm begging you."

Eliza glanced up at the sky. Almost twenty years ago she had received a direct call from the Master. *She hath done what she could. From this day will I bless thee.* She knew what her duty was as a servant of Christ. "Well, there might be another option, but—"

"Anything, Miss Frew. Anything would be better for him than what I could offer."

"Well, Mr McKellar, sometimes circumstances are such that the best thing we can do for the poor lambs is to send them somewhere they're assured a better future. Somewhere they'll be schooled and trained, and given employment, so that by the time they turn eighteen, they're fit and ready to set forth and live good Christian lives."

Mr McKellar opened his eyes wide. "That's exactly what I want for him, Miss Frew. Exactly!" He put his hand on his son's head and ruffled his hair. "You hear that, Hugh? You'd get training and a job."

"But the thing is – that place is Canada."

Mr McKellar took a step backwards. "Canada?"

"Yes. I've seen off tens of boys – and some girls – over the years. They've all had unspeakable blessings conferred upon them as a result of the change. Where once they lived in squalor and misery, now they're well-to-do farmers and respectable tradesmen. In fact, one of our boys, now a fine young man, works in a hospital in America and has ambitions to become an M.D. I have their letters and photographs in my study, if you'd like to see them."

Mr McKellar leaned forwards. "How long would it be for? Canada."

"Well, as I said, they're schooled and trained, and given employment, and by the time they turn eighteen, they're fit and ready to—"

"Eighteen? But that's, that's ... ten years," Mr McKellar spluttered.

"As I was saying—"

"But I was thinking it would just be for a wee while, then I could—"

"Mr McKellar." Eliza folded her arms.

"You ken, and once I get sorted out I could maybe—"

"Gowanlea is for homeless and friendless children who have no one to care for them. They're admitted without payment or the promise of a fee."

"I ken that," he replied, curtly.

"And in the event of such an admission, the nearest relative must sign an agreement giving me the power to send the child, or children ..." Winnie and Hugh were now quaking. "... to any situation either in this country or abroad or dispose of in any way I think best for their future good. Other needy cases who—"

"Aye, but Miss Frew, I can't—"

Eliza raised her palm to stop him. "Other needy cases, who may just have one parent, or friends, to support them, are admitted, it's true, but only when vacancies occur, and then a maintenance fee must be paid regularly. In advance. Such children can be removed from the Home at a later stage by giving a week's notice and paying maintenance up to the date of departure."

"But I've no money, Miss Frew, that's what I'm trying to tell you!" Mr McKellar cried. "If I had money, I'd no' be here, would I?"

"Well, sir, all I can advise is that you'll have to decide whether your children are homeless with no one to care for them or simply needy. If it's the latter, then you'll also need to find a guarantor for your payments."

Mr McKellar clenched his fists, looked heavenwards then kicked the doorstep. "I told you. I've nothing and I can't care for them! I've no' got any money!" he shouted.

A gobbet of his spit landed on Eliza's shoulder. He hung his head, breathing quickly and heavily. She waited until he looked at her again and slowly took a handkerchief from the pocket of her dress to wipe it away. Then she stared at the wretched man until it dawned on him what she was waiting for.

"Begging your pardon, Miss Frew. I didn't mean to ... it's just that, you ken, I'm at the end o' my tether wi' everything that's happened and—" He put his hand up and covered his eyes.

Eliza squeezed his arm. "It's all right, Mr McKellar, I completely understand. I've seen your situation before. It'll be all right."

She stepped into the hall. From the brass collection plate on the table she lifted a few of the pennies that had been donated by the Bridge of Allan Sabbath School as pin money for the children.

When she returned to the doorstep, Mr McKellar had composed himself and was looking at her expectantly. She held out the coins to Hugh. "Why don't you take your sister up to Bow Street for an ice at Bertolini's?"

Hugh glanced at his father and, when he gave permission with a nod, accepted the money. Then the boy looked at Eliza. "Is Canada near the Hillfoots?"

Mr McKellar gave a jolt then lightly cuffed the back of his son's head. "Mind your manners. What do you say to Miss Frew for giving you the money?" Hugh mumbled a thank you. "Right, well, you heard her now. Get going. But mind and don't be going up Broad Street. Bertolini's and straight back. You hear me?"

"Aye." Hugh took Winnie's hand and pulled her along behind him as he set off down the drive.

"And take your time. Me and Miss Frew have things to talk about," Mr McKellar called after them. Then he stepped over the threshold into Gowanlea.

Between dealing with Mr McKellar, then feeding and settling the children for the evening, it was dusk by the time Eliza returned to the *Dundee Advertiser*. The Gowanlea feature was by far the most expansive of the articles on the front page, taking up three of its eight columns. Indeed, three of seven, were one to discount the advertisements for Carter's Liver Pills, Frazer's Tablets and *The People's Friend*. Which reminded her, a copy of that would be on its way tomorrow courtesy of Mrs Risk of Snowdon Place, who faithfully handed in each issue once she'd read it.

Eliza scanned the page again. The only piece which came close in length to hers (though at barely half a column, not very close), was a report on additional accommodation at the post office in Wick. And to be fair, the building in the accompanying sketch looked very fine. As it should, in its 'Renaissance style with ashlar of local stone and dressings of freestone from Eday in Orkney'. It was certainly opulent compared to Gowanlea, the drawing of which, nevertheless, was twice the size.

She leaned back in her chair and reached down to scratch Jackie's head. Perhaps she should commission those Aberdeen architects for a second opinion, given they seemed to have done such a splendid job in Wick. They would surely have greater expertise than Messrs. Rankine & Roberts, who had suggested she dispose of Gowanlea and erect a larger house on the outskirts of town. She leaned forward and ran the tip of her index finger over the sketch of the Home at the head of the article. The outskirts of town, indeed. How would she rescue

Christ's lambs from the slums? How would the destitute find their way to her? And how would the depraved hear her prayers? Still, the Messrs. had provided their services free of charge so she oughtn't be too judgemental. She had her calling, they had theirs. And, although certainly not recommending it, they hadn't deemed an extension to Gowanlea entirely out of the question. It remained a possibility, and that was all Eliza needed. She closed her eyes and pressed her palms together in prayer: "Before they call I will answer, and while they are yet speaking I will hear."

Yes. God would provide, as He always did.

CHAPTER 2

THE ROW of mature trees on the street outside the town house had kept Jane Knight so occupied during the week-long stay at her aunt's that she'd reached the last page of her sketch pad. Aunt Alice said that her many drawings 'showed promise' and that she should stick at it, since nowadays women could not only go to art school, but could even, according to the daughter of a Primrose League contact in Glasgow, take classes alongside men. "Except, of course," Aunt Alice had said with a wink, "life classes." Jane didn't know what she'd meant initially, but eventually her aunt had explained it on the condition Jane didn't tell her mother what they'd been talking about.

The prospect of sketching another person naked was shocking at first. But when Aunt Alice had described how it could improve the observation skills of artists and make them think about technique, Jane agreed that there might be benefits to such a disquieting practice. "And by the time you're old enough," Aunt Alice had even predicted, "women will be taking life classes along with men. You'll see. It might be too late for me but you should stick at it. Just don't tell your mother I said so." Jane giggled, thinking about the customary statement Aunt Alice always ended on when she talked to her and her brother about anything that might be considered unseemly for young ears.

"What are you laughing at?" RJ said, looking up from his book.

"Nothing. I was just thinking about Aunt Alice."

"What's she told you not to tell Mother now?"

"Oh, nothing new."

"Look – she's given me this to read," he said, turning the book's spine towards Jane.

She tilted her head to read it. "*Barrack Room Ballads & Other Verses* by Rudyard Kipling. Is it good?"

"It's quite funny. Listen to this." Her brother sat up on the sofa, then cleared his throat. "'O the oont, O the oont, O the Gawd-forsaken oont!'"

"What on earth?"

He got to his feet and began to walk around the drawing room, hands flailing. "'The 'orse 'e knows above a but, the bullock's but a fool, The elephant's a gentleman, the battery-mule's a mule; But the commissariat cam-u-el, when all is said an' done. 'E's a devil an' a ostrich an' a orphan child in one.'"

Jane laughed and laid her sketchpad on the table. "What on earth are you talking about?"

RJ closed the book and flopped back down. "An 'oont'. It's a camel!"

"And?"

"And the military use animals to carry things," he said, as if it were obvious. "You know, elephants and horses. Well, Kipling's talking about camels."

Aunt Alice swept into the room, pulling on her gloves. "Yes, Robert, you are correct. The Empire is not supported by men alone. But perhaps that poem isn't one to recite to your mother. She might not approve of some of the expressions."

Jane and RJ looked at each other and laughed.

"What are the pair of you concocting now?" Aunt Alice

said. "Honestly, you're thick as thieves. If I didn't know better, I'd swear you weren't siblings. Your father and I did nothing but quarrel when we were your age. Whereas you pair ... Anyway, get yourselves ready because we're going out."

"Excellent!" Jane closed her sketch pad and got up. Staying with their aunt wasn't only fun because of her conversation: she also took them places their parents (between father's work and mother's delicate constitution) couldn't. So far on this visit, Aunt Alice had taken them to the Wallace Monument, the Airthrey Mineral Springs and the Lake of Menteith. And they'd travelled by train and tramcar, and by steamer on the River Forth.

"We're going into town to call on Miss Frew at Gowanlea."

"Who's Miss Frew?" Jane said, not recognising the name.

"She runs the children's home."

"Oh." The destination wasn't quite as exciting as Jane was hoping for.

"I have to take her the last of my district's collection monies. By my reckoning I'm on course to exceed last year's total by sixteen shillings. That's the highest it's been since I've been District Collector." Aunt Alice looked in the wall mirror to arrange her hat and neck-tie. "We'll be topped by District VI, of course. I mean, we can't hope to exceed the amount donated by the ladies and gentlemen of Clarendon Place and Victoria Square. But when you consider, too, how much we collected at the sale of work last month – it was quite the success – then I'm sure that, when Gowanlea's Annual Report comes out, your Aunt Alice and District IX will feature prominently. So fear not – the Knight family honour will not be besmirched." She turned to Jane and RJ. "How does my hat look?"

"Fine," they both said.

"Good. Now ..." She clapped her hands. "... chop-chop. We're going to the Top of the Town."

"Oh! Can we go to Bertolini's for ice-cream?" Jane said.

"And the castle to see the soldiers?"

"Yes, after I've seen Miss Frew. Just don't tell your mother. The thought of you in that part of town would make her swoon."

The route from Aunt Alice's house in Park Terrace to Gowanlea took them through the heart of the commercial district, its streets filled with banks, business premises, hotels, tea rooms, shops of every kind, and churches. Every so often Aunt Alice paused at a building to explain who currently occupied it, who had occupied it previously and who might occupy it in future.

At the junction of Murray Place and King Street, she stopped in front of the British Linen Bank, with its carved columns topped with stone harps. "This used to be the Stirling Tract Enterprise, founded by Mr Peter Drummond, now late of this parish, although you may still find some of his pamphlets at Gowanlea. Miss Frew is an admirer. As she also is of his nephew, Mr Henry Drummond, who was born just along from me in Park Place. That Mr Drummond was active with the American evangelists, Mr Moody and Mr Sankey. If there's time before you go back home, I may tell you about when Miss Frew and I went to hear them preach at the Erskine Church. It was standing room only and those who couldn't get in crowded at the windows to watch." Aunt Alice stared up King Street towards the Athenaeum and its statue of William Wallace. "Yes, what a couple of days those were."

"Why? What happened?" Jane said.

Her aunt gave a little sniff, then walked briskly on. "Come on. I don't want to keep Miss Frew waiting."

Upper Bridge Street was a secluded, sloping avenue with trees along one side and ivied walls on the other. The entrance to Gowanlea was on the right, along a driveway that ascended gently for about a hundred yards and was lined by thick bushes. A large evergreen tree stood to the right of the stone staircase that led to a gleaming black door.

Before Aunt Alice was able to put a foot on the first step,

the door opened wide. Jane stopped at the sight of the severe-looking woman from head to toe in black, with greying brown hair pulled tightly back and small silver spectacles perched on her sharp nose.

"Ah, Alice." The gentleness in her smile and kindness in her blue eyes took Jane by surprise. "Good day to you." Her voice was soft, with an accent Jane couldn't place.

"And to you, Eliza," Aunt Alice said, stroking the black and white collie that came down the steps in greeting.

"And who are your companions, Alice?" she said, eyeing Jane and RJ.

"These are my nephew and niece, Robert and Jane Knight, from Perth. My brother's two. They're staying with me for the week while their parents are away."

"Ah. Good day, Master and Miss Knight."

"This is Miss Frew," Aunt Alice said.

RJ gave a little bow, Jane the hint of a curtsy, and they both mumbled a greeting.

"It's very nice to meet you. Are you twins?"

"No, but you're not the first to think so," Aunt Alice said. "And, I grant you, they do look alike. But no, Robert's fifteen and Jane's fourteen."

Jane smiled, RJ frowned – it annoyed him when he wasn't recognised as the older sibling.

"Well, I hope you're enjoying your stay with your aunt and that she's taking good care of you." Miss Frew paused. "Not leading you too much astray." Jane and RJ stifled a giggle. "Anyway, while she and I attend to some business, why don't you wait in the garden? The gate's just past the fir tree. Some of the children are there and they always like to play with visitors. You can take Jackie around too," she said, glancing at the collie. "His red ball should be somewhere. He likes you to throw it for him."

"Come on then!" RJ patted his thigh to attract Jackie, and

the dog and Jane went after him along the path at the side of the house.

The garden was bordered by a high hedge and Jane heard the children before she saw them. She followed RJ through a wrought-iron gate which led to an extensive piece of sloping land. About a dozen small boys and girls were dancing around a maypole in the middle of the grassy area. Next to them, a couple of boys rocked up and down on a see-saw and a little girl dangled on a swing. At the far end of the grounds was a vegetable patch, bisected by a row of apple trees. Beyond the boundary wall to the left, the Gowan Hills led steeply up to Ballengeich Cemetery and then to Stirling Castle, and, to the right, the view extended across town to the River Forth, the Wallace Monument and the Ochil Hills beyond.

RJ kicked the red ball onto the grass. Jackie bounded after it, pushing it on with his nose towards the swing. Then the dog slumped on the ground and gave RJ a look that left no doubt about what was required next.

"It seems we're the ones who've to do the fetching," he said, going over to the dog and picking up the ball. When he threw it at the wall, the little girl got down from the swing and tugged the back of his jacket. Never knowing what to say to little ones, he gave Jane a pleading look. She came to his rescue.

"Hello. I'm Jane. Who are you?"

The girl let go of RJ and stared up at her. She had warm brown eyes and neatly brushed short hair the colour of straw. "Are you the new teacher?"

RJ laughed. "As if!"

"Wheesht!" Jane squatted so that she was level with the girl. "No, I'm just visiting. We're waiting here for our aunt. She's talking to Miss Frew."

The girl looked from Jane to RJ then back again. "Is he your brother?"

"Yes. That's RJ. Well, Robert John, really, but I call him RJ. You can call him that, too. He's my—"

The girl's face suddenly crumpled and tears streamed down her cheeks.

"Oh! Whatever's the matter?" The girl fell forward and buried her face in Jane's armpit. Jane embraced her while RJ took a step back. "There, there. It's all right. Now whatever is it? Hmm?" Jane looked to RJ for support but he shrugged his shoulders and picked up the ball Jackie had actually retrieved. "Shush now, it's all right." Jane rocked the girl to soothe her, then wiped her running nose. "There, that's better now, isn't it?"

"I've a brother too."

"Have you? All right. Do you want him to come over?" Jane looked at the groups of children in the garden. "Which one is he?" She pointed at a little boy by the maypole who had the same colour of hair. "Is that him?" The girl shook her head. "What about that one?" Jane pointed to one of the boys on the see-saw.

"Naw."

"Then how about ...?" Jane scanned the rest of the children.

"He's no' here."

"Oh. Is he out on an errand?"

The girl took a photograph out of her smock and handed it to Jane. Pictured beside three travel trunks were three boys of around eight or nine with cropped hair and sticky-out ears. Each of the troop wore identical shorts and long-sleeved shirts, thick dark socks and leather boots. The boy on the right, looking directly at the camera, was standing tall, one hand on the holdall that was on top of his trunk. The middle boy, who was looking at the camera too, had clambered onto the holdall atop his trunk and was holding a small dog. The boy on the left was sitting rigidly on his trunk, looking away, his hands clutched together. The girl put a finger over the boy on the left. "Hugh."

"That's your brother?"

"Let me see," RJ said, abandoning his game of fetch.

Jane passed him the photograph, then put her hand on the little girl's shoulder. "And what's your name?"

"Winnie."

"Oh. We've an Aunt Winifred. Not the one we're visiting here – she's our father's sister. But another one. One of our mother's sisters."

"My mother's up there," Winnie said, pointing in the direction of the castle. "The place wi' the stones."

Jane exchanged a glance with RJ. "You mean Ballengeich Cemetery?"

"Aye. Ballengeich," Winnie struggled to pronounce. "But she's no' got a stone. She's in the bit wi' no stones. Next to the wall."

Jane's thighs were starting to ache. She stood up and led Winnie back to the swing. RJ shuffled over, still looking at the photograph. "And where's Hugh?" he said.

Winnie wrapped her arm around the chain. "Canada."

"Canada?" Jane and RJ said in unison.

"He was sent to be ..." Winnie tilted her face upwards and projected her voice. "... 'a good citizen able to support himself'." She sighed. Her shoulders slumped forwards. "They wouldn't let me go wi' him. The doctor said I had a bad chest. And Miss Frew said nobody in Canada would want a lassie wi' a bad chest. Nobody'd pick me and they'd send me home, so it would be better to stay here. Hugh said if I wasn't going then he wasn't going either but they made him." Winnie pushed off the ground, then swung back and forwards. "So that he could become *a good citizen able to support himself*."

RJ gave Jane back the photograph. She stared at Hugh, wondering what he'd been thinking that day.

Her brother leaned in and whispered. "If that had been us, I would've run away before they sent me from you."

"If that'd been us and they'd sent you from me, I would've run away and followed you."

There was a shout from behind. "Jane! RJ!" Aunt Alice was standing on the other side of the garden gate, beckoning them. "Time to go."

Jane bent down and put the photograph back into Winnie's smock. "We have to go now, I'm afraid."

"Will you come back and see me?"

"Well, we're just visiting, but if we—"

"I wish you were my sister."

Jane put her hand to her mouth, then walked away before Winnie could see the tears gathering in her eyes.

CHAPTER 3

December 1899

JANE DROPPED her pencil onto the tartan travel rug that was draped over her legs. She leaned back and squinted at her sketch of the leafless willow that marked the furthest boundary of the garden. Not bad. She reached under the chair for her previous drawings of the same subject and flicked through them. This latest one was a definite improvement.

The Elements of Drawing lay open on the little stool to her left; she looked down and re-read the penultimate paragraph: *'You cannot do too many studies of this kind: every one will give you some new notion about trees.'* It was true. The more you looked at something, the more you saw its essence; and the more you practised your art, the closer you came to mastery. She scrawled her initials on the bottom of the paper and placed the latest in her growing arboreal opus on top of the others.

She reached for her shawl, which had slipped down her back, and wrapped it around her shoulders again, giving a little shiver; not because the setting of the winter sun was chilling the air, but in rising anticipation of sharing with her father RJ's letter about his journey to the Cape Colony.

19

She took the envelope out of her dress pocket and ran her index finger over her name and address written in her brother's elegant hand. Then she dabbed the British Army Field Post Office stamp. To think that just a few weeks ago it had been on the other side of the world. To think that RJ was on the other side of the world now. It was astonishing.

She took the letter out of the envelope and read it for the fifth time in as many hours.

Dearest Janey – 18 November – Cape Town, Janey! We've finally arrived. Can you believe it? I didn't write during the voyage as it was seldom calm enough to hold the pen still on the paper! My decision not to consider the navy has been vindicated as it seems I have inherited Father's tendency to mal de mer. As I lay wherever I could find space to relieve my discomfort, I thought many times of his tales of leaning over the railings during his travels to and from India. It was so bad that some of the men say they're going to settle here because they don't want to face the journey back home. Although my desperation didn't quite reach that point, I must confess to understanding their feelings. But don't worry, I wouldn't abandon you like that!

Fortunately, there were some fine fellows from the Army Medical Corps on board who were a great help. Although they hail from York, one of their chaps, would you believe, is from Stirling, where his parents live close to Aunt Alice. He was most kind to me when I was suffering and I tell you, Janey, if you weren't already engaged to Harold, and he wasn't my dearest friend, I would have no hesitation in recommending the gentleman to you as someone of the highest calibre, not to mention an excellent medical man.

24 November – I'm sorry about the smudge on the paper. It's very warm here – we've now reached Durban – and sweat is dripping from my face. I expect you're starting to shiver back home and that with the nights drawing in you'll be spending less time outside sketching. Although I imagine that, unless it's very inclement, you'll still be sitting out with that hideous old rug on your lap, and Mother will still be nagging you to go inside to the warmth. I certainly hope you are and that you'll make enquiries about attending the School of Art. You must remain determined in the midst of Mother and Father's opposition. Your work deserves greater profile than the Fine Arts Association, commendable though it is, can offer. I'm looking forward already to seeing all the sketches you'll be doing in my absence.

I think you'd appreciate the light quality here. Painting en plein air *would be a very different experience for you, though I suspect you might tire eventually of the constancy of the sun.*

Jane looked up and wondered what the Durban sky looked like. She put her hand to her mouth and swallowed. What did the battlefield sky look like?

27 November – We're being sent to the front, Janey, so I must hand this letter over to the Post Office Corps and hope they manage to get it to you as soon as humanly possible. I'm told it will take around fourteen days from Cape Town. Isn't it amazing that the paper I'm holding now will be in your hands in just a few weeks? When you get it, please hold it to your heart and pass it to Mother and Father to do the same. That way we'll be together. You're always with me, of course, and the photograph of the family I carry brings comfort. And the faith I have in our Lord gives me the belief that we'll triumph soon for Queen and country.

*Is it too much to hope that this war will be over soon and I'll
make it home for your wedding? I'll write again when I can.*

With love and prayers
Your devoted brother
RJ

Jane held the letter to her cheek, then clutched it to her
breast, sighing. RJ had touched it, folded it in two, perhaps
even kissed it before he'd slid it into the envelope. And now it
was in her hands. Even though he was thousands of miles
away, she was still connected to him. She would have to write
back quickly so he had something of hers that he could hold
close to his heart too.

She knew it would be a few hours yet until her father was
home from work but she still opened her pocket watch to
check the time. How delighted he was going to be to hear of
the battalion's safe arrival, and how amused he'd be to learn of
RJ's experience of sailing. She could already hear him saying 'I
told you so', for his advice to RJ over the years had been
constant. "Whatever career you choose, my boy, make sure it's
on terra firma. The Knights aren't suited to a life at sea." But
more than amused, her father would be proud and the
additions to the scrapbook he had started about the campaign
would doubtless burgeon.

Each day he scoured the newspapers, not just the *Perthshire
Advertiser* but the *Scotsman*, too, for clippings. Then after
dinner, he invited Jane to join him in his study to review RJ's
itinerary. They'd begun by looking at the globe and plotting
the sea voyage to Africa; now they were consulting a detailed
map in the *Victoria Regina Atlas*, looking for the places
mentioned in the newspapers and studying the red, green and
yellow lines that represented the borders of the Cape Colony,
Basuto, and the Orange Free State.

Tonight Jane would regard that map differently, places she

had only recently heard of no longer far-off corners of the imagination but places whose ground RJ had stood on and whose air he'd breathed. She shivered again, this time with fear. The Africa of the newspapers was now real.

When the final sliver of sun sank behind liquid grey cloud, Jane gathered her things, then folded up her deckchair. As she carried it over to the little porch that extended from the back of the house, she saw a figure inside – her father was standing on the threshold, staring at her. She smiled and waved, then hesitated when she saw the sternness of his face. He walked to the back door, and she held her breath as he opened it.

"Please come inside, Jane." He looked at the ground.

"Why are you home early?"

He turned and went back into the house.

Jane hurriedly propped the deckchair against the porch, leaving her sketch pad and drawings on top of the boot stand just inside.

When she entered the drawing room, she gasped. Her mother, hands clasped together on her lap, was sitting by the fireplace, leaning forward, staring at the flames. Her father stood at the other side of the fireplace, not even trying to conceal the glass of whisky he cradled in his hands. It was full to the brim.

"Father, what is it?"

He put his glass on the mantelpiece next to the Indian brass vase and cleared his throat. "Please sit down."

"Why are you home from work?"

He went over, gently took her arm and led her to the couch. "Sit down, Jane."

"What is it?" Jane looked at her mother for an answer but she remained still.

Her father returned to the fireplace and took a document from the inside pocket of his jacket. "I just got this," he said. Holding the paper in both hands, he spoke in a flat tone. "Your brother has been killed in action."

Jane's mouth went dry. There was a thump in her chest. "What?"

"Your brother has been killed in action."

She looked again at her mother, who remained unmoved, then back at her father. "No!" She laughed and shook her head. "No!"

Her father folded the telegram and put it back in his jacket. "Jane ..."

"No, no, you see ..." She retrieved RJ's letter from the pocket of her dress and went over to her father. "He's not. This came today. See!" She offered him the letter. Her father shook his head. "No, no. Listen. RJ says ..." She scanned the letter and began to gabble. "He says ... he's fine, that the sea journey was rough. He talks about your sea-sickness on your trip to India. That he met a young medical man from Stirling who lives near Aunt Alice and who helped him with his sea-sickness. That it's very hot in Durban, that—"

Her father grasped her wrists. "Jane. It's true. RJ—"

"No! No! It can't be. It's a mistake. It must be." She took a step back and resumed reading the letter. "See, here – he says he hopes he'll be home in time for the wedding and ..." The writing was starting to look blurred through her tears. "... and ..." She waved the letter at her mother, whose impassive face glowed orange. "Isn't that right, Mother? You've read it."

"Jane," her father said. "RJ is dead. At Magersfontein."

"No!" She thrust the letter into his hands. "This came only today. Look – look, read it."

"Jane!"

"He can't be! No!" She clenched her fist and thumped her father's right arm, stumbling as she did. "He can't be. He can't be."

"Come, my darling, come ..." Her father guided her back to the couch.

When her legs buckled, Jane clung to him. Then she put her head against his chest and screamed as she never had before.

CHAPTER 4

WHEN JANE WOKE UP, her back and legs weighed on the mattress as if pinned there by the heaviest force on earth. Was it day or was it night? She didn't know. With huge effort, she raised her head an inch from the pillow and grimaced at the cracking of her bones when she turned her neck. The blinds were fully drawn over her bedroom windows but, as she continued to stare, the blackness in the room gradually turned to grey and she saw the outline of her dressing table and wardrobe in the dimness. She groaned and let her head fall back. Then her memory jolted her. She pulled the blanket over her head and sobbed until she was numb. She thought she might be half-dead herself.

Dead. RJ was dead. This wasn't a nightmare from which she would wake up in relief. This was a living nightmare from which she would never wake. Was she even awake now? Words, images, fragments flashed through her mind: her father, calling her name, wafting smelling salts under her nose; Dr Bell, holding her wrist and counting her pulse; there she was, clinging onto the legs of the table, howling like a wounded animal. Her mother, staring into the fire. Jane touched her neckline and realised she was wearing her nightdress. Had her mother put her to bed? An image – Dr Bell by the bedside giving her something to drink. And then darkness.

It was still dark. How much time had passed? Had they had the funeral? Jane breathed in sharply at the realisation there would be no funeral. She covered her face with her hands. There would be no funeral, no hearse, no mourning carriage, and no grave to visit. What would happen to RJ? She pushed herself up, furious, and slammed back against the headboard. Would he be cast aside in some mass grave after having his teeth removed? Or would he simply be left to decay in the African sun? At Magersfontein. Where even was Magersfontein?

Her mother came in, a black dress over her arm and in her hands a pair of black shoes and a black hat. "Ah, Jane. It's good to see you finally sitting up." She laid the clothes at the foot of the bed, then turned the switch for the gaslight. As the globes slowly brightened on her mother swathed in black silk and crape, Jane gasped – she had never seen her look better than she did now. Her face seemed drained of tension, her skin glowing.

"Mother!" Jane said, anxiously. "What will happen to RJ?"

"Best not to think about it, dear." She held up the dress. "This has just been delivered for you. Mrs Young still has your measurements from the gown you got for your cousin Peter's wedding, but she said if any adjustments are needed she'll come to the house immediately."

"What?"

Her mother put the dress down and lifted up the shoes and hat. "And these are very elegant, don't you think?"

Jane threw the crimson bedclothes off and swung her legs over the side of the bed. "Mother! How can you be like this?"

Her mother inhaled deeply. "Because the worst has happened now. I no longer need to fear it."

"What?" Jane didn't understand. "But how can you ...?"

Her mother took a pair of black gloves out of the hat and raised her eyebrows, as if inviting an opinion on their stylishness.

How could she be so serene, the woman who normally took to bed at the slightest physical or mental discomfort? "Your son has just ..."

Her mother held the gloves up to her cheeks. "They're so soft."

Jane got to her feet. "Have you even shed a tear? How you can be so ... so ..." She was spitting as she spoke. "It's unseemly."

Her mother stiffened, but remained calm. "I'll tell you what's unseemly – you wallowing here instead of honouring your brother's memory. Harold is downstairs. He called on you yesterday, and the day before. So what you need to do is get dressed, receive him and start behaving like a fiancée, like a sister, and like a daughter, should." Jane stared at her mother, unable to believe what she was hearing. "Do you think your brother would have approved of this conduct?"

Jane flopped back onto the bed, tears streaming down her cheeks. Her mother came and stood directly in front of her. "You will not speak to me like you just did. I'll make an allowance today since you've suffered a terrible shock. But you will never speak to me like that again." Jane didn't look up when her mother opened the bedroom door. "Now, I expect to see you downstairs in fifteen minutes. Harold's waiting in your father's study. And for goodness' sake, splash some water on your face – your eyes are puffy. And put some powder on to conceal these blotches. Your face is the colour of the bedspread."

When her mother left the room, Jane remained in bed for a few minutes. She could either stay where she was, risking a repeat performance from her mother, or she could suffer in silence and do what was expected. There was nothing else for it. She got up and dressed in a trance, then went downstairs.

Harold stood in her father's book-lined study, swaying from foot to foot and wringing his hands. When she entered, he stood still, looking at her with tears in his eyes. Jane swallowed hard. She'd made a mistake coming down. She wasn't ready to receive Harold. When she looked at him, she saw not her fiancé, but RJ's closest friend. He wasn't a comfort, he was a torment. She turned to go but he grabbed her arm.

"Jane! Jane. Please."

She bit her lip, trying not to weep. "I can't bear it. I'm sorry, Harold, I can't bear to see you. It—"

"My dearest Jane, I completely understand." He pulled her back into the room. "Just for a moment. Please."

He opened his arms and she walked into his embrace, not caring if her parents interrupted and saw them being so intimate. At least Harold understood what it was to lose RJ. How could he not? As boys they had played together, stayed together, holidayed together and planned to have careers together. They were as close as could be without being brothers.

He stroked her hair with a black-gloved hand and leaned his chin on the top of her head. "Better?"

Jane almost managed a smile. "Yes, better."

He took her elbow and steered her over to the leather armchair where her father liked to read. Then he pulled over the chair from the desk and sat opposite her. "Jane, I am so so sorry. You must be bereft. As am I. I loved him." When he took her hands in his, tears filled his eyes. "I loved him so much."

"We all did."

Harold was shaking his head. "No, you don't understand. I loved him."

The way he said *loved* made her lean forward. "What do you mean?"

"Oh, Jane. Jane ..." He got up and began to pace around the room. "What do I mean? Well, I understand how hard it is for you to look at me, because I feel the same looking at you."

"What?"

He carried on pacing.

"Harold, please sit down. You're upsetting me."

He rushed back over and took her hand in his. "My darling, that is the last thing I want to do but ..." A tear ran down his cheek.

Jane looked away to give him time to wipe his face. But when she turned back to him, there were more tears. "Harold. What is it?" She had never seen a man cry before.

"Jane, Jane, I am sorry." He removed one of his gloves, took a handkerchief from his jacket pocket and dabbed his eyes. "Please forgive me."

"Of course. It's only natural." She touched his cheek. "You were like brothers."

He nodded. "That's the thing."

"What?"

"He wanted so much for you and me to be married and I ... I wanted to be as close to him as I could ... and this was the closest I could be without ... and now that he's gone, I ..." Harold began to blub again.

Jane felt a thump in her chest and held her breath. Surely he wasn't suggesting ... he couldn't be. "What are you saying?"

"Oh, Jane! I didn't mean for it to come out like this or today. But I can only speak from the heart and I can't lie to you. I—"

She fell into her father's armchair, knocked over by the realisation of the truth. Harold rushed over and kneeled before her. "Jane! I'm so sorry. I should have told you what I felt for RJ and that I—"

She thrust her palms up to stop him. "Don't say it! I can't bear to hear it."

He tried to grab her hands but she recoiled from him. "Jane! I can't lie to you any more, it wouldn't be fair."

She stiffened and stared past him to the rows of green leather-bound books on the shelves, trying with what little strength she had left to contain the flow of tears that were pricking her eyes. "Yet if RJ had lived you were going to lie to me for years, until death parted us," she said coldly.

"Yes ... well ... no, I ..."

"And what you're trying so hard not to say is that ..." Her voice cracked but she pushed through. "... now RJ is no longer with us, you have no reason to marry me."

"I ..."

"That I was just the respectable gateway to him." She exhaled with relief that she had managed to get out the words.

"It wasn't like that, Jane. He didn't love me in the same way I loved him. And he never would. I knew that."

When Harold paused, Jane glanced at him. "But?"

He tugged his black cravat. "I don't know. I knew it was wrong, Jane, to propose to you, but I didn't know how to ... and RJ would have been so disappointed, and I didn't want to risk losing both him and you if ... I'm so sorry, Jane."

She leaned forward, a hint of sympathy rising in her. "Oh, Harold."

He got to his feet and shook his hand at her. "No, Jane, I don't deserve your compassion. No." He started to pace again. "You owe me nothing but contempt. My behaviour has been despicable. So I'll do whatever you want. Whatever you want, I'll go along with it. Whatever it is. I owe you that much. You can say I've been unfaithful to you or that I favour another. That I've behaved badly or that you've fallen out of love with me, or that we're merely postponing the wedding while we grieve. Whatever will make you feel less wretched, I'll go along with. Even the truth." He was pacing faster. "Yes, even the truth. Ruin me if you wish. I deserve whatever condemnation comes to me for treating you this way. I'll do anything."

Jane looked up at the ceiling and sighed. "Except marry me."

Harold stopped in his tracks. She got up and went over to her father's desk. The atlas was open at the usual page and some newspaper cuttings lay on top of the scrapbook. She sensed Harold backing towards the door.

"So will I wait until you tell me how you wish to proceed?" he said. "It might be better if you write than if I call again. I can tell your parents I have to go out of town on business for a few days so it doesn't look too strange that I'm not being attentive to you in your grief."

"Yes, you do that," she said flatly, without looking round.

"And you'll write to me with your decision?"

She nodded almost imperceptibly.

Once he'd left the room, Jane turned to the index of the *Victoria Regina Atlas* and ran her finger down the list of M's in search of 'Magersfontein'. But after 'Mageroe' came only 'Mages'. The place her brother was fighting over didn't even merit a mention in a list of names that ran to a hundred and forty pages.

She picked up one of the newspaper cuttings that her father hadn't yet glued into his scrapbook.

THE BATTLE OF MAGERSFONTEIN
DESCRIPTIVE ACCOUNTS
THE LOSSES OF THE HIGHLANDERS

At midnight on Sunday the Highland Brigade, under Major-General Wauchope, consisting of the 1st Highland Light Infantry, the 1st Argyll and Sutherland Highlanders, the 2nd Royal Highlanders, and the 2nd Seaforth Highlanders, were ordered to move on the enemy's position. They were escorted by guides through night, the darkness of which was intensified by heavy rainfall. At twenty minutes past three, while they were still in quarter column, they encountered a terrific fire from the trenches at the base of the kopjes in the occupation of the Boers. Although it was not yet daylight, the enemy's volleys came at a point-blank range of 300 yards. Our casualties were, as was inevitable in the circumstances,

*extremely heavy; but the failure of the attack was not due to
any lack of bravery on the part of those who made it. The
conduct of both officers and men under the withering fire to
which they were exposed for so many hours was, indeed,
beyond praise. Twelve ambulances under a flag of truce
collected the wounded and buried the dead. General
Wauchope's body was found near a trench. He had been shot
through the chest and thigh and was buried at Modder River.*

Jane set the article to one side and lifted a long, narrow
cutting which listed the fatalities and casualties from
Magersfontein. Marked with a small 'x' in the black ink of her
father's pen was 'Robert John Knight'.

She took a sheet from the pile of black-edged writing paper
at the side of the scrapbook and picked up the pen.

*Dearest Aunt Alice – There is nothing else to say except that
my heart is broken in a hundred pieces. I cannot bear to relay
the details, but, suffice to say, I am unable to function at home
with such anguish and desolation in the air. I long to honour
the memory of my beloved brother but fear that I will not be
able to do so unless I have some respite from this suffocating
grief. I wonder if I might come to stay with you for a while,
therefore? A different atmosphere may be the only thing that
will quell my desperation. I fear that without such a change in
circumstances, I may never recover.*

Your loving niece, Jane

CHAPTER 5

APRIL–JUNE 1900

ELIZA SNIFFED the cold air and looked around at the group of almost a hundred people who were gathered on the driveway in front of the Home. Her prayers had been answered again. First, the building contractors had completed the work on the new wing ahead of time, and now, this Tuesday in April was milder than she could have hoped for. With no chill or showers to contend with, the opening ceremony was taking place as planned. The Lord had heard the voice of the righteous and had shown them mercy. It was a new century and a new era for Gowanlea.

They were all standing before her, the great and good of the parish and beyond. Provosts, bailies, councillors, Justices of the Peace, board members, benefactors and newspaper men; a more impressive display of civic finery, feathers and chains she had seldom seen. But while ostentation might be forgiven in the Home's benefactors, it was not appropriate either for Eliza or for Gowanlea. A plain black dress had served her well all these years and there was no reason to change her custom now. In any case, she couldn't afford to dress any other way – she

33

relied on charity as much as the children did, for she took no wage. Without Gowanlea, she would have no roof over her head and no food in her stomach. But she had earned her shelter and sustenance. For these she had worked tirelessly over the years in the service of her Master. That no one could deny. Nor, she was sure, was there any contention that, without Eliza Frew, there would be no Gowanlea.

She raised her hand and touched her mother's gold cameo brooch pinned to the bodice of her dress. Eliza wasn't wearing it for vanity or ostentation, she was wearing it in honour of her family, all of whom had been called by the Lord. Would they ever have believed, when Eliza had first taken the four-roomed house in Broad Street as a refuge for homeless and outcast women, that she would have ended up overseeing an enterprise such as Gowanlea? If they had thought those women unworthy of kindly treatment, surely they could have no moral cause to criticise the divine call that had led their daughter and sister to the service of little lambs threatened by moral perdition and physical suffering. The event that was about to begin was testament to her whole-hearted devotion.

As many children as could fit on the front steps of the new extension were arranged behind Eliza and the three church ministers. Mr Alexander Morgan, the single biggest donor, was standing to the side, waiting to be called upon to give a short address. When the bells of the town below struck three, The Reverend Forsyth introduced the singing of Psalm 121 and engaged in prayer, before inviting Morgan to speak.

"Thank you, Reverend Forsyth." Mr Morgan rubbed his hands together and took a deep breath. "Miss Frew, Reverend Buchanan, Reverend Clark, ladies and gentlemen – it is my pleasure and honour to be invited today to open the extension to this venerable institution. This splendid new wing has only been made possible by the faith and determination of one woman – Miss Frew." Some gentle applause rippled in the crowd. Eliza bowed her head. "The work carried out here by

Miss Frew and her committed helpers is an instance of the wonderful sympathy shown towards the waifs and strays of humanity, the homeless and the destitute, who would otherwise go uncared for." He made a half-turn so that he could address alternately the audience and Eliza. "Here is a woman, almost single-handedly, finding joy and satisfaction in tending, without fee or material recompense, the little ones who presently find shelter in her nest." He was so close she could smell the stale whisky on his breath. "Gowanlea has been a source of incalculable blessing to scores of little children, and with the creation of this fine new wing, I have no doubt that many more of them will be rescued from squalor, dirt and misery. Little children who, but for Miss Frew's merciful intervention, might, and in all probability would, grow up to be a curse on themselves as well as society."

Some of the children shuffled on the steps behind Eliza. Sensing Mr Morgan looking at her, she stared into the crowd. While she appreciated his very generous financial contributions, without which the extension could not have proceeded as quickly as it had, and sweet as he might be on her, Eliza sincerely hoped his position as the most significant benefactor might one day be usurped by someone of more temperate character.

"Those of you who have been invited today have made your own offerings. Love moves many hearts to aid the homeless and destitute. Love also moves the hearts of those who tend the rickety waifs and wasted items of humanity. We pray and bless Miss Frew and wish her all success in her noble and praiseworthy work."

Mr Morgan instigated some further applause and, when he didn't move aside, Eliza put a hand on his back and gave him a gentle push, allowing The Reverend Buchanan to move into position to lead the singing of 'Praise God From Whom All Blessings Flow'. Next, and not a moment too soon for Eliza, The Reverend Clark raised his hand and pronounced the benediction. The new wing, between fund-raising and construction five years in the making, was less than ten minutes in the opening.

She shooed the children from the steps, sending them inside to populate the building in advance of the tours that would be run for the benefactors. If they thought that its three storeys were impressive from the outside, wait until they saw the new schoolroom, playroom and washing house on the ground floor, the accommodation for fourteen infants, day and night nurseries, nurses' room, first-floor kitchen and bathroom, and the two large dormitories – one for girls and one for boys – on the top floor. And then, when they saw that the roof of the original house had been raised and the attics converted into airy spaces to be used as sick or isolation rooms, they would surely be in no doubt that their donations had been worth it and the money well-spent. It had been a long journey for Eliza but she'd finally reached her intended destination. The best and noblest work of God was done brick by brick.

"Eliza! A wonderful day and a wonderful achievement."

Alice Knight was before her, accompanied by her niece, both of them in mourning dress. Eliza hadn't seen the girl in years but still recalled how alike she and her brother had been as children, with the same brown hair and eyes, the same dimples and the same shy smile.

"Thank you, Alice. Many people – yourself included, and all the other collectors and volunteers – have made it possible." Eliza turned to the niece. "Miss Knight, my sincere condolences on the recent loss of your brother. He bequeathed his glory to alien soil and made the extreme sacrifice. I hope the knowledge that his Master has taken him to a higher service might offer you some comfort in these difficult days when he will be so sorely missed."

Miss Knight looked down as she spoke. "Thank you, Miss Frew."

Eliza glanced at Alice, who raised her eyebrows.

"Your aunt tells me you're an accomplished artist, Miss Knight, and make fine sketches of the natural world."

"Well, I certainly enjoy sketching, although I haven't done so much of it since ... of late."

Eliza glanced again at Alice, who gave her a nod of encouragement.

"The reason I mention it is that Miss Paterson, who volunteered with us and delivered excellent nature classes, has recently moved away with her new husband. The children so loved their field trips with her and miss them dearly. I was wondering if you might do us a very great favour and perhaps spend some time with the children? Take them on nature walks and perhaps give some drawing classes to those who show talent."

"Oh, I don't ..." Miss Knight shifted on the spot and cleared her throat. "I don't think I have sufficient experience to—"

"Nonsense, dear!" Alice said. "It's not about experience, it's about commitment. There are lots of volunteers who didn't have experience when they started. Instead they had an interest or talent in something."

"Your aunt's right," Eliza said. "There's Miss Hunter, who comes and does physical drills with the children, and Miss MacDougall, who provides a range of different recreations. And Miss Wilson, of course, who takes music and singing classes."

"Oh yes, Miss Wilson," Alice said. "A very fine soprano. Very fine indeed. So what do you think, Jane?"

When Miss Knight said nothing, Eliza stepped in. "I know you're mourning your brother, and of course, you'll mourn him for the rest of your life. Believe me, I know what it is to mourn a sibling. I lost my dear sister over twenty years ago and miss her still every day. But gradually, you return to society. And when you do, there are many things a talented young lady such as yourself could contribute. As well as prayer, activity in any sphere can be a very good thing for helping one adjust to unfortunate circumstances."

"How true," Alice said.

"And, of course, you must consider what your dear brother would have wished for you. I'm sure a young man who chose to serve Queen and country would have wanted you to make the most of your talent and in so doing make a valuable contribution to the welfare of the less fortunate."

There was a pause. For a moment, Eliza wasn't sure whether Miss Knight would collapse in grief or explode with anger.

"Thank you, Miss Frew. I'm most flattered by your kind invitation and assure you that I'll consider it most carefully," she eventually said.

Alice put her arm through her niece's. "Excellent. Now, shall we go and inspect the new wing, Jane?"

"Please do," Eliza said, nodding to acknowledge the others passing by on their way inside.

As the last of the guests were heading into the building, Eliza spotted a young man of about twenty-one step out of the bushes bordering the driveway. Well-dressed in a dark suit and hat, he wasn't a tramp or one of the ne'er-do-wells who occasionally made their way to Gowanlea in search of a handout.

He brushed the lapels of his jacket with his fingers as he approached her, then reached out in greeting. "Miss Frew. It's an honour to finally meet you."

Eliza shook his hand without thinking. She didn't recognise him, which meant he wasn't a former charge, because she never forgot a face. Although he did look somewhat familiar. Perhaps he was a gentleman of the press whom she'd seen at a previous function.

"I'm Thomas Keith. Thomas William Keith."

Eliza gave a jolt. She studied the young man's face more closely. She had known a William Keith many years ago and, like the young man before her, he had black hair, blue eyes and a turned-up nose. Surely this couldn't be ...

He smiled at her and nodded. "Yes, that William Keith. I believe you were a close ..." He stroked his chin. "... well, let's say, *acquaintance* of my late father." Eliza raised her hand to her mouth. "I'm sorry to shock you with news of his death, Miss Frew. But in the end it was a blessing for his suffering to be over." Eliza spread her feet further apart on the ground as she began to sway. "Before his passing, things were weighing heavily on his conscience. He revealed certain matters to me, which, I must say, came as something of a shock, particularly when I see for myself the lady you are now."

Eliza composed herself. "I really don't know what you're talking about, Mr Keith. Now, if you don't mind, I must go inside and mingle with the dignitaries."

He laughed, then shook his finger at her. "Now now, Miss Frew, thou shalt not bear false witness."

"I beg your pardon?" she said sharply.

"Although I thought you might say such a thing ..." He reached into his jacket pocket. "... so I brought this." He pulled out an envelope and held it up for Eliza to examine. She felt a wrench in her stomach. "Are you going to repeat your untruth, Miss Frew? Is that not my father's name and address written in your own fair hand? Or do you wish me to take the letter out and read it to you?"

Eliza snatched at the envelope but Mr Keith took a step back, too quick for her. She looked over her shoulder lest anyone was watching, then faced him, the anger rising. "What do you want?"

"That's better, Miss Frew. Much better."

She put her hands on her hips. "Well?"

"What does anyone want?" he said, turning his palms up.

"I don't know, I—"

"Oh, Miss Frew!" He laughed again. "You're such a card with your frugal look and humble lifestyle. Money, of course!"

"What?"

"Yes. I'm afraid, for reasons I don't need to disclose, I've fallen on hard times. So it's quite simple – that is what I want. Money."

For a moment, Eliza was relieved. "Well, I don't have any money, Mr Keith. I rely on charity, just like the children. So I'm afraid you'll have to go elsewhere."

"Oh, I know *you* don't have any money, Miss Frew."

"Well then."

"But the Home does."

Eliza jerked her head. "What? But I can't—"

"You see, I understand you are, among other things, quite the businesswoman. How else would you have been able to attract such significant investment, thousands and thousands of pounds, and persuade everyone from the tinker to the Lord-Lieutenant to part with their money?"

"But I can't use the Home's money for ... anything!" she insisted.

"I'm sure, Miss Frew, with all the notes and coins that come your way from your collectors and from other daily donations, it's in your gift to, shall we say, divert these in a direction other than the Home's coffers. That way there'll be no accounting for them. You see, I'm not entirely unsympathetic. I do understand there's a board and an auditor you have to report to and certain procedures you'll have to navigate. So until you're able to work out a way around these, I'll accept small, but regular, amounts to help with my day-to-day expenses. But in due course, I'll need several hundred pounds to—"

"Several hundred pounds?" Eliza stumbled sideways and Mr Keith grabbed her arm to steady her. When she found her feet, she pushed him away and looked him straight in the eye. "How dare you? Whatever your father said to you ... I'm certain he wouldn't want this. And he most certainly wouldn't approve of your abominable behaviour towards me."

"That may be true. But he's no longer here to protect your

honour, if that is indeed what he did for all those years. Though perhaps he was just protecting himself. That would certainly have been more his way of things."

Eliza closed her eyes. This auspicious day that she'd been waiting for, for years, had turned into a day that for years she'd been dreading.

"Miss Frew?"

She turned around in a panic at the sound of a female voice. Winnie McKellar was standing in the doorway of the new wing. "Yes?"

"Mr Morgan sent me to ask if you'll join him upstairs. He has some questions he'd like to ask you about the dormitories. And the entertainment's about to begin," she called.

"Tell him I'll be there directly," Eliza said, turning back to Mr Keith, whose eyes were on Winnie.

"What a charming young lady," he said, looking to the door after she'd disappeared back inside. "Is she a servant or one of your children?"

Winnie was both but that was no business of Mr Keith's. Eliza was breathing heavily. "Mr Keith, I must insist you leave now. The town's Provost is in the building, along with a number of Sheriffs, Justices of the Peace, parish and county councillors, and countless other gentlemen who would be only too willing to remove you more forcibly should I enlist their assistance."

The snarl on Mr Keith's face spread to a smile. "Father said you could be feisty."

Eliza's heart was beating ever faster and there was a pulsing in her throat. All she wanted was to turn and flee. She closed her eyes, willing herself to find the strength to act. *Those who are engaged in the Lord's work must suffer persecution. No painful thing can come into the life of an earnest discipline without God's permission. There is meaning for every trial and disappointment.* She opened her eyes and folded her arms over her chest. "Mr Keith – you have thirty seconds to leave."

He stared at her for a moment, then looked away. "I've said what I came to say Miss Frew. I'm more than content to leave you now to think about it. But make no mistake, I'll be back." He waved the envelope at her. "And unless you want the whole town knowing what you did, you'd be advised to give me what I want." He tucked it back inside his jacket and gave a little bow. Then he cocked his head in the direction of the new wing. "Please give my regards to all your gentlemen admirers. Good day, madam."

CHAPTER 6

THAT HER MOTHER hadn't asked for – and Jane hadn't volunteered – any information about a return date to Perth was why she was still in Stirling, sitting in Miss Frew's cluttered office at Gowanlea. It wasn't as if they hadn't had the opportunity to discuss the matter; they had. But, instead of doing so, her mother's weekly letters were full only of news about the house remodelling (*every room, except your father's study, which is* verboten), a project which she seemed to have taken to with uncharacteristic gusto. Jane was equally culpable, her short replies only outlining the mundane routine she'd fallen into, which her aunt now seemed determined to pull her out of. It wasn't that Aunt Alice was unsympathetic to her grief, for she also felt the loss of RJ keenly, it was simply that she discerned a purpose in life that Jane no longer did.

Everyone's assumption that when she returned home she would marry Harold also weighed on her. His regular letters, intended to maintain the pretence that their engagement would survive the postponement – which everyone had been so understanding about – were becoming an irritation. But she would smile and assure Aunt Alice that all would be well.

"A short postponement is understandable, Jane, but don't let it drift too long otherwise it might never happen."

"Love should be strong enough that separation shouldn't undermine it. Mother survived father being away in India, after all."

"Yes dear, but they were already married, so your mother didn't have any choice but to endure it."

"Well, Harold and I are quite comfortable with the arrangement. We believe the postponement appropriate. It will allow us both time to grieve so that we can start married life when our hearts are less sore. You know they were as close as brothers. Even though he's a man and couldn't show it, Harold was deeply affected by RJ's death. Deeply."

Too deeply.

"I know, dear. But life must go on."

So between her mother's indifference and her aunt's subtle mithering that she occupy herself more productively, volunteering at Gowanlea might at least buy Jane some time to continue putting off her mother and gain approval with Aunt Alice.

How Miss Frew could operate in such a jumble as the office Jane was sitting in was unfathomable. There had to be the surface of a desk under the expanse of newspapers, ledgers and accounts books, but Jane couldn't see it. Which wasn't at all what she'd been expecting, given her childhood impression of Miss Frew and, more recently, the immaculate state the Home was in at the opening of the extension. But Jane's father said of his own study: 'Everyone needs a place where they can just be themselves.' Perhaps this was Miss Frew's.

Not only was the desk completely covered, so were the walls, with hardly a piece of wallpaper visible beneath the hundreds of photographs. There were babies, toddlers, older children, youths and even some adults. Present and past residents, Jane assumed. She stood up to take a closer look at the twin images in some of the frames which, she guessed, showed the child who had been admitted to Gowanlea and the adult they'd become. As she sidled along the walls scanning the gallery, she recalled the photograph that sad little girl had shown her and RJ of her brother and his two companions who'd all been sent to Canada. What had become of them? Jane wondered. She surveyed the images more purposefully in case the very photograph happened to be there. Those poor children – Winnie and Hugh were their names – first admitted to a home then separated. Jane swallowed at the sudden memory of RJ whispering in her ear that he would have run away before anyone sent him from her. In the end, he had chosen to leave. Had Winnie ever been reunited with her brother? Or was he still in another part of the world?

Miss Frew bustled in. Jane was grateful for the interruption to her reminiscing – it didn't do to dwell on the past, that's what everyone kept telling her.

"Apologies for keeping you waiting, Miss Knight. I'm afraid the office of Gowanlea occupies me more than the children these days, when it seems I am more secretary than superintendent."

"That's quite all right." Jane returned to the chair in the corner of the room. "I was just admiring your photographs."

"Ah, yes." Miss Frew gazed at them with pride.

"And actually, I was wondering ..."

Miss Frew brushed by her and swept her arm along the wall. "Every child who has graced us is up here." She pointed up to the top row. "You see that girl on the far left? She was our very first inmate. Little Annie. She was five when that was taken."

Jane approached the oval photograph that was set in bevelled card. A plump girl in a dark dress with white collar and cuffs stood with one hand on a velvet stool and holding a doll in the other. Her thick hair, bowl-cut high above her forehead, emphasised the roundness of her face.

Miss Frew folded her arms, still staring at Little Annie.

"When I was coming down the Back Walk one night after a prayer meeting, I heard the cry of a child in the bushes. And there she was. I waited for her mother, or at least someone, to appear, but no one came. So I took her back to town and she stayed with me overnight. The next day I found out that her mother was in prison. She'd left Annie in the bushes while she went back to town for more drink. Annie was just nine months old and bore every outward sign of criminal neglect – she'd been starved, drugged, kicked about, and exposed to the night air. Her mother died in prison a few days later. So we took Annie in permanently. And with patient toil and motherly care, she improved rapidly. After a few years she was sent to Canada, where she found a happy Christian home."

"Goodness." Jane shook her head. "It's difficult to conceive of such neglect. But how wonderful that Annie was eventually able to thrive."

"Alas," Miss Frew sighed, "her days weren't to be many. She fell into consumption and departed this earth when she was just twelve."

"Oh." Jane bowed her head and returned to her chair.

"But her legacy is all around us," Miss Frew chirped. "A legacy which, I hope, you are considering making a contribution to, Miss Knight."

"Well, if there's anything of value I can offer, I most certainly will."

"Excellent." Miss Frew lifted some papers from the desk and unearthed a pile of booklets. "Miss Paterson started a nature club with some of the children. She called it the Honour Bright Club and its purpose is to give children a love of nature. And I must say that already I've noticed it's had a beneficial effect in purifying the thoughts and language of those involved, as well as giving them a new interest in the world around them. The club works in connection with Cornell University, New York."

"New York? Goodness."

Miss Frew handed the booklets to Jane. The top one was entitled 'The Moth and the Butterfly'. "These are the monthly leaflets they send us from America. After studying them, the children write to the leader at the University about what they've learned. They enjoy looking for specimens so they can tell him what they've collected. He's known to them as 'Uncle John' and he always writes back to say how pleased he is to hear from them. He's even referenced us at a Teachers' Institute in Albany, where the children's letters were read out."

Jane flicked through the booklet. "Well, goodness me." There were children at Gowanlea who probably hadn't been beyond the boundaries of Stirling town and yet here they were getting an education from someone thousands of miles away.

"Our Lord Jesus was a lover of nature. As a child, He gathered the wild flowers in Galilee. If you will do us the honour of taking on the nature club, Miss Knight, know that our Heavenly Father is at the helm."

Despite her growing anxiety that Miss Frew's expectations of her were on the high side, Jane smiled. It almost embarrassed her to ask about more practical matters. "When would you require me to take the club, Miss Frew?"

"Saturdays. Lessons take precedence during the week and the children also have classes every Sabbath afternoon. Would Saturdays be convenient?"

"Perfectly." It wasn't as if Jane had any other social commitments.

"Good. Then why don't you take these booklets away to familiarise yourself with matters? And when you're ready to begin, just let me know. The children will be delighted." Miss Frew clapped her hands, then got up and opened the office door. A little grey dog came trotting in.

"Oh!" It was the same one in the photograph Winnie had shown Jane. And, judging from the enthusiastic tail-wagging, it was still going strong.

"This is Rona," Miss Frew said. "Her mission in life is to get under everyone's feet and be in the middle of everything."

"Ah! I recognise her."

"Really?"

"Yes. Do you recall some years ago, my aunt came to call on you and brought my late brother and me with her?"

"Of course."

"Well, that day, while you and Aunt Alice were discussing matters, he and I met a little girl in the garden, Winnie, who told us her brother had been sent to Canada. And she showed us a photograph of him with two other boys and Rona."

"Ah yes."

"Do you know what became of them?"

"Winnie and Hugh McKellar? Of course I know what became of them!" Miss Frew beckoned Jane over to the window wall and pointed out the photograph she had just described.

"That's it!" Jane said, stepping forward for a closer look.

"And that's Winnie there," Miss Frew said, running her finger down a few photographs, pressing it against one of the girl dressed up and posing in the garden. It looked like it had been taken around the same period as her brother's. Perhaps it had even been taken on the same day, for Winnie wasn't smiling. "Yes, Hugh went to Canada, where he's thriving, working on a farm, and well on his way to being a good citizen able to support himself."

"And Winnie?" Jane asked, still studying the photograph.

"Winnie? I'm surprised you didn't notice her at the opening of the new wing, although I expect you wouldn't have recognised her. She's quite changed."

Jane gasped. "She's still here?"

"Yes, she's still here. And quite refined now."

"But isn't she—"

"Yes, she is, if what you were about to say is that she's past the age to leave. Normally girls her age would go straight into service, and naturally I would make sure they secure good and safe positions with people who've been vouched for. But with Winnie, well, in truth, I think she may be above that and could perhaps secure a higher position somewhere. So I suggested she stay on and earn her keep as a housemaid while she acquires further skills that will stand her in good stead to make something better of her life than might have otherwise been anticipated."

"What you do for these orphans, Miss Frew, is very admirable."

"Kind of you to say so, Miss Knight, but it's the divine hand which is at the helm steering the daily course of life. And Winnie wasn't an orphan, at least not when she first came to us. Though I'm afraid her poor father hardly saw another year after he handed the children over to us."

"Oh. How sad."

"Yes, but the Lord is our strength," Miss Frew said, opening the study door in invitation for Jane to leave. "If you'll excuse me, Miss Knight, there are a few things I have to attend to, one of which is securing an escort to accompany two of our boys to Canada in a few weeks. Unfortunately, the one I had engaged has taken ill and is unlikely to be able to carry out the role."

"I'm sorry to hear that."

"Yes. Tell me – you don't by any chance have a desire to be a chaperone, do you?"

"What?" Jane said, alarmed.

"Don't worry, I'm teasing."

"Of course. And just as well. We're not renowned in our family for our sea legs."

Miss Frew smiled. "Rest assured, I shall look elsewhere then." She took a step out of the office and looked down the hall. "Ah, here is the girl herself. Winnie! Will you show our visitor out? You may not remember her but she remembers you. You see, you were always one to watch."

An attractive girl of around fourteen or fifteen arrived at

the office door. Her fair hair was neatly arranged in a bun and the clear skin on her face glowed with health. But for her warm brown eyes, Jane wouldn't have recognised her as the sad child she'd met in the garden.

"Please see Miss Knight out," Miss Frew said. "She's joining the Gowanlea family, I'm delighted to say, taking over the Honour Bright Club from Miss Paterson." She turned to Jane. "Winnie here is an enthusiastic naturalist and also enjoys drawing those specimens she finds."

"Really?" Jane said.

"Yes, miss." Winnie gave a half curtsy.

"Well, perhaps you might show me your drawings some time. I enjoy sketching, myself."

"Yes, miss."

Jane gave a little sigh, realising that Winnie would only engage with her now if spoken to. No longer were they children who might overlook each other's stations for the joy of conversation or play. "Well thank you, Miss Frew. I'll read the information with interest and hope to call on you again soon. Good day."

"And a very good day to you, Miss Knight. Please give my regards to your aunt."

Jane followed Winnie to the main entrance in silence. When the girl opened the front door and stood to the side, Jane stepped onto the doormat, then paused and turned back. "It's good to see you looking so well. Do you by any chance remember when we met? You were very young so it wouldn't be surprising if you didn't."

Winnie looked down before answering. "Yes. You never did come back to see me. I know you didn't promise to, but ... I thought you might. I hoped you might." She gave a dismissive laugh. "But I was only seven then. I mean, what do you know when you're seven?" She reached for the door handle. "I know better now, though."

Jane felt her face redden. Yet she really oughtn't feel guilty.

After all, she'd only been visiting – by chance, at that – from another town, a distant town; and she and RJ only visited Aunt Alice a couple of times a year. But it was true, she had never in any visits to Stirling since that day returned to Gowanlea to see Winnie. She had thought about her though. For days afterwards she had thought about her. But she herself had only been fourteen. And what did you know at fourteen? Granted more than at seven, but still not much. Mind, Winnie was around that age now and probably knew more about life than Jane ever would.

"No. I'm sorry I didn't. You see, we lived in Perth and only visited my aunt a couple of times a year and when we did visit there were lots of other things arranged, and we would only have been able to come if my aunt had been coming, and she didn't visit again while we stayed with her."

"You could have asked her to bring you," Winnie said quietly. "Did you ever even ask?"

Jane bristled. "Anyway. Miss Frew tells me that both you and your brother are thriving."

"Well, *I* may be."

"What do you mean? Miss Frew said your brother – Hugh, isn't it? – your brother is doing well in Canada and—"

"On his way *to being a good citizen able to support himself*?"

"Actually yes."

"As far as Miss Frew knows, he is."

"But?"

Winnie glanced along the hall. "But Miss Frew doesn't know all the facts."

"What do you mean?"

Winnie pushed the door so that Jane had to exit. "I'm sorry, I have to return to my duties now." She gave another half curtsy. "Good day, Miss Knight."

She closed the door firmly.

CHAPTER 7

IT WAS ONLY ONCE the little group of children she was leading veered down the slope of Shore Road towards the harbour that Jane felt the tension in her body ease. Surely now they were out of sight of Gowanlea's hilly vantage point and its superintendent's gaze?

It was understandable, of course, that Miss Frew wanted to ensure her new volunteer's first field trip went strictly as planned, and that all her little lambs returned sound of body and pure of mind. Indeed, initially, it had seemed as if the proposed destination of the Cambuskenneth Orchards might be vetoed, on the basis that in 1848 Mr Peter Drummond had been prompted to publish the first of his tracts in condemnation of those who disrespected the Sabbath by picking fruit there. However, Jane had prevailed with her argument that there could be no better place for the children to see in real life what they had learned in the classroom about the apple tree, courtesy of a study leaflet from Cornell University. Also, wouldn't Uncle John, himself a fruit grower, be impressed to receive letters in the coming months demonstrating the children's knowledge and telling of their invaluable experience of the natural world? And, in any case, the trip wouldn't be on the Sabbath, it would be on a Saturday.

There was a fleeting moment, before Miss Frew finally pronounced on the matter, when Jane thought she might be harbouring second thoughts about her new volunteer. But eventually, she conceded that a trip just over the river to the orchards would be 'excellent practical and physical exercise' for the members of the Honour Bright Club.

"But Winnie will accompany you, Miss Knight. She knows the route, can deal with the ferryman and will be able to give you insights into the children's temperaments."

At first Jane was a tad insulted that Miss Frew considered she needed not just an escort but one who was seven years her junior. However, when Jane looked over her shoulder to where Winnie was bringing up the rear like an old hand, she felt only relief to be accompanied by someone so self-assured in her surroundings. So when they reached Abbey Road, it was Winnie who suggested which side to walk on to avoid the horses and carts that might be coming out of the cooperage and brass works. It was also Winnie who made sure that the boys in the group didn't stray too far from view. Nothing had been said about their conversation at Gowanlea the previous week, and for that Jane was grateful.

The route began to peter out as they approached the river and Jane had to lift her skirts a few inches above her shoes to avoid them being smeared by dust and dry muck. She stopped at the rickety wooden planks of the pier that led down the gentle gradient of the grass slope, then over the sloppy mud to the water's edge.

There was a rowing boat tied up on the Cambuskenneth side of the river. She glanced back and saw Winnie already making her way forward. "Should we go to the waiting area?" Jane asked, looking at the open-fronted hut on the grassy area.

"Not if you want to stay clean. No, just a moment." Then

Winnie strode assuredly to the end of the pier, cupped her mouth with her hands and shouted across the water: "Boat!"

After a few moments, a figure appeared from a house just behind the pier on the opposite bank. Winnie made her way back to Jane. "That's the ferryman coming now. He'll need to make two crossings because there are too many of us for just one. Don't listen to him if he says otherwise. You take four of the girls first, then I'll bring the rest of them. I'll collect the tickets."

Jane nodded, happy for Winnie to take charge, at least of this part of the trip.

By the time the ferryman had (albeit reluctantly) completed the two trips, the sun was beginning to break through the clouds. Following Winnie's directions, Jane took the path along the riverbank that led past two streets of cottages, then went east into Ferry Orchard.

At the sight of so many apple trees the children shrieked, and Jane, in turn, experienced for the first time in months a flurry of joy at the prospect of sketching such a lovely scene.

The two boys in the group started to kick their way through the long grass. "Fred! Albert! Wait until Miss Knight's given you your instructions," Winnie shouted, cuffing one of the twins on the shoulder when they returned to the fold.

Jane gathered the children around her and began her address. The girls, pretty in light blue dresses and straw hats, listened rapt, while the boys nudged each other mischievously. "Explore the orchard and pick a tree to write about. Write down how tall you think it is, how thick its trunk is and how many branches divide off it. Then look around you. How far apart are the apple trees from each other? Are there other fruit trees or bushes here? Sketch a blossom. How many petals does it have and how are they arranged? Write down everything you see, hear and smell, and we'll discuss your findings back at Gowanlea." She clasped her hands together. "Right – off you go, and come back here when you've finished."

The girls skipped away in pairs and the boys sprinted off to play tig. Winnie pointed to a wooden bench next to the path; Jane nodded with approval. It would be an ideal vantage point from which to watch the children and make a few sketches. Not only that, it offered splendid views of the Wallace Monument atop Abbey Craig and the Ochil Hills to the east. And, behind the trees at the other end of the village, there was also a glimpse of Cambuskenneth Abbey.

They worked in silence, Jane attempting a panorama of the orchard, Winnie concentrating on a single tree. Jane was impressed with Winnie's eye for detail, and the intricacy with which she captured the bark, gnarls and buds. "Your drawing's very accomplished, Winnie. You're developing quite a talent there."

"Thank you, Miss Knight. That's very generous of you to say so."

"It's not generous in the slightest. You're very talented."

"I meant in the circumstances, miss," Winnie said, continuing to sketch.

"Ah." Jane knew exactly what Winnie meant. It seemed she hadn't been the only one reflecting on their recent exchange.

Winnie lifted her pencil from the paper. "I shouldn't have said what I did, miss. It wasn't my place. I'm sorry."

Jane put her pad down on the bench. "You've no reason to be sorry. I think I understand what you were feeling after everything that's happened. But thank you, anyway, for your apology, even if it wasn't necessary. Now let's put it behind us. Look forward, not back." She retrieved her pad and began to draw again. "Although I must say that your development at Gowanlea is very commendable. The difference between when I first saw you and now ... well, it's not just that you're older, you're so capable and so refined in your behaviour. And your speech."

Winnie laughed. "Miss Frew says talking properly will help girls like me get on in life and get good positions. So, as well as reading and writing lessons, I had elocution lessons. Not everyone does, and Miss Frew doesn't mind that, as long as she can stamp out the bad language that some bring in with them."

"Bad language?"

Winnie looked out over the orchard. "You see Fred and Albert there? When they first came, well, you should've heard them. They didn't speak the Queen's English, Miss Frew said, but *the language of the gutter*. She said that, even though the bad habits of the parents had been passed down to the boys, she was going to – what was it now? – yes, 'snap asunder the link that binds them to evil associations and find the jewel within them'."

"And it seems she has," Jane said, watching the boys exploring some bushes near the far end of the orchard. "I don't think anyone looking at them now would suspect otherwise."

"No." Winnie bit her lip. "I just hope they can stay together when they go to Canada."

"They're the ones going to Canada? When?"

"Yes, soon. But Miss Frew is having difficulties engaging an escort. The one she usually relies on has taken ill."

"She mentioned that. Do they want to go?"

"Oh, yes. They're very excited at the idea of crossing the ocean. They think it would be great fun to see the sailors kill a whale."

Jane made a few scribbles below her sketch, pondering whether or not to ask Winnie the question that had been on her mind. *Nothing ventured, nothing gained*, Aunt Alice would have told her. "Not like Hugh, then?" When Winnie put her pencil down, Jane followed suit. "What you said to me the other day about Miss Frew not having all the facts about Hugh – what did you mean by it?"

Winnie swallowed. "It started off all right. He was chosen by a nice family. He was getting schooling and he worked on the farm. Then about a year ago, the farmer died and his wife sold up and moved away. She couldn't take Hugh with her, so he was sent to another place. And now ... this other farmer ... he doesn't let Hugh go to school any more, he makes him sleep in the barn, he doesn't give him enough food. Some of the other workers call him names and mistreat him. He said the farmer keeps wages from him. And now I don't know what's happening. I haven't heard from Hugh for months. But something's terribly wrong. I know it. He wouldn't not write to me."

"Have you told Miss Frew?"

"I can't. And you mustn't either. When Hugh writes to her, he mentions nothing of his predicament."

"But if she knew, then surely she—"

"Please! No. They won't believe him. It'll just cause more trouble and do more harm than good."

"But if Miss Frew knew, she could surely—"

"What could she do?" Winnie flicked her wrist dismissively. "What can she do when he's in Canada and she's in Stirling?" She sighed. "If I could, I'd escort Fred and Albert myself and go and get Hugh away from that place."

Jane looked across the orchard to where the brothers were climbing a tree. "I know you would, Winnie. I know you would."

The return trip to Gowanlea seemed to take only half the time, so keen were the children to get back to show off the grass, leaves and flowers they'd collected. As they trooped into the house, Jane heard voices in the garden. She paused at the foot of the front steps.

"I cannot and I will not." It sounded like Miss Frew, though speaking in a tone Jane hadn't heard before. She went past the fir tree to the path and peered through a gap in the hedge. Miss Frew was by the maypole with a well-dressed young man, who was standing very close to her speaking in a low voice. Judging from the wan look on Miss Frew's face, he was not delivering good news.

When Miss Frew shook her head and he went to grab her wrist, Jane scurried along to the gate and lifted the latch very deliberately, making sure it clanked. "Miss Frew?"

The man stepped abruptly away from her; Miss Frew trotted over to the gate. "Ah, Miss Knight. You're back. Excellent. How was the field trip?"

"It went well, I think." Jane looked past her to the young man, who was now by the wall, gazing out over the town. "Is everything all right?"

"Yes, yes." Miss Frew tugged at her cuffs. "And the children behaved themselves?"

"Oh yes, they were all extremely well-behaved." The young man was showing no signs of leaving, so Jane spoke louder. "They're just taking the specimens they collected to the classroom. They're so excited for you to see them ..." She turned her head towards the visitor to ensure her words reached him. "... if you've finished your business here."

Miss Frew seemed relieved. "Yes, indeed I have." She put her arm in Jane's and took a few paces towards him. "Mr Keith was just leaving. He just stopped by to pass on some news about his father."

Mr Keith stepped away from the garden wall and came over. When he tipped his hat at Jane, she saw a shock of black hair. "Miss."

Jane acknowledged him with the slightest of nods, determined not to look into his piercing blue eyes.

"And Miss Frew – it was nice to talk to you about my father. I look forward to seeing you again to continue our reminiscing. Good day."

Miss Frew stood silently, holding Jane's arm, until Mr Keith started down the driveway.

"Are you sure everything's – *you're* – all right?"

"Yes, yes. It was just a surprise, a bit of a shock, to meet the young man. That's all. And to hear of the passing of his father."

"Oh, I'm sorry to hear about that. He's clearly still affected by it. Did you know his father well?"

Miss Frew stepped away from her. "He was once engaged to be married to my sister."

"Oh?" Jane's interest was piqued. "But they didn't marry?"

"Ultimately, no."

"Oh. And did—"

"Yes, it was many years ago. Now, shall we go and inspect these specimens?"

Without waiting for a reply, Miss Frew turned on her heels and went from the garden.

CHAPTER 8

THE REGULAR MONTHLY meeting of Gowanlea's Board of Trustees was always a pleasant affair. Chair, ex-Provost Brown, hosted it in the large, bright drawing room of his villa in Victoria Square. When the business was concluded, afternoon tea was served. It was during the mingling which followed that the real business was done.

Mr Rennie, the Home's new solicitor, moseyed over to Eliza as she stood in the bay window gazing out at the spreading oak trees that lined one side of the square. He took a sip of tea, placed the cup gently back on its saucer, then leaned towards her. "I wouldn't worry, Miss Frew. I know Lord Miller through my father and he is a man with values similar to your own. I didn't want to be so unequivocal during the meeting, but I have no doubt the Court of Session will refuse the petition."

"Thank you," Eliza said. Although if Mr Rennie thought she was worried about an impending custody hearing, he had a lot to learn. She had no doubt either that Mrs Duncan's petition to have her two children returned would be refused by the Court of Session. After all, the little mites required careful attention and good clothing. Not to mention wholesome nourishing food and education suitable to their years and health, none of which they would receive from the petitioner. The man on the street would see that as plainly as the nose on his face; Lord Miller, she was sure, would have little difficulty ruling in her favour. It was unconscionable that two illegitimate children who had been brought to Gowanlea over three years ago, sickly and starved, could be removed. Not to mention that their mother hadn't once seen fit to visit them and had made no payment for their care. And how could she care for them when she'd be out of the house all day working? Eliza had faith that God – and Lord Miller – would do the right thing. Yes, Mr Rennie had a lot to learn, not just about how Gowanlea worked but about how the law of the land worked. Still, he was a pleasant and eager young man who had come highly recommended by Mr Allan, who, until last year, had been Eliza's legal counsel for almost a quarter of a century. And Mr Rennie had done a good enough job with the necessaries surrounding the completion of the extension. It would simply take time to educate him in the ways of the world in a manner no legal texts could. "Yes, Mr Rennie, I'm sure you're right. I've also had dealings with Lord Miller and he is indeed a man of great wisdom and warmth. As I said earlier in the meeting, I'll have my written answer ready in the next day or so."

"Thank you, Miss Frew. I'm sure I'll have very little to add to it. Mr Allan told me you're extremely well-versed and fluent in your court submissions."

Eliza laughed. "Well, with practice comes proficiency. But kind of Mr Allan to say so. Although I think in praising me he's really praising himself, for everything I know about the law, I learned from him."

"I hope in due course you'll also learn things from me, Miss Frew."

Eliza smiled. She had probably appeared in court more times than young Mr Rennie. "Of course."

"But now, if you'll excuse me, Miss Frew, I need to have a word with Mr Smith about the auditing of the accounts."

"Certainly."

Eliza sat down at the little table in the bay window and sipped her tea. Victoria Square was one of the finest addresses in town and, when she visited, she sometimes allowed herself to daydream about what life might have been like had she married someone, like ex-Provost Brown, who would have kept her in the manner to which she'd become accustomed as a girl. She hadn't seen any more of the house than the entrance hall and drawing room but she was sure the other rooms would be similarly large and elegant. It wasn't that she had any regrets about her calling, but in years gone by, before the extension, when she'd had two children's cots in her bedroom due to lack of space, Eliza had wondered what it might be like to sleep in a spacious bedroom and to look out over the square of a morning as she was served breakfast. And during difficult periods, she had sometimes feared that as time went on she might become less able to withstand the pressures that came with running Gowanlea. But when she had feared, she had prayed and had faith that God would provide what was needed.

As she put her cup and saucer on the table, she noticed a movement at one of the oak trees. A figure stepped out from behind it, looked over to the window and waved at her. Eliza caught her breath and glanced over her shoulder lest the other board members had seen the exchange. But they were too busy conversing to have noticed. She got up hastily, said her thanks and farewells, then bustled out of the house.

When she was certain there was no one on the street, she crossed over to the grassy square where Thomas Keith was. "What are you doing here?" she rasped. "How dare you? How did you know I was here?"

He pushed away from the tree. "Your maid. Winnie, is it? A—"

"You stay away from her!" Eliza said, taking a step towards him.

"Charming girl. And pretty too. Yes. Very pretty. She was most helpful. When I explained that I was keen to become a benefactor and wished to bequeath a significant sum to the Home, she was most eager to tell me you were at a board meeting at the ex-Provost's house and would be back in the afternoon. But I thought, why wait until then? Why not go and see Miss Frew there and perhaps meet some of the trustees and see how much they know about her past?"

Eliza stepped behind the tree so she couldn't be seen from the drawing room. "What do you want? I told you, I don't have anything to give you."

"And I told you, Miss Frew, that I'd be back. I've given you more than enough time to gather a modest amount. As I said before, I'm not an unreasonable man."

Eliza slouched. She'd hoped the threat of the great and the good of Stirling drumming him out of town would have been enough to warn Mr Keith off. But it seemed the young man had more backbone than his father ever did. Or perhaps it was simply that, as his father before him, he had a good conceit of himself.

"Now, I'm prepared to give you one last chance," he said, standing closer to her. "I believe the Home's annual concert is taking place soon at the Albert Halls." Eliza glared at him. His blue eyes shone. "And from all accounts, it's usually a most enjoyable evening – patronised by everyone who's anyone in town. It sounds like something I shouldn't miss."

"You wouldn't!"

"Yes. I'm very much looking forward to hearing the little ones you care for sing. I'm sure they do so beautifully."

"You can't!"

"So you have until then."

"You mustn't!"

"And unless you bring me a first instalment before the end

of the concert, I'll make sure I introduce myself to your board members and talk to as many of the audience as I can about their beloved Miss Frew." He grasped her arm. "Do you hear me?" Eliza looked at the ground to hide her fear and nodded. "Good. For, I swear – it's your last chance."

As he walked away from her, she keeked around the tree and over to the bay window. Through the reflections of the branches in the glass, she could see figures still standing chatting, tea cups in hand. Her encounter with Thomas Keith seemed to have passed unseen, at least by that group of the great and the good.

She crept along behind the trees towards the town side of the square. As she turned into Clarendon Place she started to trot, not stopping until she reached the junction with Dumbarton Road, which she crossed diagonally to avoid facing the Episcopal Church. To return home, she could either take the main thoroughfare and risk meeting people, or the Back Walk, and hope to get there without being apprehended. At least that was an easy choice. Unlike the one Thomas Keith had given her. Just as William had left her with no good choice in 1874, now his son had done the same.

When she arrived back at Gowanlea, via the Back Walk, Eliza went straight to her study and closed the door. She reached across her heaped desk, and from the stack of annual reports on the little wall shelf extracted the one from 1898. She opened the back cover, took out the banknotes and put them to one side before reading the statement printed on the last page.

> *Miss Frew's numerous friends will be sorry to hear that she*
> *has come through a serious illness, and that she is still far*
> *from strong. In the past ten years, she has borne the strain,*
> *not only of managing the Home, but also of getting the money*

*to maintain it. This has been an arduous work, very bravely
and successfully done during this long period; but it is now
telling on her health. Many friends, from time to time, have
urged Miss Frew to take a salary, but this she has never
consented to, preferring to trust God for all her personal
needs. Under these circumstances it has given a few friends
very real pleasure to hand over £30 to Miss Frew as a small
expression of their sympathy and appreciation of her work, in
the hope that she will take a longer and much needed rest than
she has as yet taken, and by that means be fitted to carry on
her life work for many years to come.*

James Brown, Daniel Allan, Trustees

The money had been in the report for two years. Although
Eliza had gratefully accepted it at the time, her intention was
that it would only ever be used, if needed, to support
Gowanlea, not her. But there was no doubt that it had been a
personal gift to her, so it was for her to decide how best to
make use of it. The concert was soon and she couldn't risk
calling Thomas Keith's bluff again. If she gave him a token
amount, that might buy her some time to consider how best to
go forward.

Rona and Jackie barked in the hall. Eliza closed the annual
report, put it back with the rest and slipped the money into the
pocket of her dress. She heard Winnie invite a visitor to step
inside. Then there came a knock on her study door. The girl
stuck her head around.

"Miss Frew? Miss Alice Knight is here and would like to
speak with you, if you have a moment."

"Oh." Eliza checked that the annual reports looked
undisturbed on the shelf. "Yes, of course. Bring her through."

She had barely got to her feet when Alice came bustling in,
clutching some pamphlets in one hand and an envelope in the
other. "Eliza, good afternoon! I won't keep you but I just

wanted to let you know that all the arrangements have been made now for transporting the children to the spring fete. I've managed to secure – not that it was that difficult, since everyone was competing to see how much they could do for you – enough carriages for everyone from Gowanlea and they're at your disposal for the duration. Obviously, the League is waiving admission fees for your party, and I promise you, Eliza, there will be no speeches, just entertainments. We have marionettes, jugglers, ventriloquists, conjurors, swings, pony rides, shooting galleries and, most exciting as far as the children will be concerned, a carousel."

"Yes, I'd heard you were hoping to—"

"And if Dame President Mrs Irvine is still insisting on reciting some poetry ..." Alice raised her eyebrows. "... I'll ensure there's nothing by Kipling, nothing political at all. We'll leave that to Lord Salisbury."

"Well, I—"

"Now, I know what you're going to say, Eliza – 'Make sure no written material is given to the children.' So while there may be a few pamphlets blowing in the wind ..." Alice waved the ones in her hand at Eliza. "... I cannot be accountable for all the League's members. But if there are a few pamphlets, they'll be very discreet. As the Secretary for the National Union of Conservative Associations recently said, 'The Primrose League is not a Tory party organisation, it is pledged to no party and it is only a device of the wicked Gladstonians to call them such.' And, in any case, Eliza, although you're always at pains not to be seen to favour one political side or the other, I know you're equally capable of overlooking politics when there's a prospect of a donation to the Gowanlea coffers." She winked and proferred one of the pamphlets but Eliza shook her head. "Yes, you're an astute businesswoman and one of your greatest skills is making politicians on all sides believe you're secretly on theirs. Don't worry, though. Your secret's safe with me." Alice laughed. "All your secrets are!"

"What?" Eliza took a sharp breath.

"Yes, that's what I said to Jane. 'Just you watch, dear, that receipt book of Miss Frew's will be working very hard at the fete, believe you me.' Talking of Jane, she told me William Keith has died."

Eliza turned away and made to shuffle some paperwork on her desk. "Yes."

"How strange after all this time that his son came to tell you."

"Well, I believe he was passing through on business so thought he'd call." Eliza pressed the tip of her index finger into her thumbnail. "Out of respect for Catherine, I presume."

"But it was such a very long time ago. Although I always suspected William still held a candle for Catherine, even after they separated. But it wasn't to be, so there we are."

"Yes, there we are." Eliza bit her cheek and lifted and laid a few things. "Anyway, I'm sure you still have a lot to do to prepare for the fete and I've also got things to attend to, so ..."

"Which reminds me. Here ..." Alice cast the envelope she'd been holding onto the desk. "It's from Mr Risk. I met him on the way here, and when I mentioned I was calling, he insisted on sending me off with a donation."

"Thank you. I'll be sure to send him a receipt."

"And just you wait ..." Alice patted her on the back. "... the whole town will be at the fete so your coffers are sure to be bulging afterwards. There's a lot more where that came from."

Eliza's head dropped. That was precisely what she was worried about.

CHAPTER 9

JANE GAZED out over the expanse of lawn at the refreshment marquee, carousel, stalls, and the roped-off area where the brass band was setting up. Hundreds of people from all classes and walks of life were milling around the attractions.

Almost every other person who passed seemed to know Aunt Alice. After they'd moved on, her aunt regaled Jane with their names and what their stations in life were. There seemed to be a rash of tradesmen, many without female companions or children, whose interest in the fete had surprised Jane, until Aunt Alice had explained *sotto voce*: "The working man can't risk being boycotted. Not that such a thing would ever happen, of course. The Primrose League is about fighting for free enterprise, not destroying it."

The official platform, bedecked with yellow primroses, was to the left. Miss Frew had allowed only those children who were members of the Honour Bright Club to accept the gift of a flower, and even then, only on the basis that it would be used as nothing more than a study specimen. *The only sermons given to our little lambs are the Lord's.* Jane smiled, reflecting on the friendly friction between Aunt Alice and Gowanlea's matriarch.

She turned to Aunt Alice in the next deckchair. Her eyes were closed and her face raised to the sun. "Have you always known Miss Frew?"

"Hmm?" Aunt Alice opened her eyes and leaned towards Jane. "Miss Frew? Ha! Yes. Since we were girls. Her family came here when she was seven."

"Did you know her sister well, too?"

"Catherine? Yes, I knew her fairly well. God rest her poor soul."

"What happened to her?"

"Consumption. She was just twenty-five."

"How sad. Was she older than Miss Frew?"

"Yes, but there was only a year between them."

Jane swallowed. The same as between her and RJ. "And you'd know then, I suppose, her fiancé, the late Mr Keith. Do you know why they didn't marry?"

"Oh yes, I knew William Keith." Aunt Alice reclined again and clasped her hands together on her lap. "Yes. He was quite the dashing young man, although I always thought him shallow. He and Miss Frew's sister were well-suited in that regard." Jane raised her eyebrows. "Yes. They were engaged for a time but it was called off. Although I think perhaps he came to regret it. You see, that's what I mean about you and Harold making sure you don't extend your engagement too long. It can give time for doubt to creep in, then bad decisions are made, and before you know it it's too late."

"Well, if Mr Keith's and Miss Frew's sister's love wasn't sufficiently deep to survive a break, then it was probably as well they called it off," Jane said, reflecting that she now had a useful precedent for her plan to use the current separation from Harold as grounds for breaking their engagement.

"I'm not sure love had much to do with it, dear. Certainly, they seemed happy for a while, but they parted ways not long after Mr Keith's father experienced difficulties in his business. William didn't have much of a head for money either. He rather more enjoyed social than business affairs. They moved away soon after that to Glasgow, I think, and we didn't hear any more about them. Strange his son came to tell Eliza. After all, it's been twenty-five years and it's not as if he knew her."

"Perhaps, as you say, Mr Keith senior regretted parting with Catherine and his son knew that. Or perhaps Mr Keith junior has plans to re-establish the family enterprise in Stirling and was reconnecting with his father's former acquaintances."

"If he does have such plans, let us only hope he's a better businessman than his grandfather and father were." Aunt Alice struggled out of her deckchair, groaning. "Anyway, I see the Dame President over there. I have a delicate matter I need to speak to her about so I'll catch her while she's on her own. After that, I'll fetch Eliza and we can go for afternoon tea."

Jane watched Aunt Alice elbow her way through the crowd to reach Mrs Irvine, then she set off down the garden to the carousel. Winnie was standing at the base of the steps to the ride, waving at each member of the Gowanlea party as they did a round on the brightly painted wooden horses. Fred and Albert were on adjacent ones and called to Jane when they saw her. To think that only a year or so ago they'd been sleeping out on the Gowan Hills with their mother, a homeless prostitute.

"It's lovely to see them having such fun," Jane said.

"Yes, but they're all going to be very dizzy before the day's out. I fear I'll be wiping up sick on the way home."

Jane started to laugh, then stopped, realising her insensitivity. "Winnie, I've been thinking a lot about our conversation the other day. What you said about Hugh. I really think you should tell Miss Frew. She might be able to—"

"No! I told you. I can't. Please, Miss Knight. I wouldn't have trusted you if I'd thought you'd tell anyone. Especially Miss Frew."

"But there must be something someone can do?"

The ride stopped and Fred and Albert came bounding

down the steps. "Can we go again?" They were jiggling on the spot. "Please, Miss McKellar! Can we go again?"

"Yes, but make this the last time for now. The jugglers are performing soon and you wanted to see them, didn't you?" Fred and Albert nodded enthusiastically. "Right, off you go then. One more time." The boys bolted to the end of the queue, waving as they went. After the ride started up, Winnie turned again to Jane. "There is something someone could do."

"What's that?"

"In fact there's something you could do, Miss Knight."

"Me?" Jane touched her chest and laughed. "What could I do?"

Winnie glanced at the spinning carousel, then spoke matter-of-factly. "You could go to Canada with Fred and Albert and check on Hugh."

"What?"

"Go to Canada. Check on Hugh while you're there."

"I couldn't go to Canada!" Jane said, flabbergasted.

"You could! You could be Fred and Albert's escort! They'd love that. You could—"

"Don't be ridiculous. I don't know anything about Canada or about being an escort. In any case, I'm only volunteering at Gowanlea for a short time. I'm just visiting."

Winnie folded her arms. "Yes, just like you were in 1893."

Jane felt herself flush with rage. "How dare you! You have no business speaking to me like that. Who do you think you are?"

"You have to go, Miss Knight. You're his only hope!" Winnie pulled a piece of paper out of her skirt pocket and thrust it at Jane. "I can't lose him, I can't! If you don't, if you won't go, then ... well, he'll be in God's hands."

"What are you talking about?"

She pointed at the letter, her finger trembling. "Read that. Just read that!"

"Winnie, I—"

"You of all people should know what it's like to lose a brother!"

Winnie rushed off, leaving Jane rocking on her heels. She stared at the piece of paper, not quite believing what had happened. Then she unfolded it and read what was written neatly in black ink.

Dear Winnie – I hate to write to you like this but I'm fearful
if I don't and something happens, you'll never know the
truth. Things have worsened. I fear if the master doesn't do it
to me, I'll kill him first. I'll spare you the details because
you'll be distraught enough. But I have to act soon. So in case
I never see you again, I must tell you I love you and miss you
and wish we'd never been separated. But whatever happens
here, I want you to be strong. If it's fate that we never see each
other again, I'll be comforted knowing you love me too.
Whatever happens, make something of your life, Winnie,
for me.

With all my love forever, Hugh

Panic rose in Jane. Feeling faint, she staggered to the carousel steps to sit down. Her head swam and stars flashed before her eyes. She put her head between her knees. Sweating all over, her body turned hot then cold. The ride behind her stopped, and she clung to the bannister as a procession of children skipped by.

"Are you all right, Miss Knight?" Fred and Albert were looking down at her.

Jane jumped up and wiped her brow. "Yes, yes, I'm fine. I was just taking a breather. It's so hot. Anyway, never mind me – did you enjoy yourselves?"

"Aye!"

"Aye! Can we go again?"

"Maybe later, but you heard what Miss McKellar said. Go

and join the others now. D'you see them over there?" She pointed in the general direction of the jugglers.

"Oh, aye. All right. And after, can we have another go on the carousel?"

"We'll see. Now off you go."

"Are you no' comin wi' us, Miss Knight?"

"Eventually. I'm just going to get a glass of water first."

"All right!"

The boys tore off. Jane waited until they were with the other Gowanlea children before skirting along the back of the crowd and heading into the marquee.

A troop of women in blue uniforms with yellow facings, and with blue and yellow ribbons on their hats, stood to attention as they waited for their next customers. The smell of scones and cakes was delightful, but Jane felt too nauseous to eat. About half the places were occupied, but Aunt Alice and Miss Frew weren't there yet. Jane sat at a table on the perimeter, glad that the canvas muffled the hum of the crowds outside and intercepted the glare of the sun. There was a little blue vase of yellow primroses on the table, and underneath it a piece of paper, face down. Jane tipped the lip of the vase, slid the paper out, and turned it over.

WHY ARE WE AT WAR WITH THE BOERS?
To protect our fellow subjects from ignorance and oppression;
to maintain the authority of our Queen and country;
for equal political and civil rights for all;
and to lay the foundations of a lasting peace.

Tears pricked her eyes. She crumpled up the handbill before hurling it under the table. Then she turned her chair and stared at the wall of the marquee so that no one would notice her distress.

She should have known better than to come to the fete. It was too much. Certainly Aunt Alice had been circumspect about her Primrose League activities. She didn't share the discussions of the meetings she attended and she hadn't taken part in the celebrations for each battle won. Not even those for the relief of Ladysmith, when the council had brought forward the official opening of the town's electricity supply and switched on the new electric lamps in King Street, arranging a panel of bulbs on the Athenaeum to spell out 'Lord Roberts'.

Yet Jane couldn't kid herself any longer. Although she hadn't been able to face the celebrations, she understood them. After all, it was easy to celebrate when it was other people's brothers who had made the ultimate sacrifice. And the unedifying truth was that, had it been someone else's brother who had fallen at Magersfontein, and had her brother still been involved in the fray, Jane would also have been out in the streets celebrating. RJ would have expected nothing less. He had volunteered with gusto and believed in the cause. He had probably believed, too, that he would willingly die for it, as young men were wont to when they thought it would never happen to them. Aunt Alice had said that the victories belonged to every soldier wherever they'd fought. "Each battle, whether won or lost, leads to the end of the war. Without Magersfontein, there would have been no Ladysmith. Your brother is part of every victory."

Jane took a primrose from the vase and pulled off all its petals. RJ might have been part of every victory but what did it count for now? Honour and glory were of no consequence to the dead. If only he hadn't been sent to Magersfontein. If only he hadn't gone to Africa. She lifted the vase then slammed it down on the table. She would have done anything to save him, to bring him back home. Just as Winnie was trying to do for her brother.

"Jane, dear!" Aunt Alice was coming towards her, accompanied by Miss Frew. Jane quickly swept the torn petals to the ground, then dabbed her eyes and face with her handkerchief. "Yes, it is rather hot and stuffy, isn't it?" Aunt

Alice plonked down while Miss Frew stood scanning the marquee, no doubt for prospective donors. "Who are you looking for, Eliza?"

"No one," she said, somewhat distractedly.

"Well, take a seat then. Have a rest and let's have some tea. You hardly need to seek people out. Goodness! If anything, you need to hide from them."

Miss Frew turned sharply. "What do you mean by that?"

Aunt Alice laughed. "Well, I know I'd be exhausted if I was constantly approached by people feting me and pressing money into my hands."

Miss Frew cast another look around the marquee. "Oh, I see. Of course, yes."

"Even if they mean well."

She finally sat down. "They're not all beneficent and complimentary, I can assure you of that, Alice."

"Yes, but the ones who matter are, Eliza, so that's the main thing. Now, I'm famished. What shall we have? Mrs Irvine's scones are quite delicious with a little of her raspberry jam. Are you hungry, Jane?"

"Not really."

"Oh? I'd have thought you would be. It's hours since you had anything. You have to eat, dear. I can't have you going back to your parents a shadow of your former self. Although your father wrote to me the other day saying he may have to spend a couple of months on some business in London, and wondering if I might accommodate you for a while yet. It seems your mother's thinking of going with him and making a little holiday of it."

"Mother's decided to go with him to London?"

"Apparently, yes."

Jane furrowed her brow. "With her constitution?"

"It surprised me too. But a change of scene would be good for her, I think. And if so, your father doesn't want you staying in Perth on your own."

"So they're just upping sticks and abandoning me? What if I had plans to ...?"

Jane slumped in her chair. Plans to what? She couldn't go back to Gowanlea, not now that she knew about Hugh. How could she be with Winnie after what had happened? And how could she keep such a secret from Miss Frew? No, she couldn't stay any longer in Stirling. Yet now it seemed she couldn't go home either.

Miss Frew put her hand on top of Jane's. "If it's any consolation, Miss Knight, I, for one, will be glad if you remain with us for a good while yet, even if we don't feature in your long-term plans. Your aunt tells me you have ambitions to attend the School of Art?"

Jane harrumphed. Yes, she had ambitions to attend the School of Art, and the greatest champion of that ambition had been RJ. He had wanted her to make something of her life, just as Hugh did for Winnie.

"But until you take off to follow your passion, we will cherish the time you do spend with us," Miss Frew added.

Jane shook her head. How could she follow her passion and leave Winnie not knowing what had become of her brother? How could Jane, of all people, let her suffer like that?

"Yes, I keep saying to her, Eliza, that young ladies these days have so many more opportunities open to them than we ever did. And the means to take advantage of them."

"Not every young lady," Jane said. Winnie didn't have the means to travel to Canada to be reunited with Hugh.

"Well of course not, dear. But fortunately you do."

"You're right, Aunt Alice. "

"Amn't I always, dear?" Aunt Alice and Miss Frew laughed.

"I do have the means, don't I?" Jane sat forward and clasped her hands together, as if to hold in her grasp the plan she'd just formulated. There *was* somewhere she could go and there *was* something she could do. Something that mattered.

She might have been powerless to bring RJ home, but she wasn't powerless to help Winnie and Hugh McKellar. She took a deep breath to try and calm her racing heart. "Miss Frew?"

"Yes, Miss Knight?"

"I was wondering ..." Jane's voice faltered. Her chest felt like it might burst with the tension. *Fortune favours the brave, dear, fortune favours the brave.* "The thing is ... if you haven't already made alternative arrangements ..." Her mouth was completely dry. "... I'd like to offer my services as escort to Fred and Albert on their journey to Canada."

"What?" Miss Frew looked at Aunt Alice in astonishment, then back at Jane.

"What?" Aunt Alice chimed.

"Yes. I've grown very attached to them, you see, and I think it would be good for them if they travelled with someone they know."

"Well I never." Miss Frew sat back. "Miss Knight. *Jane*. That is most kind of you, really most kind. And I'm most appreciative of the sentiment. But the trip to Canada is arduous and conditions onboard won't be—"

"Exactly!" Jane retorted. "Fred and Albert are just children so they need to be with someone who'll—"

"They won't be what you're accustomed to. And the crossing can be very difficult. So no, I can't allow it."

"Miss Frew, I'm quite prepared to do whatever's necessary to accompany the boys. In fact, I need to accompany them." She stared at the remaining primroses, then raised her eyes. "You see, I think it's time to move on from my brother's death and to think of the future."

"Jane, maybe you should—"

"No, Aunt Alice, let me speak. Coming here has inspired me. You and Miss Frew have inspired me to think about others less fortunate than myself. Less fortunate than me and RJ. And how I might best serve them."

"Miss Knight, that is gratifying to hear, but really it's out of the question," Miss Frew said firmly.

Jane's shoulders dropped. "Oh."

In the silence that followed Aunt Alice ran a fingertip over her enamel lapel badge, a yellow flower, diamante at its centre, amongst blue ribbons engraved with the words '*Imperium Et Libertas*'. Two ladies then appeared, carrying trays with the afternoon tea. When they'd finished setting the plates and cups on the table, Aunt Alice waved them away and lifted the steaming tea pot herself. As she very deliberately poured Miss Frew's cup, she asked casually, "Have you secured an escort yet, Eliza?"

"Well no, I haven't but—"

"In that case, would you allow it if I went too?"

"What?" Jane managed to splutter just before Miss Frew did.

"Let Jane be the boys' escort, Eliza, and I will be hers." Jane opened her mouth to speak but Aunt Alice shushed her with a wave of her hand. "After all, I've sailed to India. I've experienced storms at sea and witnessed behaviours which, shall we say, you wouldn't wish a young lady such as my niece to be exposed to."

"Yes I know, Alice, but ..."

"But what, Eliza?"

"Alice, we've known each other for over forty years. I know you and your brother sailed to India to join your parents and I know that you're a match for anyone, man or woman. But your journey in first class was a world away from accompanying child emigrants in steerage. No, I simply can't allow it."

"Of course you can allow it," Aunt Alice said. "It's as easy as just saying 'yes'. Jane's right – what better for the boys than to travel with people they know and who care for them? Unless you're saying I'm less capable than one of your other escorts?"

"Of course not."

"Well then. As far as I can see, there are no negatives to Jane's proposal. After all, you've more than enough to be worrying about running Gowanlea in the exceptional way you do And, as you say, we've been friends since we were girls and have seen each other through difficult times."

"Yes Alice, but ..." Miss Frew looked abruptly over to the entrance of the marquee as some gentlemen came in.

"Don't look so worried, Eliza. Everything will be fine. Let Jane and I do this and remove at least that burden from your shoulders."

CHAPTER 10

April 1874

As The Reverend Goldie's booming voice echoed around the walls of the Baptist Church, Eliza opened one eye and glanced up at the platform party where Mr Henry Drummond sat, head bowed under his tall hat, hands together in prayer. It was said he'd performed excellently presiding over recent evangelistic meetings, and in the crowded Union Hall on Sunday had read requests for prayers, including one for the conversion of non-churchgoing inhabitants of the town, and another that more labourers might be sent to encourage their conversion. And that, on Tuesday, he had read a portion of scripture from the parable of the ten virgins. And now here he was at this meeting, convened especially for young converts, men and women alike.

Eliza's father had been delighted when she'd said she intended to go, her mother passive, and her sister dismissive. And when her parents were out of earshot, Catherine had said to her: "You have your sights set too high with Mr Drummond. His mind's far superior to yours and his heart will only ever belong to his beliefs and his books. You can't compete with the Lord for his heart."

"Don't be ridiculous, Catherine. I've never spoken to the gentleman, let alone contemplated a friendship with him."

"But you admire him, do you not?"

"Of course I admire him. There's much to admire. Much for anyone to admire."

"Granted. But life's generally easier when you have less lofty hopes. That way you risk less disappointment." Then her sister had laughed and added, "Look at me and William!"

"William's an ideal match for you. I think you'll be very happy together."

Catherine had shrugged and smiled. "I think so too. Our levels are similar in all manner of things. And you know father always says how important that is."

Eliza had nodded, imagining that her father's reaction would be the same as her sister's, were he ever to suspect her admiration for Mr Drummond.

The Reverend Goldie was speaking now about the difficulty that converts to Christ would experience in their daily lives. "You will be misunderstood. Misrepresented. Many of your previous friends will turn their backs upon you. There will perhaps be sneering allusions made, even in your own families." Eliza thought briefly of Catherine. "But ..." He raised his hand. "... these difficulties *without* will not trouble you compared to the difficulty of greater magnitude *within*. Which is looking into your own hearts and endeavouring to find something good there, instead of looking to the Lord Jesus Christ."

The formal proceedings ended with a rendition of a hymn written by the American, Mr Sankey, which, Eliza noticed, Mr Drummond sang along to heartily before leaving with the platform party for an after-meeting. A fine voice was another of his admirable attributes.

She left the church and started down Murray Place. After

she'd taken only a few paces, a black carriage pulled up alongside her. She looked up at the coachman, who stared ahead, holding the reins of the two black horses. One of the windows slid down and there was a loud whisper. "Eliza!" Then a louder one. "Eliza!"

She stepped closer to the carriage. Skulking in the dimness within was her sister's fiancé.

"William! What are you doing here? Don't tell me Catherine sent you to escort me home? I've told her and father that I'm perfectly capable."

He opened the carriage door and beckoned her. "Quickly! Get in!"

Eliza looked to her left and then to the right. "Why? What on earth's the matter?"

William jumped out, grabbed her arm and pushed her to the foot tread. "Please, Eliza! Just get in!"

She stumbled as she climbed into the cab, then fell over onto the bench. William hurried in behind her and closed the door.

"William, what's happened?" Even in the evening's low light, she could see his face was ashen. He pulled the silk roller blind down to cover the window. "Is it Father? Mother?" Eliza began to panic. "Surely not Catherine?" William shook his head and rubbed his hands. "Tell me!"

At her raised voice, he gave a jolt. Then he took off his hat and, with a deep sigh, placed it next to him on the bench. "Eliza, you must help me. I don't know what to do. I just don't know what to do." He slumped over and put his head in his hands.

"William! Tell me what's wrong!"

He sat upright and took a long breath. Then he reached under the bench, hauled out a large holdall and placed it on the floor between them.

Eliza moved her legs to the side and peered down. The bag was splayed open and stuffed with what looked like a blanket.

"This is what's wrong," he said. "I have to get rid of it and you're the only one I can turn to."

Eliza leaned over, tugged the blanket, then thumped back against the wall, making the carriage rock. William stared at her, eyes wide.

"Whose is it?" She glanced back down at the holdall. The baby was very still, its eyes closed. "Is it alive?"

William leaned forward and tilted his head. "Yes. I can just hear it breathing."

"Whose is it?" All he could do was look at her. "William, whose is it?"

Eliza heard him swallow.

"It's Nellie's."

"Nellie's? Who's Nellie?"

"She used to be one of our maids. She left a few months ago, before—"

"One of your maids?" Eliza spluttered. "So what are you doing with it?" William looked into his lap. "William, what are you ...?" Eliza paused, unable to stop what should have been an unthinkable scenario from entering her head. "It's not ...? It's not yours, is it? William?"

He took her hands in his and started to ramble. "It's not what you think ... well, I mean, I did, it is ... but I ... I didn't force her, she ... I wouldn't do that! How could you think I could ...? No, she wanted ... she didn't stop me ... I know I shouldn't have but ... and now—"

"She was hardly going to stop the man who puts a roof over her head and pays her wages," Eliza said stiffly.

"No, it wasn't like that either ... I ... Nellie ... we ..."

"Don't be ridiculous, William, that's exactly what it was like."

"No, I—"

"Where's Nellie now anyway? How is she? What does she ..?"

William let go of Eliza's hands and sat back. "Gone. She left the house a few months ago. I didn't know about the ... I had no idea. Then she turned up today, left it with me and fled."

"It? Do you not know if your bastard child is a girl or a boy?"

William looked at her, shocked. "Eliza!"

"What is it? Did I say something inaccurate?" she said calmly.

He shook his head, then gabbled on. "Then father found me and said that if I didn't get rid of it, he'd disown me. That he didn't want to hear another word about it as long as he lived. That I wasn't to come back unless, *until*, the problem was sorted out. If he disowns me, I'll have nothing. And Catherine won't—"

"Catherine! You think Catherine will marry you after this?"

"She can't know, Eliza! No one can know. I can't do that to your sister. *You* can't do that to your sister. Imagine the shame it would bring on her, on your parents, on your whole family. By association. And more than that, do you want her heart broken because of a silly mistake on my part that meant nothing?"

"For a silly mistake that meant nothing, you've ruined at least one life and seem about to ruin another."

"What do you mean?"

"William, I can take nothing to do with getting rid of a child. How could you ever think I could?"

"No, no! No. I don't mean getting rid of it, of harming it. Of course not." His smile was one of terror. "No. You see, I wondered if you knew any kindly families who might yearn to take care of a child. Or of any Christian association who might take it in and care for it."

Eliza shook her head, then folded her arms. "And what would you have me do, even if I did know of such facilities? Which, by the way, I do not. Knock on their doors and tell them where I got the child from?"

"Of course not."

"Then what would you have me tell them?"

"I thought you could say you found it abandoned somewhere."

Eliza laughed in exasperation. "When? Where?"

"I don't know, I ..."

"So you want to involve me in your deception? You want me to be questioned by the parish? You want me to sell my soul for you?"

"Well, unless you're going to tell your sister and your family, you're already involved in my deception. Are you going to tell them, Eliza? Are you going to destroy your sister's future and your family's good name? At best you'll receive only pity. At worst ... Is that what you want for them? For yourself? What other option is there?"

"How dare you!" Eliza thumped the leather side panel with her fist. "How dare you involve me in this? How dare you? I want nothing to do with this. This has nothing to do with me."

She turned away, pulled the window blind back a little and peered out at the church. The Reverend Goldie was right – looking into her own heart, could she find anything good there? And if she did, what would be the cost? William might be a deceitful fornicator but his assessment of the matter was nonetheless right. Would Catherine thank her for bringing her betrayal and sadness? Or for taking from her the opportunity of marriage into a respectable family and to a young man with prospects? Would her parents thank her for bringing disgrace into their home? For shattering their hopes that at least one of their daughters would take a place in polite society? And what of the child? Its mother had fled and its father couldn't bring it up. What hope was there for it in such circumstances? Eliza let the blind fall back over the window and rubbed her forehead.

"What about the poorhouse?" William eventually said.

Eliza raised her eyebrows. "No. You'll be seen by the porter and night watchman. And if you're caught it'll all come out, so you'll have wasted your time."

"The entrance lodge and porter's room are on Union Street but there's a back way in off Lower Bridge Street, past the asylum towards the hospital block. We could go there and—"

"We?"

"One of us would need to keep watch while the other leaves the child at the hospital door. It won't be there long, I'm sure. And they'll take it in, and at least it might have some chance in life rather than—"

Eliza shook her head. "I'm not abandoning a child on a doorstep!"

"I'll do it. But I need you there in case someone comes. And if someone does come, I'll pretend I'm the worse for drink and scuttle away."

"Scuttle away with the child?"

"I suppose so."

"And what then?"

"We'd need to try again later."

Eliza inhaled, then blew out slowly. "I don't know, William. What if we're recognised? We can't just trot up in a carriage, ask the coachman to wait while we abandon a baby then ask him to drive us home again."

"You're right. We'll have to walk. It's not far."

"But what if—?"

"What other choice is there, Eliza? Tell me. What other choice do we have?"

There it was again – *we*. Not only was William a deceitful fornicator, he was *manipulative*. Eliza wondered if Nellie had felt the same way as she did at that moment – that whatever she chose to do was a bad choice. While Nellie had fled to who knows where, that option wasn't open to Eliza. But wherever the two of them ended up, they would both pay for their sins for the rest of their lives, of that Eliza was sure.

She and William got out of the carriage, dismissed the coachman, then walked the short distance north to the junction of Lower Bridge and Union Streets. Eliza had her shawl wrapped around her head and shoulders while William, head bowed, walked behind her, clutching the holdall to his chest. The child still made no sound but Eliza couldn't bring herself to look at it. She was already burdened with too much knowledge.

It began to drizzle as they skirted the west boundary of the Stirling Poorhouse. Eliza glanced back at William, who pulled the blanket over the child to protect it from the elements. As they passed the rear of the pauper lunatic asylum, staying close to the perimeter wall, the foul smell from the nearby cattle market made Eliza gag.

"Here," William said. "Stop." Some stones had collapsed from the wall leaving a low gap. He pointed to the building on the left of the asylum. "That's the back of the hospital. I'll go straight across that area in front and leave it ... the bag ... at the door. I'll be quick. If you see anyone coming, em ... can you whistle?"

Eliza puckered her lips but blew out only air.

"Never mind. Just shout. Shout .... em ... no, just scream. Yes, scream. They'll think at first it's coming from up there." He nodded in the direction of the Gowan Hills looming over the poorhouse. "And when they realise it's from closer, I'll have escaped."

Eliza glanced up and shuddered. Heaven only knew what might be going on up there. She'd read reports in the newspapers of gambling and drunkenness, and even of women selling themselves. And now here she was, at the bottom of these Hills, conspiring in another sin.

"Eliza? Do you understand what I'm saying? If you see someone, the night watchman, anyone, you must scream. Eliza?"

She nodded, then took off her shawl. "Take that. Cover yourself with it then put it on top of the blanket to keep the child warm until it's discovered."

William gave her his hat in return, then wrapped the shawl

around his head and shoulders. "Right, I'll be back in two minutes. That's all. I swear to you." He put the holdall on the ground and embraced her. "Thank you. I don't know how I can ever repay you."

Eliza pushed him away. "Just go, William. Go."

She put his hat on and crouched down against the wall, gazing up at the Hills. She wouldn't look out for him and she wouldn't scream for him if someone came; this was down to William.

It could have been two minutes or it could have been two hours when Eliza's trance was broken by him grabbing her arm and pulling her up. "Come on. Quickly. It's done."

She knew she'd have to behave normally, despite her dread that there would be a knock at the door and she'd be detained by the county constabulary. But after a week, no one had come – the child must have been found and taken in; William must have gone unseen. Perhaps her actions had been the correct ones. After all, what choice had she had? Still, she had a leaden feeling in her stomach.

When she went down to breakfast, Catherine was already at the table. Now that their father had left for work, the *Stirling Observer* was spread out untidily next to her ('No reading at the table' was one of his many rules).

"Even if no one else is there?" Catherine would query.

"Even if no one else is there. Standards must be upheld in private as well as in public, otherwise they are not standards at all."

Eliza gave a little shiver; if her father thought reading at the table unconscionable, what would he think of his youngest daughter's unholy actions? He must never know, no one could ever know. She must find a moment to speak to William to cement their secrecy.

"Oh, there you are. Finally," Catherine said. "I wondered whether you were going to make it before luncheon."

Eliza sat down. "I've been feeling a little tired of late."

"Well, it's all that gadding about you've been doing to your evangelistic meetings." She prodded the newspaper with her finger. "There's a report of them here."

"They're not *my* evangelistic meetings. There were a great many more people than just me there." Eliza buttered a piece of cold toast, then took a bite.

"Oh, and there's mention of your Mr Henry Drummond," Catherine teased. "Several mentions, in fact."

"He's not *my* Mr Drummond," Eliza said, playfully hitting her sister's arm. "Let me see!" She snatched the newspaper and ran her finger down the page in search of the report. Before she was able to locate it, however, a different headline made her go cold.

Abandoned Baby Dies

She read the first few sentences, dropped her piece of toast and covered her mouth with her napkin. Then Eliza got up and scurried from the dining room before she was sick on her father's table.

89

CHAPTER 11

July 1900

The sea was calm and the sky blue, the land in the distance green. Jane leaned against the railings and gazed back across the water towards the harbour at Moville, just outside of which their steamer was moored. The approaching tender was carrying mail and passengers from Londonderry and, once they were offloaded, the *Neapolitan* would resume its journey across the Atlantic uninterrupted. The leg from Glasgow so far was probably less than a twentieth of the entire route, but already Jane felt as if she were thousands of miles from Scotland. And how good it felt. Not only had she left home behind, she had left behind the person she was there.

She closed her eyes, tilted her head and stretched her neck, enjoying the warmth of the late afternoon sun. Her back muscles ached, it was true, but that was only to be expected after a night in unfamiliar quarters. Nor could she refute that the third-class cabin she was sharing with Fred, Albert and Aunt Alice was spartan and disagreeable: its bunks were hard, its bedding rough, its furnishings minimal and its facilities basic. Yet Jane's exhilaration at being in a new environment trumped any of its discomforts, just as her conviction to travel to Canada had trumped Miss Frew's initial doubts about the trip. Her *significant* initial doubts. But gradually, that resistance had waned, though her insistence that the party must not under any circumstances travel first class, despite Jane's clumsy, though well-intentioned, offer to pay (her parents had left her a decent allowance while they gadded about London), did not. "I won't hear of it. The boys must be treated the same as others of their kind. Setting them apart on the journey would be wrong. Nor can you give them false expectations." Aunt Alice had also said it was a foolish idea, and had made it abundantly clear what to expect of third class, lest her niece harboured any romantic illusions.

"Then I'll accompany the boys in third and you must take a first-class cabin, Aunt Alice," Jane had retorted.

"Don't be ridiculous, dear. I can't escort you from first class. In any event, your parents would never forgive me if I abandoned you to third class. Not that we'll tell them of our little adventure. No, we'll be there and back long before they return from London. You can just write to them and Harold before we leave to say that you and I may be taking a trip to the coast – which, of course, is true – and that your regular letters may be delayed. That will save them worrying when they don't hear from you."

"Oh, I don't imagine they'll worry," Jane had said blithely, before adding, in case her aunt became suspicious, "and Harold is so busy at work at the moment, I doubt he'll even notice any absence of correspondence."

Aunt Alice had seemed dubious but not sufficiently so to question Jane further. Not only that, but she had also, after careful consideration – very careful consideration – agreed not to tell Miss Frew of Jane's intention to check on Hugh's welfare. "I'm not saying he is, dear, but what if he's exaggerating or being untruthful? We don't want to cause bad feeling or blacken anyone's reputation until we know what's really going on. And don't raise his sister's hopes either."

"Of course not, Aunt Alice." And Jane hadn't, although it had taken much to quell Winnie's excitement once she discovered that the Misses Knight would be accompanying the boys to Canada.

"Your aunt is a very ... interesting lady," Winnie had said once her astonishment at the news had lessened.

"That she is."

That she was, and Jane didn't know how she'd have managed without her these past months. From giving her refuge in Stirling, to encouraging her to volunteer at Gowanlea, and now facilitating this potentially foolhardy odyssey, her aunt was both saviour and guardian angel. Not that she was above giving her niece a good ticking off, if circumstances warranted it. Just that morning when they'd risen and Jane was congratulating herself on having easily survived the night in third class, Aunt Alice had put her firmly in her place. "Don't get carried away, dear. Remember that sub-standard conditions are only tolerable if they're fleeting, or all you've ever known."

Jane opened her eyes and looked towards the bow on the starboard side of the main deck, where Aunt Alice was sitting on a bench. Fred and Albert were nearby, watching some crew members prepare to remove the fore hatch to receive the goods and luggage from the tender that would soon be drawing alongside the *Neapolitan*. One of the seamen, a splendid fellow from Hamilton called Mr Naylor, seemed to have endless patience for explaining the ship's operations, and already the boys had acquired some technical knowledge which they were enjoying showing off.

"Miss Knight! Miss Jane! D'you ken the orlop's the lowest deck on the ship and that it's below the water? Miss Knight! Miss Jane! D'you ken what 'Heave short' means? We do!"

When Mr Naylor and his fellow crew member

disappeared below deck, Fred and Albert returned to her side. They looked so smart in their dark suits, collar and tie, and shiny boots, all supplied by Miss Frew especially for their journey.

"Miss Jane! Miss Jane! Mr Naylor's away down into the orlop. All the things from the tender are going down there. D'you ken what a tender is, Miss Jane?"

"Why don't you tell me, Fred?"

"It's a boat that helps other boats and brings all the cargo in."

"I see. That's very interesting."

"Miss Jane?" Albert joined in. "I'll maybe be a sailor instead of a farmer when I grow up. Mr Naylor says that ..."

At the sudden rumble from below, Jane and the boys looked back to the hatch. Seconds later there was a loud swoosh, immediately followed by an explosion which blew a furious cloud of dust and smoke into the air. Jane pushed the boys down and covered their heads as some heavy shards landed only a few feet away. When the deck shook again, she hauled them towards the stern. "Come on!"

The deck shook. Everyone froze, anticipating another blast. That brief, eerie silence was broken by screaming. A figure, blackened by soot, hair and clothes on fire, emerged from the fore hatch, then hurled himself over the railings.

Jane hurried to the wheelhouse, where groups of terrified passengers were mustering. The captain pushed against the crowds, and above the hubbub, bellowed for the hoses to be applied. "All hands! Flood the hold! Flood the hold!"

She found a nook in the railings and manhandled her charges to the ground. White faces and wide eyes betrayed their shock. "Fred? Albert? Are you all right?" She shook them until they acknowledged her with the tiniest of nods. "Are you hurt? Did anything strike you?" She looked them up and down. Their limbs all seemed present and intact, their hands and faces free of wounds. "Fred! Albert!" she shouted, which seemed to wake them from their stupors as if from a dream. "Are you all right?"

"Aye!"

"We're all right, Miss Jane!"

"Thank God."

"I prayed to Jesus to be saved. That's what Miss Frew's always telling us to do," Fred said.

Jane hugged him, praying that the flames crackling below deck wouldn't make their way up through the gaps in the boards.

A grey cloud of smoke hung from midships to the bow. Jane searched for a glimpse of a royal blue dress, a navy hat and matching shoes, or a red and cream carpet bag. But there was nothing of Aunt Alice in the scrum of arms, legs and heads in the surrounding blur. *Pray to Jesus she was saved.*

"Listen. I have to go and find Miss Knight and bring her here where it's safe." Fred and Albert looked at her in alarm. "It'll be all right, but you have to stay here." Albert's lip wobbled. "I won't be long, I promise. Just look out at the water. Don't look anywhere else and don't go anywhere else. Understand?" The boys held each other's hands and Jane embraced them again. "Everything's going to be fine. Just remember what Miss Frew told you. Pray to Jesus."

She hauled herself along the railings, squeezing through groups of people, some tending to wounds, others comforting their fellows. The deck was littered with debris and she kicked aside purses, caps, books and dolls. As she stepped over a man's brown glove, she realised with horror it was still covering a severed hand. She flopped onto the railings and retched, trying to shut out the cries of, "Look away! Oh Lord, look away!" coming from somewhere nearby. She stared down at the water lapping the hull; would it be easier just to plummet into the water? Jane screamed, then steeled herself. She had to find Aunt Alice, no matter what horror she might see. She had to know Aunt Alice was alive. She grasped the railings and, still facing out to sea, side-stepped her way to the bow.

When she reached the benches on the port side, she turned and looked across to where Aunt Alice had been sitting. "Oh God!" She was lying on the deck, a man crouched beside her.

Jane ran over and dropped to her knees. "Aunt Alice!" she cried, shaking her. "Are you all right?"

Her aunt let out a howl. The young man pushed Jane's hand away. "Don't touch her there! Her shoulder's dislocated!"

"What? Aunt Alice? Are you all right?"

Aunt Alice groaned and rubbed her arm. "I'm fine, dear, just a bit shaken, that's all. I was knocked off the bench in all the kerfuffle and landed on my shoulder. Which this young man has kindly put back in."

The man deftly made a sling from a stray headscarf and gently manoeuvred Aunt Alice's arm into it. When he stretched the silk around her elbow, she yelped again.

"Are you a doctor?" Jane said sharply.

"Of course he's a doctor, dear. Do you think I'd permit just anyone to put my shoulder back in?

The man helped Aunt Alice up, steering her to the bench, where her carpet bag still sat. "There we are. Hopefully after a few weeks, it'll be right as rain."

"This is Dr Clarke, dear."

"My apologies, doctor," Jane said. "I was just so anxious about finding my aunt and so worried in case anything had happened to her that—"

"It's quite all right, miss. I think in the circumstances we can all be forgiven for being a tad fraught."

"Are you the ship's doctor?"

"Jane! Stop asking questions!"

"No, no. I'm just heading home with some colleagues. We were at a conference for surgeons in Glasgow."

"And I for one am very glad you were on board," Aunt Alice said.

"Well, if you're all right now, I'll leave you in the capable hands of your niece and go and see if there are others who need my help. There may be passengers with more serious injuries."

"I'm afraid there are," Jane said, on the verge of tears.

"But it goes without saying, if I can be of any further assistance, please don't hesitate to ask. It will be my pleasure to assist you in any way I can. Ladies." Dr Clarke quickly took his leave, disappearing into the wafting smoke, going towards who knew what hellish scenes.

"Oh, Aunt Alice!" Jane hugged the uninjured side of her aunt's body. "I'm so relieved you're all right. It's awful. Some people have been very seriously hurt, maybe killed. And when I saw you lying there, I thought at first …" Jane began to sob.

"That I was dead?" Aunt Alice put her arm around her. "Oh, it'll take more than a little explosion to kill me, dear."

"It's terrible, Aunt Alice, terrible. I don't know if—"

"But where are the boys, Jane? Are they all right?" Aunt Alice stood up.

"They're fine. They're safe. They're by the wheelhouse. I told them not to move while I came to find you."

"Well, that's where we must be too, dear. Come!"

When Jane and Aunt Alice reached the boys, true to their words, they were in exactly the same spot. Captain Bremner pushed past them and stood on the top step of the wheelhouse.

"Ladies and gentlemen," he shouted. "Can I have your attention, please?" A hush instantly descended. All eyes turned to him. "We will be evacuating the ship. I repeat, we are evacuating the ship. The mail tender will take you ashore. The wounded will be removed first, along with women and children."

Fred tugged Jane's arm. "Does that mean us, Miss Jane? Are we getting off?"

"I sincerely hope so." The smoke coming from the fore hatch had turned from white to black and it surely wouldn't be long until there was another explosion, perhaps even worse than they'd already experienced.

"Please remain calm and obey the crew's orders while you wait to board the tender."

"Three cheers for Captain Bremner," someone called out. "Hip hip ..."

Jane, Aunt Alice, Fred and Albert, as one, gave three hearty hoorays, Jane's the loudest of them all.

Whether it was the proximity of land, the arrival of the tender, or the captain's reassuring words, the panic that had initially taken over the ship subsided, despite the smoke continuing to billow from the holds.

The crew went around the passengers, selecting those who were to form the first troop to board the tender, and Jane's party shuffled slowly to the transfer point. In front of them was a woman rocking a baby: "I've found God. When that blast came, I relived every sin I've committed. The most awful one was having rejected our Lord Jesus Christ. But he saved me. So I've turned to him now and I'll never turn away from him again."

"Miss Frew always says that too," Fred noted.

Over three hundred passengers were led onto the mail tender. Jane regretted having asked the boys to count them, in an attempt to keep them occupied. For the boat hardly seemed large enough to accommodate two hundred. She shivered; surely they weren't going to survive an explosion only to drown in a sinking?

She focused on the very welcome sight of Moville pier, which came closer and closer. Close enough to swim to, should the tender go down at the last minute.

Aunt Alice tapped her. "Are you all right, dear?"

"What?"

"You're shaking."

"Am I?" Jane felt the tears coming again and turned away. "It must be the chill of standing about waiting."

"Right, boys, let's all huddle together. Miss Jane's feeling a bit cold."

As they embraced her, Jane became completely overcome. Whatever did she think she was doing embarking on this journey? Fred and Albert could have been standing near the hatch and been blown to smithereens. Aunt Alice could've been maimed by flying debris, or killed. The explosion could have happened far out in the mid-Atlantic, and they could've sunk slowly to watery graves. Just what had she been thinking? Third class accommodation should have been the least of her worries. But she had been determined. Not, in truth, for Winnie, or Hugh, or Fred and Albert – no, this was about RJ. Yet she could travel the world and it wouldn't bring him back.

As Jane sobbed harder, Aunt Alice stroked her hair.

"It's all right, dear. It's going to be all right. You're safe, the boys are safe, we're all safe. And the Lord is with us."

CHAPTER 12

E‑IZA LED Mr Lee upstairs to the playroom, where Ann and Susan Duncan were waiting to be questioned. So far the visit seemed to be going well, with Mr Lee impressed by Gowanlea and commenting favourably on the comfort of the Home and the keen intelligence of the children he'd observed in the classroom. As the advocate appointed by the court to enquire into the facts set out in Mrs Duncan's custody petition, he had to appear impartial. Indeed, he had adeptly passed over Eliza's subtle attempts to find out how his unannounced visit to Mrs Duncan's one-room house had fared. But, however objective he might profess to be, he surely couldn't think that Ann and Susan would be better off living in such surroundings. And with a woman no less, who, to all intents and purposes, had abandoned her children. Surely not.

"Mr Lee?" Eliza said, when they reached the first-floor landing. "Will part of your enquiries be into the abandonment by Mrs Duncan of Ann and Susan? After all, it was she who entrusted her children to me – most enthusiastically, I might add – in a quite deplorable condition of health. Perhaps their Lordships might find it helpful for their deliberations to hear—"

"Miss Frew, it is not in dispute that the petitioner, in utter want, was glad to entrust her children to anyone who could keep them. That she had the sense and goodness of heart to bring them to you and to a place where she knew they would receive love and care should count in her favour. At least she didn't leave them in the hills, exposed to the elements, or on a doorstep somewhere."

Eliza winced. Her eyes blazed momentarily at Mr Lee. But of course, he didn't know what she and William had done all those years ago. He couldn't know. She coughed in order to cover her embarrassment at her error of judgement in opening herself up to such criticism. "Excuse me."

"So, no, that will not form any part of my enquiries. I'm considering only the present character, conduct and circumstances of the petitioner, and her present fitness and willingness to support her children."

"Yes, of course. And I'm sure your report will be scrupulously fair and accurate, Mr Lee." He smiled, which Eliza hoped meant she had recovered the situation somewhat. "Now, the children are in here. Please follow me."

When she opened the door of the playroom, Ann and Susan immediately looked up from their dolls. They beamed at her. How pretty the girls looked, freshly bathed, fair hair neatly brushed, and each wearing a new dress selected from the recent generous donation from the Busy Bee Club of Bridge of Allan, who were well on their way to surpassing last year's donation of 131 newly-made articles of clothing.

"Miss Frew!" they squealed in unison.

Eliza held out her arms and, as they walked into her embrace, she gave each one a quick squeeze. "You remember I told you that a gentleman would be coming to talk to you about how you like living here and how you would feel about going back to stay with your mother in her little house?" The girls nodded earnestly. "Well, this is the gentleman, Mr Lee." Ann and Susan curtsied and greeted him politely. "The judges who'll decide what happens have asked him to speak to you, and to me, and to your mother. Once he's spoken to us all, he'll tell the judges what we've said and then they'll make their final decision. And ..."

"We have to do what they say," Susan said.

"That's right. We all have to do what the judges say."

"Even you, Miss Frew?"

Eliza laughed. "Yes, even me."

"Even God?" said Ann.

Eliza smiled proudly at Mr Lee.

"Because you always say God's master of all and that 'the Divine's hand's at the helm steering the daily course of life'."

"That's very true." Eliza cleared her throat. "And I'm sure the judges will take it into account. But before they do, Mr Lee needs to talk to you. All right?"

"Yes, Miss Frew."

"Yes, Miss Frew."

"Excellent. Then I'll leave you to it." Eliza turned to Mr Lee. "When you're finished, Ann and Susan can escort you back to my study. Won't you, girls?"

"Yes, Miss Frew."

"Yes, Miss Frew."

"Now, why don't you take Mr Lee over to the table to have a chat? And afterwards, I'm sure he'd be interested in hearing about the lovely outfits you've made for your dolls." Ann and Susan puffed their chests out. "You see, Mr Lee, these lovely china dolls are two of twelve kindly provided by the Misses Haldane of Dollar, who have also supervised the girls' handiwork. Now that all the dolls have been beautifully dressed, they're ready for emigration and will be sent with our love to the Church of Scotland's Women's Association, for the Girls' School in Calcutta and our sisters there. No matter how grateful the children here are for everything they have, each of them also knows, that it is more blessed to give than to receive."

"And the children made the outfits?" Mr Lee said.

"Oh, yes. Both boys and girls here are taught to knit and sew. Why, just this morning, little Patrick, who is only six, sewed a button onto his jacket. And our eldest boy, Dick, could compete with any woman in darning."

"Very commendable, Miss Frew. But shall we get on?" Mr Lee said, glancing over to the table.

"Of course, yes. I mustn't keep you from your duties. Right girls."

Ann and Susan, cradling their dolls, trotted over to the table, usually used for card games and drawing. Once Mr Lee had settled down beside them, Eliza left the room and pulled the door slowly shut. She paused outside the playroom and looked along the corridor towards the landing. No one was nearby. Then she held her breath and put her ear to the door.

Between the thump of her own heartbeat in her ears and the girls' soft voices, it was difficult to make out full sentences. Was that 'comfortable' Ann just said? And 'happy'? And was that a 'yes' from Susan when Mr Lee said Eliza's name? She hadn't directly tutored Ann and Susan in what to say, of course not – she hadn't had to. Because since the day they'd arrived at Gowanlea, they had feared a return to the misery of their prior life. The care and attention Eliza had bestowed upon them these last three years would speak for itself. God, in His love and mercy, had interposed to bring the girls to her and He would interpose to allow them to remain.

She moved away from the playroom and started downstairs. As she reached the ground floor, the front door burst open and Winnie rushed in waving a folded newspaper.

"Miss Frew! Miss Frew! It's terrible. Look!" She thrust the paper into Eliza's hands and prodded at the headline printed in large, bold capitals.

TERRIBLE EXPLOSION ON GLASGOW STEAMER
TWO KILLED AND TWENTY FIVE INJURED

"Oh, my Lord ... oh, my Lord." Winnie was going from foot to foot. "What if it's Miss Jane, and Fred or Albert? Or Miss Knight? What will we do if they've—"

"Shush, girl! You'll rouse the children." Eliza pulled Winnie into the study and closed the door. "Sit down and calm yourself while I read it." She plonked Winnie at the desk and put on her spectacles.

A terrible explosion has occurred on board the steamer the Neapolitan, *departing Glasgow for Quebec and Montreal and having on board a general cargo, 63 cabin, 432 intermediate and steerage passengers, and a crew of 100. The liner put into Moville at three o'clock yesterday afternoon for mails and passengers. Shortly after calling there, a dreadful explosion took place of such force that two persons were killed and about 25 injured.*

Four hundred of the passengers were brought up to Derry and were detained for a considerable time in open sheds along the quay. Ten of the injured were subsequently removed to the county infirmary, their injuries being so serious that medical aid was indispensable. Some of those who have sustained injuries are not expected to recover. The local agent did everything in his power to render the sufferers assistance and provide accommodation for their fellow passengers.

Attempts were, it is stated, made to sink the vessel but up to the despatch of our telegram from Londonderry they had proved futile. The liner, which is well-known on the Québec and Montréal route, was under the command of Captain Bremner, an officer of good experience and standing. At over 4376 gross tonnage and 400 feet long, it is in every respect one of the best and substantially equipped vessels engaged in the trade.

Eliza put the newspaper face down on her desk and sat in one of the chairs usually reserved for visitors or applicants. She stared at the photograph of Fred and Albert on the wall to the right of the door. It was hardly two days since she'd seen them off, so smart in their suits and caps, excited little men heading off for a better life in Canada. The other children had gathered in the driveway to wave farewell as they'd left for the railway station, some of them joking about stowing away in the boys' trunks, which seemed so large they might house a small child. Miss Knight was in good form too, glowing, distracted from her grief by a new purpose, and raring to embark on her first ever journey beyond the confines of Perth and Stirling counties. And Alice was – well, Alice was just Alice: steady, sensible and kind, the same she'd been for as long as Eliza had known her. Together, the four of them seemed an ideal blend of innocence, energy, enthusiasm and experience. If anything had happened to them, Eliza would never forgive herself.

She lifted the newspaper and re-read the article, conscious of Winnie's eyes boring into her as the girl studiously awaited guidance and comfort. "This is indeed terrible. We must ..." When Eliza looked up, there were tears streaming down Winnie's cheeks. She went over and put her arms around her. "We must pray to God and trust in Him that our dear friends are safe. This is truly a terrible thing to have happened." Winnie leaned against Eliza and sobbed. "We must be strong and believe they're safe and that no ill has befallen them. Over four hundred were saved. Odds are that our intrepid band are among them."

Eliza sniffed and looked up at the ceiling, as Winnie wiped her nose. The girl had grown close to Miss Knight in the past weeks and was more confident and assured because of it. Eliza was equally sure that Miss Knight, even if she wouldn't admit it, was learning much from the young charge who was so ably assisting her with the Honour Bright Club. Despite their difference in age, life and background, they were a good match. "Yes, if anything had befallen them, we would have heard, I'm sure," Eliza said when Winnie had composed herself. "However, let's send a telegram asking for news. Although doubtless the newspapers will provide more details in the coming days that will give us reassurance."

As Eliza lifted a piece of writing paper and a pen to begin the message, the dogs barked outside in the hall. Then there came a knock on the front door. Eliza tutted. "Who is that now? Go and tell them I'm indisposed. Whoever it is. Well, unless it's the Queen. Or someone coming to bequeath a hundred pounds." Winnie smiled. "No, no, on second thoughts, tell them I'm not in. Yes, that would be better. Take a message and tell them I'll contact them when I'm home."

"Yes, Miss Frew." Winnie went to open the door.

"Oh. Wait a moment." Eliza put her hand to her chest. The shock of the news had temporarily erased other concerns from her mind. She reached into the pocket of her dress and took out a sealed, brown envelope. "If it's Mr Keith, please give him this."

Winnie glanced at the envelope, then accepted it. Although Eliza knew she would carry out the instruction unquestioningly, and that no explanation was expected or required, shame compelled her to offer one. "Yes, you see, there was a biblical reference he was asking about when I last saw him. He couldn't quite place it. So I said I would look it up and write it down for him and also give him a note of some other passages that might provide him with comfort. You see, em, yes, his father recently died and I, em ..." Although she knew she was rambling, she couldn't stop. "... suggested that the good book has always been an excellent source of consolation for me and that when my father died it gave me

solace and the strength to, em ... carry on in the face of – "
Winnie was looking at her quizzically. "Anyway." Eliza
smoothed her dress down. "If it's Mr Keith, say I'm out but
that I left this for him in case he called."

"Yes, Miss Frew."

"Yes, good. Right. On you go now. Close the door behind
you and make sure you tell him I'm not here. Do you
understand? I don't want anyone, any visitors, in the house
when we're dealing with this." Eliza rustled the newspaper,
and Winnie looked as if she might weep again. "On you go
then."

"Yes, Miss Frew."

Once the door was closed, Eliza closed her eyes, shook her
head and slumped on her desk. Then, in a whisper, she recited:
"Therefore I say unto you, what things soever ye desire when
ye pray, believe that ye receive them, and ye shall have them.
And when ye stand praying, forgive if ye have ought against
any; that your Father also which is in heaven may forgive you
your trespasses. But if ye do not forgive, neither will your
Father, which is in heaven, forgive your trespasses."

CHAPTER 13

Sailing on a tender back down the Foyle to Moville, less than thirty-six hours after taking it up the water to Londonderry in the darkness of a drizzly night, was to Fred and Albert simply another fantastic element in what was turning out to be a more exciting adventure than they had been led to anticipate.

Their initial shock at the explosion had waned, and far from the dull monotony of a sea passage punctuated only by meals and prayers, the start of their journey had turned into an epic, stuffed with heroics and derring-do. From the sailors who'd hauled the passengers to safety on ropes, to the German man who'd found a baby and reunited it with its mother, to the doctors who'd treated burns, broken bones and far worse in the make-shift cover of the Moville coal store, all had fed the boys' exhilaration. And how Jane envied their resilience.

Aunt Alice, as ever, was more concerned with practical matters. *A telegram must be sent to Miss Frew to ease her worries. Essential items must be purchased lest their trunks hadn't survived the explosion.* "Let that be a lesson to you, Jane. When travelling, always keep money and valuables on your person. You never know what might befall you." And given the uncommon circumstances, Aunt Alice had also deemed that, not only would it be permissible, it would be required, to use her resources to make sure the boys' needs were catered for, even if some of the other child emigrants would have to accept handouts to replace items lost. "That will leave more provisions for those who really need them and who have no means of replacing what they've lost. Even Eliza would approve of that."

As for Jane – exhilaration was only for those who didn't yet have any sense of their own mortality, and occupation only for those who'd come to terms with it. Over two sleepless nights in a Londonderry hotel, she had thought more than once of heading straight to the city quay and taking a steamship back to Glasgow. And in between those thoughts of flight had come thoughts of RJ, who had departed from Dublin. Londonderry was a long way from Dublin, of course it was, but it was tempting to get on a train to go and see for herself the barracks he'd left with such optimism and the platform where his regiment had been so feted. To stand in his footsteps, the last footsteps he'd taken in the United Kingdom of Great Britain and Ireland. *Oh, RJ.* She would never know his final resting place, never visit his grave, and never be able to say goodbye. When Winnie had said goodbye to Hugh, had she ever conceived they wouldn't stand again on the same soil?

Jane pulled her shawl over her shoulders and yawned. The tender for Moville had departed early from Londonderry and the sun was just beginning to rise. A replacement steamer had been sent by the shipping company from Glasgow and would be departing with those who wished to continue to Canada at nine-thirty. Not everyone did, that was clear from the number of people who were milling around the deck.

Among those on board, however, was a group of boys from a children's home in Glasgow and Fred and Albert were getting acquainted with their fellow emigrants. Jane tilted her head towards them to eavesdrop on the tales being exchanged.

"I didn't think we'd be put up in a hotel. I thought we'd just bed down in the sheds by the harbour."

"I can't wait to write and tell them all what happened and how we escaped. They'll no' believe it."

"I hope my trunk's been lost so I'll no' have to read my Bible. And that I'll no' have any paper so I'll no' have to write letters."

"I bet you'll no' get out of prayers even if you have lost your Bible. You ken what it's like."

"Aye."

The boys sounded at the same time like children and elders, young in years but old in experience, excited to break free of some conventions but resigned to the certainty of others. In the days to come, would they pause to consider just how close they'd come to death? Or, with lives already consumed by simply surviving, would it just be another ordeal they'd faced and moved on from? There was something to be said for living in the moment the way these boys had had to. If not their circumstances, Jane envied their apparent peace of mind.

"Good morning, miss."

She gave a start. "Oh. Good morning, Dr Clarke."

He tipped his hat. "I thought perhaps we should introduce ourselves properly now things are calmer."

"Of course, yes."

He held out his hand. "Dr Stephen Clarke, at your service."

"Jane Knight. Miss Jane Knight."

"Delighted, I'm sure."

When he gave her hand a little squeeze, Jane lowered her eyes. "Likewise."

Now that she had a moment to consider him, Jane thought he must be around thirty. There was a hint of grey in the brown hair at his temples and, when he smiled, a wrinkle or two under his brown eyes. "And I must thank you again for helping my aunt. We really are most grateful to you for tending to her."

"Again, Miss Knight, it was my absolute pleasure. And how are you both now?" He gave a tired smile. "It's been a harrowing time."

"Oh, I'm quite …" She was about to give the polite answer, that she was just fine, none the worse for the ordeal. But looking into the gentleman's eyes, she knew he wouldn't believe it. "Well, let's just say that, like most of us, I've experienced better days than the last two." She looked away as the emotion started to rise in her, then managed to gather herself. "But the main thing is, we're safe."

"Indeed, yes. And your aunt? How's her shoulder? I trust she's not in too much pain?"

"Well, Dr Clarke, if she were in pain, no one would know about it."

"Yes. I imagine she's not one to complain."

"Oh, no! Ha! On the contrary – she's very much one to complain! Just not about anything that might suggest any infirmity on her part."

"Ah, I see."

"Yes. Did you not know?" Jane laughed. "Infirmity is for others, not the Knights. I'm surprised she didn't get round to telling you that while no doubt denying she needed assistance."

"Actually no, she didn't. She offered no resistance to my ministrations at all."

"That says much about your bedside manner then, Dr Clarke," Jane heard herself say.

"Oh, I think, Miss Knight, everyone's entitled to feel a bit infirm after recent events. But, as you say, we're just fortunate to have emerged uninjured, if not unscathed. There were others who weren't so fortunate." Now it was Dr Clarke's turn to glance out over the water. "No. I accompanied a number of the injured to the County Hospital in Derry and assisted the surgeons there as best I could. But I'm afraid there remain a number of people who are severely, perhaps fatally, wounded. The number of deaths may well rise above two."

Jane put her hand to her mouth. "And the two?"

"One was a crew member who'd just gone into the hold and the other a young Italian man, Giuseppe, who'd received a blow to the head. I held his hand as he ... he wasn't alone at the end."

"And the crew member – was it a Mr Naylor?"

"It was. You knew of him?"

"Yes. He was very kind to the boys I'm escorting. Very patient. He answered all manner of questions about the steamer and sailing. I'm so sorry he ..." Jane took her handkerchief from her pocket and blew her nose. "Forgive me, Dr Clarke. As you say, we may not be injured but that doesn't mean we're unscathed."

"Miss Knight, there's no need to apologise. Really." He put his hand on her arm. "I don't subscribe to your aunt's philosophy on infirmity."

Jane spluttered a laugh and wiped her eyes. "Thank you, Dr Clarke. You're very kind."

"I'm happy to be of assistance to you and your aunt, who, I must say, may find that the crossing doesn't help her shoulder. If the state of the ocean's anything like it was when I came over, she'll find herself being tossed around quite a bit. She really ought to be taking it easy with such an injury. You say you're escorting two boys to Canada? Might it be possible for them to join another group and be escorted with them? I understand there's a large contingent from Glasgow on board."

Jane looked across at Fred and Albert who were deep in conversation with their new friends. "No, I don't think—"

"Indeed I myself would be happy to supervise them, were you and your aunt to find it necessary to take your leave. Much though I would welcome a further week on board in your company, in the circumstances, it would be quite understandable."

"Oh, no, we couldn't do that. I'm sure we'll ..." Jane stopped when she realised her heart was racing at the suggestion of going home. "... manage just fine."

"Yes, I'm sure you will, Miss Knight, I'm sure you will. But the offer remains, so please bear it in mind."

"I will. Thank you, Dr Clarke. Again."

"My pleasure, Miss Knight. Again." He bowed and went to meet with some colleagues who were engaged in a confab on the other side of the deck.

How fortunate the passengers on the *Neapolitan* had these medical men on board in a time of such need. The number of fatalities would surely have been greater had they not attended the County Hospital to see to the injured. Dr Clarke seemed a fine doctor. And a fine man.

Suddenly thinking of Harold, Jane had a pang of remorse at her admiration for Dr Clarke. But she shook her head. How nonsensical it was to feel guilty about a man who had never loved her and who was only her fiancé to maintain appearances.

Aunt Alice appeared at Jane's side. "Try not to brood, dear. It won't change anything. Best to just keep busy."

"Oh, hello. Are you all right? Is your shoulder bothering you?"

Her aunt looked at her as if she had asked the most absurd question on earth. "What?"

"Your shoulder. Is it bothering you? Is your sling quite comfortable?"

"Jane, dear, there are plenty of things in life that bother me but I don't let them interfere with my way of living."

"Of course not, no. It's just that ... well, I was just thinking, you see ... if the passage is to be rough, which I believe it may be, and the vessel rolls, it might be difficult to keep our balance and there might be a risk of falling. With your shoulder the way it is, might it be better if we ...?"

Aunt Alice's eyes narrowed. "If we what?"

"Well, it's just ... I was just wondering – are you sure you should continue to Canada?" Aunt Alice looked at her as if she were certifiable. "You know, with your shoulder and everything. I mean, you wouldn't want to do it any further damage. We might find ourselves being tossed around quite a bit and you really ought to be taking it easy with such an injury."

Aunt Alice laughed. "Don't be ridiculous, dear. And leave you on your own? You know Eliza only allowed it because I was going to be with you. And events of the last couple of days have shown that anything can happen, so it'll take both of us to ensure that everything else goes smoothly. In any case," she said, patting her shoulder, "if I'm to suffer pain, I can just as easily suffer it here as at home."

"Yes, but you see, I was chatting with Dr Clarke and he—"

"Yes, I noticed. I don't think it's just my shoulder that's piquing his interest in us."

Jane ignored her aunt's insinuation. Still, she couldn't help but blush. "—he was most concerned that you should rest. In fact, he suggested, well, he *offered to* ... he said that he would be very happy to accompany the boys on our behalf and hand them over to the agent from the County Distributing Home once they arrive in Canada."

Aunt Alice's face darkened. "What?"

"Yes, or they could maybe join the other group and be accompanied to the railway station for onward travel."

Aunt Alice stiffened. "And you think that would be an appropriate way to proceed?"

"Not in normal circumstances, no, of course not. But with everything that's happened, with your injury and—"

"Don't you dare bring my shoulder into this. This has nothing to do with my shoulder and everything to do with you. You cannot seriously think about abandoning these children now? Not after everything they've already been through. And I don't simply mean in the last two days. Fred and Albert have already been abandoned by those who were meant to care for them. Are you to do the same?"

Jane felt her face flush again, this time with shame. "No, I just—"

"And what about Hugh? Are you no longer concerned about his welfare? And Winnie, what about your promise to her that you'd try to find him? What will you tell her? That the delicate, privileged Miss Knight bailed on her, too, when the going got tough?"

Jane had never seen her aunt so cold. "No! I ... I just—"

"These children are not merely pastimes you can drop when you get fed up or when things get too hard for you. Do you think that your—"

So steely. "It's not that, Aunt Alice!" Jane cried. "I'm just—"

"Do you think that your brother didn't wish, when he was marching into the fray, that he could just get on a steamer and come home? Where do you think the world would be if everyone decided to renege on their commitments? Have you any idea what Fred and Albert have been through and what they've still to go through? Or are you too busy with your own noble mission? Grow up, Jane. You're not a child any more."

Jane took a sharp intake of breath, unable to control her sobs any longer. "No, no! I'm just ..." Her chest heaved, as she sniffed. "... scared."

Aunt Alice glared at her. "Everyone's scared, Jane. But you just have to get on with it and do what's right." She lifted her carpet bag and stuffed it under her arm. "Now, I can't stop you, at your age, from doing anything. But, whatever you decide, I will be continuing to Canada to look after Fred and Albert, as I promised Eliza I would." Aunt Alice tugged at her glove. "We'll have a short period at Moville. I intend to visit the company's office with the boys to ask about our luggage and to confirm that I require passage, at least for myself and them. You have until embarkation on the substitute steamer to make up your mind."

Head down, Jane set off in the opposite direction from her aunt and made her way to the stern and as far away as possible from Dr Clarke, Fred and Albert, and the Glasgow group.

The ship's wake was the only movement in the otherwise still waters of Lough Foyle, and the rocky inlets and sandy bays at the base of the shallow sloping cliffs were twinkling. It was a far cry from the swells of the rough Atlantic. Surely even her father would be able to sail this route without falling victim to *mal de mer*. The thought of him, and her mother, gallivanting around London, oblivious to their daughter's situation, appalled Jane. How could she have gone along with Aunt Alice's exhortation not to tell them about the voyage? This wasn't some childhood day out to a less salubrious part of town, it was a potentially treacherous journey that had already threatened their lives, and ended the lives of at least two others.

But what could she do? She might want nothing more than to go home to Scotland, to Perth, to her parents' house, her childhood home, her own bedroom ... but there was nothing, and no one, there for her.

The mail tender manoeuvred alongside the pier at Moville, allowing the passengers an easy transfer to terra firma. Jane hung back as they trooped towards the harbour, where hordes still milled around. She looked out towards the Atlantic Ocean, where a large steamer was moored offshore. That would be the *Ecuadorian*, the replacement for the *Neapolitan*, ready and waiting for its passengers, as if nothing had happened. And why wouldn't it be? *Life goes on*. That was another one of Aunt Alice's sayings – it was only surprising she hadn't said it to Jane during her tirade. But her aunt was right, as she usually was. Life did go on. And whether Jane boarded the steamer or not, it would still sail for Canada with Fred and Albert. And Aunt Alice.

She walked slowly along the deck towards the wooden gangway that led down to the pier and gingerly made her way off the tender. Then she took a deep breath, before heading to the harbour to await instructions for boarding the *Ecuadorian*.

CHAPTER 14

Eliza sat up late into the night with her Bible, eventually selecting passages from Corinthians and Romans for the next day's prayers. Her faith had been tested over the years, but this test was amongst the most challenging. Not only did she have to convince herself of God's plan, she had also to ensure that the faith of Gowanlea's little lambs wasn't shaken.

In the morning, the children, solemn and earnest, listened intently and prayed for the souls of everyone on the *Neapolitan*. To quell the anxiety of those who might be taking the same journey as Fred and Albert in the coming months, she talked to them of J. Hudson Taylor and his six-month passage to Shanghai to save souls. And, of course, of Mr Henry Drummond, sadly departed from this earth three years now, who had sailed to Africa, America and Australia to spread the word of God. The same Mr Henry Drummond, she reminded them, who was born not far from Gowanlea and had declared that Christianity was what made life's burdens tolerable.

"Remember, children – 'Beareth all things, believeth all things, hopeth all things, endureth all things.'"

As the older children headed out to the Allan School, those

who were members of Scripture Union arranged to meet in the afternoon to read and pray together. The younger ones, on their way to Gowanlea's school room, promised Eliza that their bedtime prayers would be for Fred and Albert. Winnie, old enough to understand the dreadful circumstances but too young to cope with them, Eliza confined to chores in the kitchen, out of sight of bairns and visitors, lest her sobbing set off a contagion of misery.

As soon as the complimentary newspaper was delivered, Eliza opened it in the hallway and pored over the updates from Londonderry. A further two deaths were confirmed, the total now four: a poor sailor, intestines torn and face skinned; a fellow crewman, unrecognisable so blackened was his body; a young Italian, felled by flying debris; and, a poor woman whose ...

Eliza dropped her arms. It was almost unbearable. She closed her eyes and murmured: "Preserve me, O God, for in thee do I put my trust." Then she inhaled deeply and let the breath out, before raising the newspaper and starting to read again: ... and a poor woman whose head was recovered below deck. "For thou wilt not leave my soul in hell."

Further deaths were predicted among passengers who had severe burns and severed limbs. An inquest was to be opened at which the captain and coroner would be the first witnesses. Eliza glanced away from the article, catching sight of the adjacent column – births, marriages and deaths. *One generation passeth away and another generation cometh: but the earth abideth for ever.*

She folded the newspaper and tucked it under her arm. As she turned to go into her study, there was a single loud knock on the front door, which brought Jackie and Rona running into the hall from different directions. Winnie, her face blotchy, materialised from the kitchen but Eliza waved her away. "I'll get it."

"Telegram for you, Miss Frew," the post office boy said, handing her the document as soon as she opened the door.

Eliza felt a thump in her chest. "Thank you," she muttered, her hands shaking as she unfolded the piece of cream paper. Just ten words were enough to bring her the greatest relief.

Misses Knights' party well. Travelling on to Canada as planned.

Eliza's chin dropped to her chest and she put her hand over her mouth. Then she opened her eyes and read the telegram again. And again. Each time the words remained the same. *O give thanks unto the Lord; for he is good.* She kissed the paper and rushed back inside, shouting for Winnie, who was in the hall before Eliza could call her name a second time.

"They're safe!" Eliza shouted, waving the telegram at her.

"What?" Winnie grabbed it, then began to cry. "Oh, Miss Frew! Miss Frew! They're safe." Tears of joy streamed down the girl's face. Eliza held her for a moment.

"Right, that's enough. Dry your eyes and go and tell Cook and Nurse. I'll go to the schoolroom."

Winnie jumped on the spot.

"Go on then!" Eliza said.

"Yes, Miss Frew."

Everyone at Gowanlea, including those who couldn't yet read, wanted to study the telegram, so that, by the time it had been passed around them all, a little tear had appeared in the crease of its fold. Eliza flattened the paper and smoothed it down, then put it on display on the table in the hall, with a hand-written note propped beside it: *God is our refuge and strength, a very present help in trouble. Therefore we will not fear, though the earth be removed, and though the mountains be carried into the midsts of the sea; though the waters thereof roar and be troubled. Psalms 46, 1–3.*

To further mark the good news, they decided to add prayers of thanks and an additional hymn to the programme for the annual concert at the town's Albert Hall that night, even if it meant teatime would be rushed to allow for an extra rehearsal. "After all, Miss Frew," Ann Duncan said to Eliza when she arrived home from school at dinnertime, "it doesn't matter if we miss tea. You're always saying, *Verily thou shalt be fed*."

Eliza felt unusually nervous as she waited for the curtain to rise. But as soon as the children's full ensemble started singing the chorus of 'The Roll Call', she was becalmed. When the roll call was called up yonder, she would definitely be there.

Susan Duncan recited 'A Mortifying Mistake' with great intelligence and spirit, and the younger children acted out the song 'Two Hands' with such gusto that an encore was demanded. Miss Wilson herself, having schooled the children so well in their singing, gave a poignant solo rendition of 'Lead, Kindly Light', and young Mr Hill, an upcoming young baritone, delighted the audience with a selection from Gilbert & Sullivan. So sweetly did the children and the other performers sing that Eliza wasn't surprised when ex-Provost Brown announced from the stage in his vote of thanks that donations on the night had come to thirty-six pounds and eleven shillings, six pounds up on the previous year.

"This will be added to the Home treasury and spent judiciously, as usual, by Miss Frew, whom I must mention before bringing proceedings to a halt."

Eliza smiled at him from her front row seat. Then she held up her hand and shook her head in an effort to prevent him from saying more. But it was fruitless.

"This evening's fine performances by the children would not have been possible without Miss Frew, who, as ever, must be commended for the devotion and wholehearted zeal with which she carries out the noble work of child rescue. As a single woman, she bravely undertakes the highest work it is possible to engage in, the work of caring for children. In all her work, her motto is unselfishness and her badge is set forth in a wreath of smiles. Hope directs all her efforts, while love crowns each step of the path. Under such conditions, success is inevitable, as we have witnessed tonight during this quite wonderful concert. Ladies and gentlemen, Miss Eliza Frew."

When the applause started, Eliza got to her feet and turned away from the stage to acknowledge the audience on the floor. She looked up to the balcony that ran along three sides of the hall and nodded at the familiar faces of some of the faithful supporters who had championed Gowanlea since its inception: Mr Thomson Paton, from Alloa, was there; Mrs Hunter of Zetland House in Bridge of Allan; Mrs Lennox of The Station Hotel; Mr McPherson of the Barnton Joinery Works; the proprietors of the *Stirling Sentinel* and *Stirling Observer*, who would doubtless publish most complimentary reviews of the evening's proceedings. She looked up at the ceiling then closed her eyes and sighed with relief. Blessed. She was truly blessed.

Refreshments, kindly funded by Mr Mackenzie of Westerton, were provided in the Lesser Hall after the concert. When Eliza finally made her way there, after having paused en route several times to receive plaudits, ex-Provost Brown had a cup of tea waiting for her.

"Miss Frew, you have surpassed yourself. The children were magnificent. They are more of a credit to you every year. Given how anxious you must all have been about your travelling party, the achievement is even greater."

Eliza was about to speak, when she heard a voice behind her.

"Yes indeed, Miss Frew. And ..."

It couldn't be.

" ... I just wanted to tell you ..."

He wouldn't.

" ... how pleased I was to ..."

Eliza felt as if she had received a blow to the stomach from a medicine ball.

" ... hear that your party is safe and finally on the way to Canada. The children's tribute to them this evening was charming, and everyone from Gowanlea will certainly be in my prayers tonight." The reprobate turned to ex-Provost Brown and stretched out his hand in greeting. "Forgive me, I should introduce myself. Thomas Keith." Ex-Provost Brown glanced at Eliza. "Your speech at the end was most appropriate, sir. Your words very well chosen."

"Oh thank you, young man." Ex-Provost Brown shook Mr Keith's hand. "Most kind of you to say so."

"Yes, most appropriate. I must apologise for interrupting you and Miss Frew, but when I saw you together, I didn't want to lose the chance to offer you both my sincere congratulations and thanks for all the work you do for the children. And I'm sure your words, sir, about Miss Frew, captured the feelings of everyone in the hall."

When Mr Keith smiled at Eliza, she thought she might be sick. Ex-Provost Brown smiled at her too, apparently oblivious to her disquiet.

"Oh, yes. Miss Frew enjoys the support and sympathy of a large number of friends in this town," he said.

"As indeed she should, sir. As indeed she should. Yes, my late father, William, who recently passed away, was a close acquaintance of Miss Frew and her sister many years ago when his family lived in Stirling, so it has been a great pleasure to renew the family acquaintance in recent weeks."

"I'm sorry to hear about your father, sir," ex-Provost Brown said.

Eliza, silent and rooted to the spot, managed a sympathetic nod, so as not to appear ill-mannered.

"Thank you. It was certainly a sad event. However, on going through his effects, I discovered his connection with Miss Frew, which led me to come here to see for myself the wonderful work she does. I hadn't anticipated, however, that it would be quite as compelling as it is. What work you do with the poor creatures that God brings to your door, Miss Frew."

Eliza forced herself to smile and acknowledged the compliment with a slight nod.

"William Keith?" ex-Provost Brown said, stroking his chin. "Am I right, Miss Frew, that he was once engaged to be married to your sister Catherine?"

Eliza was startled by the turn the conversation was taking. "Um ..."

"Is that the William Keith of whom we are speaking?"

She clenched her fists tightly by her side until her nails dug into her palms. "Em, yes. That is correct, Provost." She cleared her throat. "But they were very young and, as is often the way with these things, over time they realised they were perhaps not best suited for a life together. Ha! Thank goodness for long engagements! And, as I recall, when they called it off, it coincided with the Keith family's move to Glasgow." Eliza glared at Thomas Keith. "Yes, were there not, Mr Keith, financial issues to be addressed which precipitated the move?"

Thomas Keith laughed heartily, brushing off her intended humiliation. "I wouldn't know, Miss Frew, since I wasn't born at that time. But certainly, for as long as I can remember, my father's business interests proved very successful. So successful, in fact, that I'm thinking of relocating to Stirling and carrying out my business interests from here."

Eliza gasped. "What?" This was too appalling for words.

"Well, Mr Keith, this town has many opportunities for those willing to work hard," ex-Provost Brown said. "If you need any advice, although I am no longer on the council ..." He looked over his shoulder, then winked at Mr Keith " ... I still have connections there."

"That's most kind of you, sir. I shall bear it in mind. But before I do that, Miss Frew, I'd be delighted to make funds available to you so the children might attend the Alloa Fair when it comes. There will be a circus, Manders' waxworks, hall of mirrors, merry-go-rounds, shooting gallery—"

"Oh, I don't think so," Eliza said, waving her hand dismissively. As if Mr Keith wasn't morally bankrupt enough, what sort of establishment did he think she ran that she would submit her charges to the influence of the rogues associated with fairs?

"... coconut shies, and all sorts of other entertainments."

"Mr Keith," she said, trying to find the words and a tone that wouldn't alert ex-Provost Brown to her animosity, "that is most kind of you. However, the children's programme is already very full at this time of year with events and excursions, and, of course, their own fund-raising efforts. In fact, we are already over-committed. So, much though I appreciate your gracious offer, I must decline." She turned to look around the Lesser Hall, as Mr Keith glared at her. "But should you wish to make an equivalent cash donation and allow us to use it as we see fit for our most needy purposes, that would be an excellent substitute. As I'm sure ex-Provost Brown will attest to, we are most shrewd in managing our finances to make the most of every penny donated."

"Indeed, yes! Miss Frew is a superb businesswoman and makes every penny count." Ex-Provost Brown glanced over Eliza's head and gave a little wave. "Please excuse me, Miss Frew, Mr Keith. I am wanted by the current Provost. Very good to meet you, sir. And, Miss Frew, what can I say? Another triumph."

Eliza and Thomas Keith waited in silence until ex-Provost Brown was out of earshot. Then in the battle to speak, Eliza got her question in first. "What on earth do you think you're doing?" She paused her planned diatribe to smile at some passers-by who had nodded at her. "This is an affront."

Mr Keith reached into his jacket pocket and pulled out a brown envelope. "I just wanted to confirm that I received your own kind donation, which was received with thanks."

"Put that away," Eliza spat.

"Yes," he said, slapping it against his palm, "and not just for the amount, which is acceptable to be going on with, but—"

"I said, put that away!" Eliza glanced around anxiously.

"... but for the lovely messenger you sent with it."

Eliza did a double-take. "What?"

Mr Keith laughed and returned the envelope to his pocket. "Yes, young Winnie. Lovely girl. I was only glad to be able to offer her something in return by way of consolation. You see, she was most upset about the news from Ireland, most anxious about the condition of her associates who were caught up in the terrible disaster."

Eliza moved closer to him and spoke coldly and deliberately. "You will have nothing to do with Winnie McKellar."

"But why ever not, Miss Frew?" Thomas Keith said in an exaggerated manner. "After all, the lady herself told me how much she appreciated my sympathy and kind words."

The anger was rising in Eliza. What a scornful, scornful man. "She is still a girl and unschooled in ... in ..."

"Miss Frew, you're not suggesting, I trust, any impropriety on my part?" Mr Keith grinned. "All I was going to suggest was that I would be very happy were Winnie, Miss McKellar, to be your chosen emissary to bring me your ... envelopes. In that way, you need not deal with me. Which, I sense, might be your preference."

Eliza put her hands on her hips. "It most certainly would be my preference, Mr Keith. But not if it means you have dealings with Miss McKellar. That I will not permit, despite my own disinclination to see you."

"As you wish, Miss Frew, as you wish. But I think you'll find Miss McKellar more open to me than you would care to think. Certainly, she was keen to visit the shows with me."

"I will not allow it. Do you hear me?"

"She is allowed time off, is she not?"

"She is. But while at Gowanlea, she must follow my rules."

"We shall see, Miss Frew, we shall see. Anyway, congratulations again on a splendid evening. I trust it has raised a great deal of money. As you know, the success of Gowanlea is very important to me. Now, a good evening to you, Miss Frew." Mr Keith bowed to her. "I shall, of course, be in touch."

CHAPTER 15

Fred and Albert pressed their faces against the window as the train pulled in.

"Is that it, Miss Jane?" Albert said, stabbing his finger on the glass in the direction of the neat brick-built house by the platform.

"No, that's just the station," Jane said. "Remember what I told you? We take a stage coach to the Home from here."

"Oh, aye. D'you think it'll be bigger than the station house, Miss Jane? D'you think it'll be as big as Gowanlea?"

"I think it will be bigger."

"Really?" A huge grin spread across his face.

"Really."

Albert elbowed his brother in the side and giggled with excitement. "Miss Jane says it'll be bigger than Gowanlea!"

Not for the first time on the journey, Jane smiled at their wonder and resilience, at these two boys who, hardly any time ago, had known only the same square mile of Stirling town. Who had now travelled thousands of miles and witnessed sea and landscapes far beyond their ken. Whose horizons, as well as ambitions, had widened. "We're no' going to be just sailors,

Miss Jane, we're going to be ship's surgeons, like Dr Clarke," was what Fred had announced on disembarking the *Ecuadorian*. It was a far cry from sleeping out on the Gowan Hills.

The group of Glasgow boys led the band of immigrants from the station to an adjacent area of ground where the horse buggies were waiting. As the group emerged from behind the building, applause broke out, and Jane stopped in her tracks at the crowd of people welcoming them to Brome County.

"My goodness, they can't often receive visitors if we're being treated as royalty!" Aunt Alice said, sidling up behind her. There was warmth and kindness on the faces of the ladies and gentlemen who were cheering them. "But how truly lovely it is to receive a welcome like this." Her aunt put her arm through Jane's; Jane could have sworn that she saw her swallow a tear.

"Look Miss Jane! Look! My trunk!"

And so it was – a bit more scraped and battered than when Jane had last seen it in the driveway at Gowanlea, but still with Fred's name neatly stencilled in the clean white paint applied by Miss Frew herself. How worried they must all have been when they'd heard about the explosion. But hopefully Aunt Alice's telegram had arrived safely, and the letter she'd written during the voyage and was just handing to the station master to post would bring further reassurance to everyone in Stirling. Stirling, *Scotland*, that was. For, as Aunt Alice had told them on several occasions since they'd left, they might find a few Stirlings in Canada, too. "But none, of course, as exceptional as the original after which they're named, my dears."

The trunks and the human cargo loaded onto the wagons, the convoy set off for the short journey to the County Distributing Home, only a few miles away. In the low sun of early evening, the mountains in the distance reminded Jane of the Ochil Hills, the gently sloping fields of the Perthshire countryside. And as the roadway ran alongside a large lake, Jane recalled trips with Aunt Alice to Loch Lomond. And trees, what glorious trees! There were the maples, cedars and firs that Miss Frew had told her to expect, as well as orchards laden with apples. So many that Jane longed to take her sketchpad and pencil from her carpet bag.

When the road veered away from the water, it continued through a glen. Then, as they emerged once again into sunlight, the wagons slowed and turned sharply up a narrow tree-lined track. Aunt Alice waved away the dust that rose from the wheels and hooves and gave a little cough. Jane peered through the cloud, which cleared as the surface of the track became smoothed by a covering of hay.

Albert leapt up. "Look, Miss Jane! The fancy house!"

"My goodness, yes."

The solid brick building was bigger than Gowanlea, all right, twice as long and just as high, with two storeys. The green shutters of its tall windows were handsome against the red tiles of the steeply sloping roof with its six chimneys. There was a striking white balcony on the first floor at one end of the building and, at ground level, a long veranda, its platform sheltered by a tin roof running two thirds of the way along. To the side was a plot of land with fruit bushes, piles of cut hay and a kitchen garden.

As the wagon came to a halt, Jane gathered her bag. A group of boys came running out to assist with the trunks, while a young lady in a navy-blue dress ushered the new arrivals and their escorts to the double entrance doors, which were splayed open in welcome. In the centre of the large, bright atrium stood a woman – of similar age to Aunt Alice and Miss Frew, Jane ventured – with open arms.

"Welcome, welcome, all of you! I am Miss Strachan, the superintendent," she declared, in a refined Scottish accent. "First of all, we must thank the good Lord for your safe passage and arrival. You have endured more than most on this journey to a new life, but now you can look forward with gladness to the good things that await you. You will be elated, I'm sure, but also tired. So tonight, before going to the dining hall to eat, then retiring to rest, we will gather briefly in the schoolroom to give prayers of thanks and to praise the Lord in song. You must rest well, because tomorrow afternoon the ladies and gentlemen will start arriving to find the little boys to whom they will offer good homes and sparkling futures. Now, follow these boys, who will show you to your places in the dormitory."

When Fred and Albert remained at her side, Jane put an arm around each of them. "You heard Miss Strachan."

They exchanged a look of apprehension.

"Are you coming too, Miss Jane?" Fred said.

Jane laughed. "Me? No! This fancy house is just for you, not for us. No, Miss Knight and I are going to the hotel in town." Fred's face crumpled. Jane ruffled his hair. "But we'll come back before we start back home to Scotland."

An older boy beckoned the twins to follow him.

"Promise?" Albert said.

Jane bit her lip. "Promise."

As they disappeared down a corridor, Aunt Alice touched Jane's arm. "They'll be fine, dear. The worst is over. Be happy. They're going to have opportunities they could never have imagined."

"You're right, of course. But ..."

"I know, dear. I know."

Miss Strachan supervised the procession of boys streaming from the hall. From behind, she could have been Miss Frew: hair in a tight bun, straight back, head slightly tilted.

When the last of the new arrivals had been ushered away to the dormitories, Miss Strachan returned to the atrium. Even the high neckline of her dark grey, belted dress was the same as Miss Frew's.

"Ladies – Miss Knight and Miss Knight?" Jane and Aunt Alice nodded. "How wonderful to meet you. Thank you for escorting the boys. I know that you stepped into the breach to assist Miss Frew, who I'm sure is most grateful. You couldn't have imagined that your journey would be quite so eventful, however."

"Indeed, no," Aunt Alice said, patting her sling.

"I trust your injury's not too severe?" Miss Strachan said.

"Not at all. I'm only wearing this to keep my niece and the doctor happy."

Jane gave her aunt an indulgent smile.

"Well, it's to your immense credit that you felt able to continue the journey after such a terrible experience."

"Oh, there was never any doubt we would carry on," Aunt Alice said. "Was there, Jane? We made a promise to the boys. And ..." She laughed. "... more than that, Eliza would never have forgiven us had we beaten a retreat!"

"Well indeed," Miss Strachan said. "Miss Frew would never let her goals for her children be thwarted by a mere explosion."

"Ah. You know her well then," Aunt Alice said.

"Our acquaintance has certainly deepened over the years. She's sent a number of children to us, all of whom have been polite, presentable and devout, and quickly chosen by those desperate to provide a loving home for them."

"What about Hugh McKellar?" Jane said more abruptly, and less diplomatically, than she had intended. But she was too tired for polite chit-chat; all she wanted was to lie down and sleep, and the sooner they found out about Hugh, the better.

"What my niece means," Aunt Alice said quickly, "is that, as well as escorting Fred and Albert, we hoped also to visit Hugh McKellar, who we understand recently had to move from his original placement."

The smile on Miss Strachan's face disappeared. "Ye-ess," she said, in a tone just short of questioning.

"Yes, you see, the boy's sister, Winnie – poor Winnie – she has a delicate constitution and has taken to worrying excessively about her brother of late. The separation has been very difficult for her. She was meant to come to Canada with him but was deemed unfit."

"Ah," Miss Strachan, said, as if that explained a great deal.

"And well," Aunt Alice continued, as if in confirmation of the assumption, "Winnie in her fragile state of mind, believes Hugh to be in trouble. Or even danger. No matter what Eliza or anyone else says to her. And so worried is Eliza now about the girl that she asked us if, while we were here, we could visit him, so that on our return we might reassure his poor sister as to his well-being."

"Miss Frew made no mention of this in her correspondence."

"No, she wouldn't have. But poor Winnie had a very unfortunate turn just a few days before we left, which convinced Eliza that action should, if possible, be taken to calm the girl's nerves." Jane remained silent; Aunt Alice was doing a better job than she could of presenting the case, embellished or not. "So of course, there was no time to write."

"Of course not, no," Miss Strachan said. "I see. Well, that's certainly most unfortunate for the girl but probably the right decision that she wasn't sent to Canada with her brother if she is so fragile. However, I can assure you, ladies, Hugh will be perfectly fine. Thriving, in fact. Yes." She started towards the double doors. "We have all kinds of checks to make sure the children are well-placed." Jane and Aunt Alice trailed behind her. "They're regularly visited by government school inspectors, and the ministers of the districts where they're placed are asked to visit to see that they attend church and Sunday school. The staff here also undertake surprise visits. There have been no reports about Hugh being in any trouble. And, while it was most unfortunate that his original placement came to a sad end, his new placement is with a man who's been known to us for some twenty years and has taken in many boys, training them all to be good farmers." Miss Strachan stopped on the threshold and gazed outside. "Mr MacLeod's character is unblemished – he came in the fifties as a baby from the islands – and he was given a very positive reference from his local minister certifying him as a suitable person to be entrusted with the care of children. He happily signed our contract and knows that there are certain obligations he must fulfil. If there were an issue, small or large, he would report it to us. And, heaven forfend, if there were an issue so irrecoverable as to require the boy to be returned, Mr MacLeod is required to give notice. And of course ultimately, we retain the right to remove any child if they happen to be disadvantageously placed or the agreed conditions aren't being met." She turned to Jane and Aunt Alice. "So I think you'll agree, Miss Knight, if there was any trouble, we would know about it. No child is lost sight of and their comfort and happiness are looked after in every way."

"Of course," Aunt Alice said, before Jane, impatient, could reply. "But still, for Winnie's sake, if arrangements could be made for us to visit Hugh in his placement, I would be – Eliza, Miss Frew, would be – most grateful." Jane curled her lip in satisfaction at her aunt's skilful handling of the matter. "And I'm sure Hugh would very much like to hear news of his sister too," she added, taking advantage of Miss Strachan's hesitation to emphasise her point. "I think you would agree that a visit would ensure everyone concerned is content."

Miss Strachan indicated to one of the coachmen to bring his wagon to the door. "It's best for the children if their escorts don't linger, ladies. We don't want to make any attachments that might have formed on the journey more difficult to let go of. And I'm sure you must be in need of some rest and sustenance yourselves."

"But we were going to come back to see Fred and Albert before we return to Scotland. I promised them we would come to say goodbye. Surely we can return to say goodbye to them?" Jane said, anxiously. "Particularly given what they've had to endure on the journey?"

Miss Strachan stepped outside and nodded to the coachman as he got down to assist Jane and Aunt Alice. "Given the exceptional circumstances, I will allow it, if it means they'll settle better in their placements when the time comes."

"Thank you," Jane said, taking the coachman's hand as she climbed into the wagon.

"And our visit to Hugh?" Aunt Alice said.

"The stagecoach passes by Mr MacLeod's farm on its route the day after tomorrow and returns the same way an hour later," Miss Strachan said flatly.

"Thank you. I'll be sure to tell Eliza and Winnie how helpful you've been." Aunt Alice held out her good arm for Jane to pull, while the coachman, in a rather ungainly and ungentlemanly fashion, manoeuvred her up from behind. It was just as well they were in the countryside.

Aunt Alice groaned as she landed heavily on the bench beside Jane. "We will, of course, report back to you, Miss Strachan."

"I'm sure you will."

Jane waited until the wagon had turned back onto the road before daring to speak. "I didn't know you were such a good liar, Aunt Alice."

"I didn't lie, dear, it was the truth in spirit. And sometimes the truth in spirit is better than the truth in fact."

Jane leaned into her aunt and closed her eyes as they made their way towards town and Cameron's Hotel – according to Miss Frew, the more suitable of its two accommodation offerings, being comfortable and well-situated near the Methodist Church (where she had suggested, strongly, they might wish to attend a service) and a small picturesque lake. There were also doctors, a dentist, a bank, a library with a reading room, and a meeting hall close by. Which all sounded very civilised. And safe, which was something Jane had come to appreciate more of late. For the first time since leaving Moville, she was calm. Despite everything, they had reached their destination and delivered Fred and Albert safely.

Now all they had to do was find Hugh.

CHAPTER 16

AFTER DROPPING Jane and Aunt Alice off, the stagecoach pulled away to continue its route around Quebec's eastern townships. Already this place felt as if it had been Jane's home for months, rather than just a few days. She gazed around the lush valley and the tree-covered slopes it bisected, feeling them familiar.

"Now, remember what I told you," Aunt Alice said, prodding her arm.

"Yes, don't worry, I'll just smile sweetly and leave it to you."

Jane waved the fan she'd borrowed from Cameron's Hotel in front of her face to try and generate some cool air. She couldn't say their lodgings were the height of luxury but they were comfortable and practical, with little touches in the rooms – like fans, and handkerchiefs – that Mrs Cameron provided.

"Visitors can be taken unawares by the conditions and we wouldn't want that, would we? I know what it's like for ladies coming to a strange place. I learned when I first came here that there are things you don't realise you'll need."

The hotel had been in her husband's family for years and she was the driving force behind its recent renovation and redecoration. "You should have seen the state of it when old

Mr Cameron passed away. I told my husband, I'll only be staying on if we turn it into somewhere people want to stay rather than somewhere they just have to put up with."

Jane imagined Mr Cameron the younger wouldn't have put up much of a fight, and that any resistance he might have staged would have been quickly quelled by his no-nonsense wife.

"They're like that, Highland women," Aunt Alice had said. "They've a lot to put up with."

But there was no question of Jane and her aunt just having to 'put up with' their present accommodation. Compared to their cabin on the *Ecuadorian* and their compartment on the train, their room on the first floor of the hotel was splendid, with a soft bed, wardrobe space for their clothes and belongings, two wooden chairs with cushions, a dressing table with a mirror, lace curtains over the big windows, and a door that opened out onto a balcony overlooking the main street and its pretty clapboard houses. There were carriages for hire outside, should they wish to take a trip – "Lake Brome's very nice at this time of year" – and the stage coaches stopped there too, making use of the blacksmith's shop next door. A bit further along, there was a general store and a bank. The Methodist Church was just a short distance down the street on the left, and Mrs Cameron had offered to accompany them to a service. "It would be good for you after the journey you've had."

Nothing, it seemed, was too much trouble for her and there was nothing she wouldn't think of to make her guests as comfortable as possible. She'd even given them canteens of water, and bannocks and cheese, for the stagecoach journey, an offering Aunt Alice had initially pooh-poohed – but two hours into the three-hour journey, she had gratefully tucked in.

Alas, there was nothing Mrs Cameron could do for Jane at the foot of the track that led to the MacLeod homestead. Her dress was sticking to her body, her hair damp under her bonnet and her feet sweating in her shoes. What she wouldn't give for an ice cream from Bertolini's. She glanced at Aunt Alice; although her dress was heavier and darker, she still looked cool. And, whereas Jane's face felt flushed, Aunt Alice remained pale.

Her aunt removed the top from her canteen of water, took an unselfconscious slug, then wiped her mouth. "What are you smiling at?"

"I was thinking about your Primrose League ladies and how appalled they'd be by your lack of manners if they could see you now."

"Pish tush, needs must," Aunt Alice said, handing Jane the canteen. "Just don't tell your mother we were swigging from a bottle like the women up the Gowan Hills!" Jane laughed, spluttering water over her chin. "Anyway, come on. You heard the coachman – we have just an hour then he'll be back for us."

Aunt Alice hitched up her skirts and set off along the track, Jane following in her footsteps to avoid potholes and ruts. There were fields on each side – one with cattle, the other with sheep – bounded by neat fences. As they got closer to the wooden farmhouse, the grazing pastures turned to fields of hay and the young men who were tilling the soil paused for a moment, silently leaning on their hoes, to watch the two strange ladies make their way to the dwelling.

"What a peculiar sight we must be," Jane said as Aunt Alice stepped over a dried-out cow pat.

"When you get to my age, dear, you no longer care how you appear to people. Now watch your footing there."

"Ha!" Aunt Alice didn't care how she appeared to people because invariably she appeared impressive.

On the left, just before the house, was a row of stables, five horses leaning out over the half-doors. Next to the stables was an open but covered barn, stacked with hay, with hens and their chicks pecking the ground in front of it. As Jane and Aunt Alice passed by, two sheepdogs bolted out from behind the bales and ran towards them, barking with excitement.

"Gracious, it's just like Gowanlea," Aunt Alice muttered, continuing undeterred.

Jane stepped around the bouncing dogs just as a man appeared in the open doorway of the house. With a single, guttural call, he shooed them away. Both animals immediately lay down, their tails pounding on the dusty ground so that little clouds rose up.

"Afternoon, ladies," he said slowly, slightly bemused. He had a rifle under one arm and a chicken under the other. His thick brown tweed trousers were held up by cream braces and his rough blue shirt was buttoned to the neck.

"And a very good afternoon to you, sir," Aunt Alice said jauntily.

When he started down the steps, a girl of around sixteen slipped out of the house and stood on the porch.

"Are you lost?" He spoke in an accent that was neither Scottish nor Canadian, but somewhere in between.

Aunt Alice stepped forward. "Mr MacLeod, is it?"

He squinted at her and tapped the toe of one of his battered, black boots on the ground. "Who wants to know?"

If this was Mr MacLeod, for a man of about fifty, he looked at least ten years older, with a long white beard and whiskers, and with strands of white hair poking out from under his straw hat.

"I am Miss Alice Knight and this is my niece, Miss Jane Knight. And no, sir, we are not lost, but we are indeed strangers. Not just to the county but to the country."

"I figured," he said, looking them up and down. Jane shifted on the spot; they must indeed look ridiculous to him.

"Yes, quite!" Aunt Alice said, laughing. "So, you are Mr MacLeod?"

"I am."

"We've come to the right place then," Aunt Alice said, as if their turning up in rural Quebec was as unremarkable as finding her way to a new tea shop in Stirling. "We've come from the County Distributing Home, to where we've just escorted two young boys from Miss Frew's home in Stirling, Gowanlea. You know of it, I presume?"

"I know of the Distributing Home."

"Indeed, so I'm led to believe. Miss Frew has sent a number of boys out to the Home over the years and she's asked us to do her a personal favour while we're here and look up a lad who will be familiar to you – Hugh McKellar."

Mr MacLeod twirled his rifle, then thumped the butt on the ground. A tabby cat, lying on the porch, which Jane hadn't until then noticed, jumped down and skulked away. "McKellar?"

"That's right, yes. Hugh McKellar. You see," Aunt Alice continued, as if it were simply a routine matter, "his poor sister, Winnie, is quite unwell and Miss Frew asked if we might visit to tell him about her and to pass on to him, in person, a gift from her." Jane glanced at Aunt Alice – *a gift*? "I know it would boost her recovery no end if we were able to tell her, when we get home, that we've seen her brother and that he's—"

"He's not here." Mr MacLeod looked over their heads towards the fields. "He's driving cattle to another town. Left this morning. It'll take him a day to get there, a day to rest and a day to get back."

"Oh, that's such a pity," Aunt Alice said.

Jane's shoulders slumped. She looked at the ground. After everything they'd been through, he wasn't here. The thought of the bumpy journey back to town without having seen him suddenly felt overwhelming.

"But he's doing well here, sir?" Aunt Alice said.

"They all do well here. I'll tell him you called, ladies."

Mr MacLeod turned away. Jane looked at her aunt in a way

she hoped would convey her desperation that something should be done. But Aunt Alice merely shrugged.

There was a movement on the porch. Jane glanced at the girl, who beckoned her with the twitch of a finger.

"Em, Mr MacLeod?" Jane said. He stopped and looked over his shoulder. Aunt Alice turned her head sharply. "I wonder, sir, if you'd be so kind as to allow us to fill our canteens for the trip back to town? We drank them dry on the way here and it's so hot. We're not quite used to such conditions. I'm sure you understand. It's the islands, isn't it, your family hails from?" She laughed. "They don't see much sunshine like this there, I'll wager."

Before Mr MacLeod could answer, the girl came down the steps. "I'll see to that for the ladies, Uncle."

Mr MacLeod grunted in assent, then walked away from them in the direction of the barn.

"Lovely to meet you, sir!" Jane called after him, her heart beating more quickly now.

The girl waved Jane and Aunt Alice up the porch and into the kitchen. The wall of coolness which met them made Jane sigh with pleasure.

"Please come in and sit down, ladies. I'm Eileen MacLeod. My father was Mr MacLeod's brother."

"Thank you, Miss MacLeod. This is most kind of you," Jane said, taking her place at the kitchen table with Aunt Alice.

"Not at all. We don't often have visitors, especially ladies on their own."

Aunt Alice laughed. "I'm sure you don't."

Eileen took the canteens and went over to the barrel of water sitting on the kitchen counter. She was a slim girl, with thick wavy brown hair that was only just contained by the clip on her head. When Jane swung back in her chair to watch her replenish the canteens, she noticed the girl's hands were trembling.

"Yes, very kind of you, indeed, Miss MacLeod. Em ..." Jane

cleared her throat. "We understand from Miss Strachan at the County Distributing Home that your uncle has been very kind over the years in giving a home to a large number of boys and in training them up to be farmers."

"Yes, I believe so," Eileen said, securing the lids of the canteens and letting the drips fall into the barrel. She brought them to the table, then went to the door and looked out into the yard. Jane craned her neck and looked out too, seeing no one except the tabby cat, which had returned to its spot on the porch. Eileen came and sat down with them at the table.

"Hugh isn't driving cattle. He's run away," she blurted, rubbing her hands together. She glanced outside again.

Jane sat forward. "What?"

"Why?" Aunt Alice said sternly.

Eileen got up and fetched a jug from the counter, then took three glasses from a cupboard next to the stove and poured them each a drink.

"It's apple juice from the fruits of our orchard. Forgive me, I should have offered it to you before."

Jane smacked her lips after her first sip, then glugged down some more. It was the best apple juice she'd ever tasted. "Thank you, it's lovely. I didn't realise just how thirsty I was."

"So Hugh ran away?" Aunt Alice said.

"Hmm," Eileen said, taking a drink. "Yes." She put the glass slowly down on the table and held onto it. "My uncle, well, he has very firm views and he takes to some of the boys more than others. If he doesn't take to you, it can be ... difficult."

"And he didn't take to Hugh?" Aunt Alice said.

"No. Nothing Hugh did was right. And when the boys don't do things right, he ... well, it got bad. He made Hugh sleep in the barn and only gave him leftover food. He stopped him going to lessons and didn't pay him properly either for his work. And the other boys, they don't mean anything by it, but if my uncle takes against someone, they have to take against him, too. And then ..." Eileen paused and hung her head.

"What dear?" Aunt Alice said. "And then what?"

Eileen's face turned pink. "My uncle thought Hugh behaved inappropriately towards me." Jane and Aunt Alice glanced at each other. "But it wasn't true! He's kind and gentle and he protected me when ... my uncle beat him, and after that Hugh said he couldn't stay. He was scared something more serious might happen and he'd end up in trouble."

"Do you know where he went? Where he is now?" Jane asked. Eileen was silent. "If you know where he is, please tell us. We've come to take him home, if that's what he wants."

"He doesn't want to go back to the Distributing Home," Eileen said quickly.

"We don't mean the Distributing Home, dear."

"What? *Home*, home? Scotland home?"

"Scotland home," Aunt Alice said, putting her hand on Eileen's. "If that's what he wants."

"That's what he wants," Eileen said after a moment.

Jane looked at Aunt Alice, who gave her a nod of encouragement. "So do you know where he is, Eileen?"

The girl looked outside again, then lowered her voice. "There's an abandoned cabin in the woods a few miles from here. I hide provisions for him near the track and he comes at night to collect them. He's asked me to leave him some money so he can take the train to the city."

Jane took her pencil from her bag and tore a page from her sketch pad. "Right. If I write a note, can you leave it for him?"

Eileen nodded.

As Jane wrote, Aunt Alice leaned in to read her words.

Dear Hugh – If you wish to go back to Winnie, please make your way to Cameron's Hotel and we'll ensure your safe passage home. We are friends of Winnie and Miss Frew and we know what's been going on. You're not in trouble. Use this money to get to town if you wish to go back to Stirling with us. If not, use it to go to the city. Winnie's doing well but misses you and worries about you. If you choose to go to the city, please write to her to let her know your situation and that you're well.

Miss Jane Knight, Miss Alice Knight, Stirling

Aunt Alice took some money from her bag and handed it to Jane, along with a postcard. "Put that in, too."

It was an image of the Wallace Monument, viewed from Stirling Castle. Jane turned it over and on the back were four words: *Your loving sister, Winnie.*

"The gift?"

Aunt Alice nodded.

Jane swallowed a tear and folded the money and postcard inside the piece of paper. Now it was her turn to glance outside. "Here," she said, sliding the message across the table to Eileen. Her heart was racing. "Will he come soon?"

"Yes." Eileen put the paper into her apron pocket. Then she sighed. "I'll never see him again, will I? Whatever he decides."

"Probably not, dear," Aunt Alice said.

"If he comes to you, will you tell him I'm sorry? And ..." She sniffed. "... that I love him?"

Aunt Alice squeezed her arm. "Of course we will, dear. Of course we will."

CHAPTER 17

THE BACK of Cameron's Hotel got the sun first thing in the morning and offered a bright spot to sit and draw the little lake that was just a hundred yards or so beyond. Although perhaps more large pond than little lake, it was no less picturesque for it. As Jane sketched the clump of trees on the far side of the water, her eye was sporadically drawn to leaping fish. So quick were their movements, she never quite managed to see one clearly, but their splashes and ripples made gentle undulations on the water and brought the otherwise still scene to life. Beyond the trees, the pointed slate spire of the Methodist Church, topped with a cross, rose into an azure sky.

Her stomach gave a growl. She glanced back towards the hotel, lest anyone else taking a stroll before breakfast might have heard, but thankfully, she alone was enjoying the view. She was peckish, however, and although she'd left her pocket watch in the bedroom, her hunger pangs suggested that she must have been sitting outside for at least an hour.

She closed her pad and got up from the wooden bench, which she reckoned must have been placed there by an artist since it offered the perfect angle for sketching. Not that her drawing had come to much, so full was her mind with thoughts of Hugh. Had he got her note yet? Had Eileen even been able to leave it for him? If he'd got it, was he on his way to them, full of hope? Or would he doubt their intentions and use the money to head to the city instead? Those were the thoughts that had kept Jane awake most of the night and which still consumed her. Aunt Alice, on the other hand, even if similarly distracted, hadn't appeared so troubled that sleep eluded her. She had dropped off in no time, despite having dozed in the stagecoach on the way back to town – "I wasn't sleeping, dear, I was just resting my eyes" – and was still in heavy repose when Jane had risen.

She headed back to the hotel, her pace quickening as the delicious smell of pancakes and bacon grew stronger. At the front door, her stomach growled again and she ran upstairs to fetch her aunt for breakfast. When she entered their room, however, the curtains remained drawn, Aunt Alice still asleep. Jane went over to the windows to let in the daylight. "Come on! Breakfast's ready and it's a glorious day. I've been out sketching already." When she returned to the bed, Aunt Alice was unmoved. Jane shook her gently. "Are you all right?"

Aunt Alice slowly opened her eyes. "Oh. It's you, dear."

Jane laughed. "Of course it's me! Who else were you expecting? It's lovely out there and Mrs Cameron's cooking up something tasty by the smell of things."

Aunt Alice raised her arm slightly, then snuggled back under the blanket. "You just go ahead, dear. I'm still ..." She yawned.

"What's the matter?" Jane had never known her aunt to linger in bed.

" ... a bit tired."

Aunt Alice was flushed. There was perspiration on her upper lip and brow. "Are you under the weather?"

"No, no. Just tired after yesterday, with the heat and the bumpy ride and all the excitement. I'll be fine, dear. You go ahead without me. I'll just have a little nap. I won't be ..." Aunt Alice closed her eyes and her head fell to the side.

"Can I get you anything?" Aunt Alice's head shook vaguely. "All right. I'll get some breakfast, then come back and see how you are. All right?" Aunt Alice was drifting off. "All right?"

"Hmm."

Jane stood up and looked down at her aunt. In her white nightdress, with her hair loose, she suddenly seemed older. Maybe things were just catching up with her. Yes, that would be it. A few hours' rest and she'd be right as rain.

Jane tip-toed from the room and went downstairs to the dining room. She took a seat at their table, already set for two, and shook out one of the crisp napkins that lay folded on it.

Mrs Cameron came bustling over. "Ah, Miss Knight. Good morning. This has arrived for you," she said, handing Jane a letter, "and there's been a message from the Distributing Home for you and your aunt. I take it your aunt will be joining you momentarily? I have some syrup for her to try which I think she'll like very much."

"Em, no. Actually, she's a bit tired after all the travelling so she's resting this morning."

"Yes, I'm not surprised it's all catching up with her now." Mrs Cameron gave a knowing nod.

"Exactly." Jane felt reassured that Mrs Cameron's assessment was the same as her own. "So, a message from the Distributing Home?"

"Yes. From Miss Strachan. She says that if you want to say goodbye to the boys, you should go this morning as they'll be leaving later."

"What? They're leaving already?"

"Apparently. But that's a good sign because it means they've been selected. And none of them wants to be in the bunch left unchosen after the first applicants. I know I wouldn't!" Mrs Cameron laughed. "Would you?"

"Well no, I suppose I wouldn't."

"Now, pancakes for you, Miss Knight? And would you like some eggs, too?"

Jane refolded the napkin and put it on the table. "I think, Mrs Cameron, if you don't mind, I'll eat something when I get back. I wouldn't want to miss the boys if they're leaving today."

"I can certainly make you up something later, Miss Knight. And for your aunt, if she fancies it."

"That's very kind of you. I'm sure she will."

"That's what I'll do then. And I'll get the maid to tell one of the coachmen you'll be wanting his services to go to the Distributing Home."

"Please do, Mrs Cameron. Thank you."

Now that Jane was becoming familiar with the area, the journey to the Home seemed much shorter and quicker than it had on the first day. *The first day* – already it seemed like weeks ago. Londonderry and Moville months, Stirling years. Perth decades.

As the coach trundled past now recognisable landmarks, Jane relaxed and opened the letter Mrs Cameron had given her.

Dear Miss Knight – I trust you're well and that the end of your journey wasn't as momentous as the start. Never again shall I hope for an adventurous journey! I trust, too, that your aunt's shoulder is healing as it should and not giving her any more trouble than might be expected.

Since I've returned to Montreal, I've thought of little else but our ocean crossing and everything we experienced together. You may have done the same. As fellow passengers, we shared

*such extraordinary events that none of us will ever forget
what we witnessed. These events, I believe, have created
bonds which in normal circumstances would have taken
years.*

*I hope, therefore, that you and your aunt won't think it
improper of me to write to you in this way and ask if I might
correspond with you in future. I also hope, notwithstanding
your forthcoming marriage, you will accept my sincere offer of
friendship.*

Yours, Dr Stephen Clarke

"Miss?"

The driver, having brought the coach to a stop at the Distributing Home's double doors, was on the ground, offering Jane his hand to climb down.

"Oh yes, yes," she said, still flustered after repeated readings of Dr Clarke's letter. She tucked it safely back in her bag, then glanced up at the house and down the driveway, still discombobulated by Aunt Alice's temporary incapacity, and Fred and Albert's imminent departure. They would be disappointed Aunt Alice wasn't with her to see them off; and she would have to face Fred and Albert, as well as Miss Strachan, without Aunt Alice's reassuring presence. Miss Strachan would surely enquire about their visit to Mr MacLeod's farm. What was Jane to say? She and Aunt Alice hadn't talked about it, hadn't anticipated that the boys' stay at the Home would be so brief. What would Aunt Alice say?

The front doors opened. Miss Strachan was on the threshold. "Good day, Miss Knight." She glanced both ways. "Are you alone today?"

Jane finally took the coachman's hand and stepped down. "Yes, my aunt's resting after our—"

"Yes, your trip to the MacLeod place. How did it go? It can

be quite arduous for the uninitiated. I do hope you took some provisions for the journey. It can be thirsty and hungry work."

"Indeed."

Jane was still mulling over what she would say about Hugh as Miss Strachan led her inside and into a receiving room off the main hall.

There was a small table in the centre of the room, with a jug of juice and some glasses set out. "Please sit down, Miss Knight. Fred and Albert will be with us in a moment. Can I offer you some apple juice while we wait?"

"Thank you, yes."

"I'm sure the boys will take some too," Miss Strachan said, filling three glasses. "Yes, they've been most fortunate in securing a home with a Mr and Mrs Menzies. They run a farm about forty miles from here and are—"

"They? Both of them? Together?"

"Yes."

Jane sighed with relief. "Thank goodness. I was so afraid they'd be separated. Which would have been difficult for them, as twins. And the Menzies are – well I'm sure they are – good people?"

"Oh yes, very good. God-fearing people. They hail originally from Fife, I believe."

"And what about Fred and Albert? Are they happy about it?"

"Very much so. But you can ask them yourself when they appear."

"I couldn't bear the thought of ... well, after everything we've been through together, I mean, after everything *they've* been through to get here, I'm delighted it seems to be working out well for them. At the moment, anyway."

Miss Strachan topped up Jane's drink. "So tell me, Miss Knight – how did you find Hugh? Well, as anticipated?"

Jane lifted her glass, slowly took a drink, then she set it

down on the table. "Mr MacLeod says so, although ..." She gave a little sniff.

"Just as we thought."

"... unfortunately, we didn't actually get to see Hugh. Mr MacLeod said he was away for a couple of days driving cattle."

"Ah yes. An important job. He must be doing well if Mr MacLeod trusts him with his cattle," Miss Strachan said, giving a nod of satisfaction. "Very good."

"Certainly that's what Mr MacLeod told us." Jane bit her lip. Miss Strachan was so certain in her beliefs, so certain of her rectitude, that Jane knew she wouldn't believe what Eileen had said.

"So when you return you can let his poor sister know that all's well with her brother."

The door opened, and Fred and Albert came into the receiving room, their faces lighting up when they saw her. "Miss Jane! Miss Jane!"

"I'll leave you to your goodbyes," Miss Strachan said.

The boys trotted over to the table. Jane stood up to receive them with a hug.

"Where's Miss Knight?" Fred said.

"She's a bit under the weather today, so she's having a rest."

"Is her shoulder bad?"

"Em, yes, I think it's maybe a bit sore. But she told me to tell you she hopes you're going to a lovely place and that she wants you both to write to her in Stirling as soon as you get there. Will you do that?"

The boys nodded.

"We're going to a big farm, Miss Jane!" Fred said.

"After the doctor checked us out, all these ladies and gentlemen came to look us over and Mr and Mrs Menzies picked us!" Albert said.

"Aye. Miss Strachan had us all lined up in the reception room and all the folk went along the line."

"And some of the laddies were puffing their chests out and saying 'Pick me, pick me, I'll be a good boy.'"

"But we didn't say anything. We just stood together and didn't speak unless we were spoken to. That's what Miss Frew always told us."

"Aye. Then, Mr and Mrs Menzies came and started asking us about ourselves and what we kent about animals and things."

"And we told them all about what we'd learnt wi' you at the Honour Bright Club about apples and insects."

"And they said we were awful smart and that they were looking for bairns just like us on their farm."

"And Mrs Menzies said we were bonnie-looking laddies."

"And Mr Menzies said we'd learn a trade wi' him and we'd go to school and we'd get money for our work."

There was excitement on the boys' faces. Had Hugh felt the same at first? Lord, Jane hoped the Menzies were good people who would look after the boys and treat them well. "So you're happy to go to live with them on their farm?"

"Oh aye!"

"Good. But listen to me," she said, patting the chairs for them to sit down at the table with her. "I want you to promise you'll write to me and tell me everything about it. All the details. And if you ever have problems, which I'm sure you won't, but if you ever were to have any problems, any problems at all, then you must write and tell me about them. And let someone here know. From time to time you'll be visited at the farm by people from the Home who'll want to know if you're doing all right. So if you're having any problems, any whatsoever, you tell them. Do you understand?"

"Yes, Miss Jane."

"Yes, Miss Jane."

"And if you ever decide to come back to Stirling, you make sure you visit Miss Knight. You never know, I might be there too."

"Next time you bring boys from Gowanlea to here, Miss Jane, will you come and visit us?" Fred asked.

She looked down. "Well, actually ... I won't be coming back. I only came with you because you are two very special little boys and I wanted to make sure you got here all right and that you go to a nice family in a nice place. That's why you must write, to let me know what you've achieved and how big and strong you're growing. You're wonderful boys and you're going to have wonderful lives. Now," she said, getting up from the table, "I'm sure there's lots to do to get ready, so I'd better leave you to it and get back to town."

Miss Strachan reappeared in the doorway. She must have been listening outside. "Is that you ready, boys? Have you said your goodbyes now? Mr and Mrs Menzies will be here soon." Jane nodded at the boys when they looked up at her for guidance. "And we need to check your trunks to make sure you've got all your things and that you haven't taken anyone else's by mistake. And Cook's preparing a picnic basket for you for the journey, and," she said, smiling broadly, "she's putting in a treat for you."

"Is it one o' them big apples?" Fred said, excited.

Miss Strachan put her hands on her hips and gave a little jiggle of her head. "It might be!"

"M'on then!" Fred said, pulling Albert's arm, and making for the door. "Bye, Miss Jane!"

The sound of them scuttling down the corridor ceased with the slamming of a door. Then there was silence.

Jane felt her eyes water. The boys' burden might be heavier than hers, but their hearts were surely lighter.

"Well," she said, opening her bag and searching for her handkerchief, "it's probably best if I leave them to it."

"Yes, as I said, when they finally leave, it's best for them if there's no one here they've had strong ties with."

Jane blew her nose. "Best for them, yes," she mumbled, then crumpled up her handkerchief and stuffed it in the pocket of her dress. "Best for everyone."

Brisk – that was the order of the day. From Miss Strachan's escorting of her to the front door, to Jane's stepping into the coach before the driver could get down to assist, to the trotting of the horses as they made their way back to town, to Jane's leaping to the ground and dashing into Cameron's Hotel. If she didn't get back to the room soon, she feared she might collapse weeping on the main street.

Mrs Cameron greeted her in the reception hall. "Miss Knight! I'm so relieved you're back." The proprietress was a bit breathless. "It's your aunt."

Jane felt a thud rise from her chest to her throat. "What?"

"We heard a noise from your room and when we went to see what had happened, there was no reply. So I took the liberty of going in. Your aunt, she must have been trying to get up to ... well, we found her on the floor. She must have fallen. She was unconscious."

"Oh, dear Lord." Jane hitched up her skirts and shot upstairs.

"I've sent for the doctor!" Mrs Cameron shouted after her.

CHAPTER 18

Eliza looked at the pile of letters Cook – Mrs McCallum – had left on the desk for her. It was always the same after the annual concert, the donations arriving in the days that followed almost equalling those given on the night. She flipped through the first of the envelopes, hoping there might be among them correspondence from Mr Rennie about the outcome of Ann and Susan Duncan's custody case. But none of those she glanced at bore the typeface used by the law firm. What was taking their Lordships so long? Mr Lee must surely have submitted his report by now.

She put the first tranche of unopened envelopes to one side, then lifted the next few from the pile. She could tell which were donations without opening them, the faint outline of the banknotes showing beneath the paper. At last she came to a more official-looking one, postmarked 'Helensburgh'. This would be information from the Inspector of the Poor, whom Eliza had asked to track down the mother of one of Gowanlea's boys, David Walker, to seek her opinion about him going to Canada. While there was no requirement for Eliza to seek Mrs Walker's permission, she preferred to make the effort, if only to avoid any time-consuming – though invariably futile – court challenges.

She reached under the newspaper for her letter opener and slit the envelope at the top. Yes, she was right, it was from Mr Crombie: *Mrs Paton, David's grandmother, says she would never think of standing in the boy's way of going to Canada. The mother is in England now. She has the two youngest and feels it takes all her time to keep them. Mrs Paton says that she will let her know but it will be all right. Yours.*

The news wasn't surprising, for David's mother hadn't been seen in Stirling since she'd completed her jail sentence. And she certainly wouldn't be back for David now she'd moved to England. He was a lively boy, full of energy, and would be well-suited to farm life in Canada. Eliza folded Mr Crombie's letter, put it back in its envelope, then dropped it into the open drawer of her desk.

"Miss Frew?" Winnie knocked on the door after opening it. "Just to let you know that we're back from our trip to the Smith Institute. The children were quite taken with the stuffed birds and they've done some drawings they're keen to show you when you have a moment. They're writing notes for Uncle John now to tell him all about it."

"Very good. I must say, Winnie, you're doing well with the Honour Bright Club in Miss Knight's absence."

The girl smiled. "Thank you, Miss Frew. When do you think the Miss Knights will return?"

"I'm not sure. It'll probably—"

"It's just … Cook said she thought there might be a letter from Canada in today's mail," Winnie said, eyeing the pile of envelopes.

"Oh." Eliza sorted through the remaining post. "I haven't looked at them all yet." The last in the bundle was thick; she immediately recognised Alice Knight's neat handwriting. "Ah, this looks like it. I'll read it, then come and let you – and Mrs McCallum – know how things are progressing."

"Thank you, Miss Frew. We've been so worried with the explosion and everything, even though we know they're safe."

"Indeed."

Winnie turned to go, then paused. "Em, Miss Frew?"

"Hmm?" Eliza said, opening Alice's letter.

"While we were at the Smith Institute, I happened to meet Mr Keith. He—"

"What? Thomas Keith?" She dropped the letter. "You met Thomas Keith?"

"Well, I didn't go to meet him, we just bumped into him. He was there looking at the paintings and—"

"Was he now?" Eliza said stiffly. She hadn't taken him as a connoisseur of art.

"Yes. He came over to speak to the children when he saw us and took great interest in the work of the Club. He said he'd be very pleased to fund a trip to the Royal Scottish Museum in Edinburgh for the children to see the natural history collection. He said it would be of great benefit to their education. I said I'd have to ask you but he said he'd already spoken to you about financial matters and was sure you'd be only too delighted to receive his donation. Especially if it was for educational and not entertainment purposes." Eliza bit the inside of her cheek. "He's such a nice gentleman and he was so kind to me the other day when he saw how distraught I was about the news from Ireland. And he was telling me today about opportunities in Glasgow for girls like me and he said he was sure I would—"

"He said what?" Eliza pushed up off her chair.

Winnie took a step back. "Yes, em, he said there were lots of companies setting up and that they were looking for girls to work in their offices and he thought an intelligent girl like me ..." She blushed and glanced at the floor. "Well, he thought I'd be good at that sort of work, and that he was setting up a business himself and I—"

"Never you mind what Mr Keith says. You've got enough

to be doing here without him putting ideas into your head." Eliza softened her tone when Winnie's face fell. "Of course you'd be good at that sort of work. You'd be good at any sort of work. But if that's the sort of work you're interested in, never mind Glasgow, I've plenty of contacts here. I'm sure you could get a good position—"

"But Mr Keith said there are lots of things going on in Glasgow and that—"

Eliza raised her hand. "Enough, Winnie! Enough."

Winnie looked bemused; it was hardly surprising that she didn't understand Eliza's intolerance of talk of Thomas Keith. Eliza, on the other hand, could only too well understand Winnie's favourable impression of him – and it angered her no end. Where the girl would see only generosity and kindness, Eliza saw manipulation and immorality. Whereas Winnie would see only an eligible young man who was surely on the up, Eliza recognised a conman when she saw one.

"Let me think about the trip to the Royal Museum of Scotland. Perhaps when Miss Knight returns, I'll discuss it with her. All right?"

Winnie looked deflated. "Yes, Miss Frew."

Eliza waved the letter from Canada at her. "I'll read this now and come and get you and Mrs McCallum when I've finished."

"Yes, Miss Frew." Winnie backed out of the study, head bowed.

When the door closed, Eliza threw the letter onto the desk and thumped down onto her chair. Thomas Keith was beginning to have her truly cornered. She couldn't tell Winnie or ex-Provost Brown about his poor moral character or his underhand tactics, for that would risk exposing her own past; yet nor could she continue to appease him by giving him money. Her savings, as well as her patience, were running out.

She picked up Alice's letter and took out the several folded sheets of writing paper from the envelope.

*Dear Eliza – Londonderry – I trust Her Majesty's Post Office
has been its usual efficient self, and you've received the
telegram I sent yesterday from Londonderry and thus been
spared a lengthy period of uncertainty about the awful news
from Moville. It was a quite terrible and terrifying incident.
Your boys were magnificent in the circumstances. I received a
small injury but nothing that time won't heal. The captain
was heroic, as indeed were all his crew. It was an anxious wait
to board the mail tender, but thankfully (and I am so very
thankful, Eliza) land wasn't far off.*

*I've thought about you a lot, Eliza, in the past twenty-four
hours, and now perhaps I understand the strength of your
faith. There was a moment on that ship when the only thing I
could do was pray to God for His mercy to let us live. I know I
wasn't alone in that.*

*Isn't it peculiar how people change with a terrible experience?
I can't stop thinking about the night you told me you were
going to dedicate your life to serving Him. I didn't quite
believe you at first. And although I agreed that Mr Moody
and Mr Sankey were most persuasive in their ministrations, I
did feel your declared commitment extreme. Or perhaps that
you were only declaring it to impress Mr Henry Drummond!
But now, Eliza, I think I understand the choice you made
then, if not the reasons for it. That you must have been driven
by something so strong that your purpose in life became clear.
That that purpose has guided everything you do. And
although I don't think I could ever devote myself as
wholeheartedly to His service as you do, I intend, when we get
back to Stirling (pray to God), to consider how I might better
serve His will.*

The Atlantic – Conditions are very calm – no mal de mer *as
yet in our party. Jane is calmer too now we're underway. Her*

state of mind is being assisted, I'm sure, by the attentions of Dr Clarke, who is most solicitous as to my well-being and is making sure that my shoulder is healing as it should. I've told him that he has no need to attend to me, but I think it gives him something to do and also provides him with a good pretext to talk to Jane, for whom I suspect he may, as they say, 'have a notion'. Given the circumstances, I am overlooking the fact that she is engaged to be married and not thinking too harshly of her for enjoying his company.

Dr Clarke almost seems disappointed that my shoulder is healing so well. I'm wondering whether or not I should injure something else to give him a reason to consort with us. I think perhaps the drama of the explosion is playing a little with everyone's emotions. Once we're back on land, normal manners, I'm sure, will return.

Jane has succumbed to the Knight's seasickness curse. I can't help wondering if she's done it on purpose so that Dr Clarke can assist, which of course he needs no encouragement to do. Fred, Albert and I are made of sterner stuff and remain unaffected.

There's much excitement on board as we're due to reach Quebec today. Dr Clarke seems somewhat subdued and has given Jane and me his card lest we need any assistance while in Canada. He resides in Montreal, which is a distance of over sixty miles from Brome County, so I can't think he really believes we'll call on him. But it's never been a crime in our great Empire to live in hope.

Canada – As you told us, Eliza, Canada at this time of year is very green and there are lots of trees for Jane to sketch. Or there will be once she's finished moping about having to say farewell to Dr Clarke. She thinks I haven't noticed.

Eliza put the paper down and looked up at the ceiling.
Then she rifled back through the letter and scanned down the
third page.

*But now, Eliza, I think perhaps I understand the choice you made
then, if not the reasons for it.*

Well, in over twenty-five years Alice Knight might not have
understood the reasons, but if Thomas Keith had his way, they
would be known by everyone soon enough.

CHAPTER 19

April 1874

When the North Church came into view at the end of Murray Place, Eliza saw a steady stream of ladies going inside for the prayer meeting that was to be presided over by Mr Moody and Mr Sankey.

She'd already heard from her parents' housekeeper about the meeting that had taken place the previous evening, and the anticipation of finally witnessing the gentlemen in the flesh was making her stomach flutter. According to Mrs McQueen, the Erskine Church, the town's largest building, had been overflowing, with people turning up two hours beforehand to make sure they got in. Every seat was taken and the passages were packed, with those who weren't admitted peering in the windows to get a glimpse of the evangelists and hear Mr Sankey's singing. Apparently, the appearance of Mr Moody in the pulpit and the music of Mr Sankey, playing his harmonium and singing hymns from his own collection, had caused quite the sensation. And, on occasion, there had been a certain lack of solemnity. "It's just as well you're going this morning, Miss

Eliza. With all the men at their work, there'll be far more decorum."

There was nothing decorous, however, about the way Eliza was trotting along the street. She'd lost time waiting for Catherine to return from taking tea at Mrs Keith's and, eventually, had headed out without her sister lest she miss the start of the proceedings. Hopefully, Catherine had made her way directly to the church and would be waiting at the entrance with Alice Knight so that all three of them could proceed directly inside and be sure of gaining a place in the pews.

As she neared the church, Eliza scanned the groups of people before catching sight of a raised arm waving in her direction. It was Alice. And, thank goodness, Catherine was standing next to her. Eliza weaved her way in and out of the shifting huddles to reach them.

"Hello, Alice." She turned to her sister. "You're here then. Where did you get to? I waited at the house as long as I could but when you didn't appear, I had to leave."

"Yes, I came straight here. I stayed longer than anticipated. Mrs Keith was distressed. I've just been telling Alice about it."

"Well, talk as you walk," Eliza said, joining a line of ladies who were heading into the building.

Catherine skipped alongside her. "You'll never believe it. They found a woman's body in the Forth the other day, down at the harbour. And it turns out it was a maid of the Keiths." Eliza almost walked into the back of the lady in front of her, who had momentarily paused. "Well, a former maid. Not that she was very recognisable. They think she'd been there a few days. But they found a watch in her pocket that had been passed down to William when his uncle died. He didn't have any sons of his own. His name and initials were engraved on the back of it. Can you believe it? She must have stolen it before she left. She left months ago and told them she was taking up a post in a house in Alloa, nearer her family. Mrs Keith's very upset. Obviously about the poor girl drowning but also because she can't understand why Nellie would steal from them. She said she'd always seemed such an honest and good worker and that—"

Eliza stopped abruptly in the aisle. "Nellie? Did you say Nellie?"

Catherine nodded. "That's right. I only met her a few times myself when I was visiting but William seemed quite fond of her. And he said she was a good worker, too. Always very obliging. She was so young. It's quite tragic."

Alice spoke from behind them. "Was it an accident ...?"

"I would think so," Catherine said.

"... or did she ..."

"Did she what?"

"You know," Alice said. She lowered her voice and stuck her head between Eliza's and Catherine's. "Do herself in."

Catherine gasped. "I hadn't even considered that. Surely not! Why would a girl of her age do that? As far as William's mother knows, she was perfectly fine when she left their employment. Eliza? Are you going to stand there all day? There are some seats a few rows down. Move yourself."

Catherine gave her a little shove. Eliza dragged herself forward, holding onto the pews in case she lost her balance. Her head was swimming and her vision blurring. She grabbed the back of a pew where there were free spaces and pulled herself in. By good fortune, when she stumbled, she ended up seated.

Catherine laughed. "What on earth are you doing? Don't tell me the excitement's gone to your head? Do I need to get my smelling salts out?"

Eliza took off a glove and deliberately dropped it on the floor so she could lower her head to try to quell the faintness which risked overcoming her. She leaned forward and rested against the back of the pew in front. Then she closed her eyes tightly and swept her hand aimlessly around on the floor. Poor Nellie.

"What are you doing under there?" Catherine said.

"Hmm?" Eliza slowly sat up. "Nothing." She lifted the Bible that was next to her on the pew, opened it at a random page and feigned reading it.

Poor, poor Nellie. What had happened to her? Had it simply been a tragic accident? Had this young girl somehow fallen into the water unnoticed and been unable to save herself? Or had she flung herself in, unable to survive the anguish of having given up her child?

The Reverend Beith and The Reverend Goldie were speaking, but Eliza couldn't concentrate on what they were saying.

And that poor child. Had Nellie discovered William had betrayed her and that the dead baby found on the doorstep of the poorhouse was hers? Did she blame herself for leaving it, not to a life of privilege, but with a father who abandoned it in the cold and dark?

Mr Sankey sang some hymns, but Eliza couldn't really make them out for the terrible, discordant melody of the ringing in her ears.

A breath caught in her throat at a sudden, awful thought – surely William hadn't anything to do with Nellie's death? It didn't bear thinking about.

No. Surely not. The deceitful, manipulative fornicator wasn't a murderer – he didn't have the stomach for it.

There was one thing Eliza was sure of, though – however it had come to pass, Nellie had been as good as killed by a woman she didn't know who hadn't sufficient moral character to do the right thing.

Eliza's body felt like it was crumpling in on itself; her head was thumping as if a hundred cannonballs were crashing into her skull. The Lord looked down at her angrily from the stained glass of the large window behind the apse, and the carved stone cherubs in the transept seemed to weep in horror.

Dear Lord, what had she and William done?

"She hath done what she could."

The sound of a strange accent roused Eliza from her dwalm. When she looked up to the pulpit, Mr Moody was addressing the congregation. She rubbed her eyes and shifted in her seat, glancing along the pew to check whether anyone had noticed her internal jousting. But everyone was watching the preacher, rapt. In his late thirties, he had a bushy dark beard and moustache, and dark hair swept back from his forehead. Shorter and stockier than Eliza had anticipated, he spoke rapidly and abruptly, though clearly and loudly.

"That is what it says in the fourteenth chapter of Mark: 'She hath done what she could.' And it was a small thing that Mary did. But she loved Him and she showed her love in acts. Her heart went with the offering. Remember, the widow had but two mites and she cast them both in. She hath done what she could. So what is the lesson here? It is that the Lord expects us to do what we can. And we can all do something. If every Christian man and woman did what Mary did, multitudes would be reached and blessed. You might think you can't do much. But if you are the means of saving just one soul, that soul may be instrumental in saving a hundred more. Three years ago, when Mr Sankey and I were in England, there was a woman who had been a nominal Christian for a good many years but who did not think she had any particular mission in the world. But that woman was stirred by Matthew 14:8. 'She hath done what she could.' So the woman thought she would try and do something for the fallen sisters in her town. She went out and talked kindly to them on the street. She hired a house and invited them to come and meet her there. And now she has rescued many fallen ones and restored them to their parents and homes. Many sisters have been reclaimed from sin and death through the efforts of one woman – one woman –

who did what she could. It is a great thing to lead one soul from the darkness of sin into the glorious light of the Gospel. I have a motto written in my Bible: 'Do all the good you can, to all the people you can, in all the ways you can, as long as you ever can.' I commend it to you. Live so that it may truthfully be said of you: 'She hath done what she could.'"

After a brief silence, The Reverend Beith rose and said a prayer, before pronouncing the benediction. Then, just as the congregation looked up, he continued: "Ladies and gentlemen, please keep your heads bowed for a moment. If you have been aroused or if you are anxious about your souls, if you are unsaved and wish help to ask Him for spiritual sight, if you are persuaded that you wish to become a committed Christian, or if you are a sinner in need of repentance, or are uncertain of your salvation, please feel free to raise your hand. If you wish personal guidance, there will follow an enquiry meeting in the hall, where a body of willing workers are keen to attend to you."

Eliza glanced around, then thrust her arm in the air.

Alice elbowed her. "What are you doing?"

"Eliza!" Catherine whispered.

"God bless you," Mr Moody said from the pulpit. More hands went up. "God bless you. And you. And you. God bless you."

Once the ministers seemed sure no one else wished to make known their intentions, the congregation filed away quietly, with conversations only starting once the faithful were outside.

"What were you doing, Eliza?" Catherine said. "I thought for a moment you were going to go forward to the enquiry room."

"Yes," Alice said. "Don't think I didn't notice that Mr Henry Drummond was among those who were going to advise the anxious."

"I don't need to go to the enquiry room for advice," Eliza said. "I know what has to be done and what I now have to do."

Catherine and Alice exchanged a look. "And what is that?" her sister said.

Eliza glanced at the Baptist Church, adjacent to the North Church, and thought of William's carriage pulling up that terrible night a few weeks ago. "Did William not notice the watch was missing all that time, Catherine?"

"What?"

"You said that the maid, Nellie, was found with his watch."

"Oh. No. He wears his own watch, not his uncle's. And in any case, you know what men are like." Catherine laughed. "He wouldn't notice it was missing until he wanted to wear it."

"You think so?"

"Of course. How else would Nellie have it?"

Eliza looked her sister straight in the eye, unsure whether the flicker it gave was one of doubt, acknowledgement or bemusement.

"Anyway, the main thing is that he has it back now and we can pass it on to our son when we have children."

Eliza baulked at the thought of it. She couldn't let Catherine marry William, not now. "Of course, yes."

"So what is it you know has to be done? What is it you have to do?" Alice said. "Has Mr Moody inspired you to *do all the good you can* then?"

"As a matter of fact he has."

"Pray tell."

"All in good time, Alice, all in good time. But first I have an errand to run. You two go ahead and I'll catch up with you."

"Are you sure you're not just hanging about for a chance to see Mr Drummond?" Catherine teased.

Eliza shook her head. "What I have to do doesn't involve Mr Drummond. Or any other gentleman for that matter. Quite the contrary."

Alice giggled and put her arm through Catherine's. Then

Eliza's sister and her dear friend moseyed along Murray Place towards the centre of town.

When she saw them pass the foot of King Street, Eliza turned in the opposite direction, crossed Station Road and carried on to Maxwell Place where the post office was situated.

Inside, she bought the cheapest paper and envelopes that were for sale, then scurried over to a table to write down the words that had been forming in her head.

Dear William – It is with horror and great sadness that I've learned about the latest casualty of your reprehensible behaviour. Which compels me to write to you in these – final – terms. I must look into my heart and find something good there. And so it is with heavy heart, William, that I say to you that you must not marry Catherine. I couldn't live with what I've been a part of if you were to become a member of our family. You must therefore find a way to let her down gently in the coming weeks. If you don't, I will reveal everything I know and confess everything I've done. In doing so, I recognise the damage that will be done on a great many fronts. But that damage will be less than that which would be wrought by your continued presence in our lives. Standards must be upheld in private as well as in public, otherwise they are not standards at all. I intend now to devote my life to righting the wrongs I have been associated with. I think it would be best in the circumstances if you destroy this letter and, in due course, completely sever connections with every member of my family.

Yours, Eliza Frew

CHAPTER 20

JULY 1900

DR AUSTIN WAS HUNCHED over Aunt Alice, taking her pulse and checking her temperature. He adjusted the compress on her forehead and ran a finger over the bruise on her right cheek. Her eyes opened briefly, weakly, then closed heavily.

"What's the matter with her?" Jane cried, unable to contain herself any more. It had been an unbearable wait for Dr Austin, who had been away on an out-of-town visit. With every passing minute, she'd feared he would arrive too late.

He gently put Aunt Alice's hand by her side on top of the blanket. "She has a fever, from an infection. And the bruise is from her fall."

Mrs Cameron nodded. "She was on the floor when we found her. We carried her back to bed."

"Is her condition the same or worse than when you found her?"

"About the same. She was in and out of consciousness."

"Do you think so? You don't think her breathing's worse?" Jane gulped. "That she's sweating more?"

"I don't, no."

Dr Austin felt Aunt Alice's cheek with the back of his palm. "Well," he pondered. He opened his faded brown leather bag and rummaged among the bottles, packets and instruments. "Hopefully, her fever is a simple one that will pass soon. But she needs hydration. I'll leave you a tonic with quinine."

"And if it doesn't pass soon?" Jane said, alarmed.

"Let's wait and see. The body has its own ways of fighting these things. And I understand from Mrs Cameron that your aunt is what we might term a 'fighter'. So that is all to the good."

Jane looked at her listless aunt; she had never seen her look less of a fighter.

"Oh, yes, Miss Knight's quite the character, Doctor." Mrs Cameron put her arm around Jane. "Don't worry, dear, she'll be all right, I'm sure. The fever will break and she'll be right as rain. I've seen it often in guests from across the water."

"Were they all 'right as rain'?"

Mrs Cameron hesitated. "The ones like your aunt, who are determined and have strong faith, they were."

Jane glanced over to the window. The lace curtains wafted in the breeze. What good were determination and faith? They hadn't helped RJ. Why would they help Aunt Alice?

"Now," Dr Austin said, "I suggest you wipe down the furniture so bacteria can't gain a hold. And keep the window open to ensure a constant flow of air." He put a tincture bottle on the bedside table. "Put a few drops of this in some water and try and get her to take some. If she can't, pour a little into the side of her mouth. I'll come back tomorrow. But if—"

"You're going?" Jane said, aghast. Dr Clarke wouldn't leave his patients. He would stay with them until the bitter end.

"Yes. But if you need me in the night, you know where I am. And try not to worry, Miss Knight. Take comfort from your aunt's faith. Good day, ladies."

Try not to worry? Take comfort? Jane stomped over to the dressing table and dipped a towel in the water basin. Then, increasingly frantic, she wiped down the mirror, the wardrobe, the chairs, the windows, and every object in the room. When she'd worked her way back to the bed, Mrs Cameron took her hand. "Dr Austin's an excellent doctor. He has the confidence of the entire town."

Jane scrubbed the headboard more vigorously. She should send a telegraph to Dr Clarke to seek a second opinion, that's what she should do. After all, he was a surgeon in Montreal, not some small-town quack.

"Really. I would trust him with my life."

Jane paused at the sincerity in Mrs Cameron's voice and pulled a chair up. "You say you've seen this before in visitors and that they've been right as rain? Did Dr Austin treat them too?"

"Yes, dear. Yes he did. I wouldn't just say that to make you feel better."

"No, I don't believe you would."

"There's no room for sugar-coating things in these parts. But I could tell you countless lives he's saved. Not that your aunt's in that position, of course," Mrs Cameron quickly added.

Jane looked at her aunt. It was true, she wasn't worse. She was presenting much the same as before. "No."

"So how about I bring you up something to eat? You can't look after your aunt if you don't look after yourself."

"That would be very good of you." Perhaps Jane wouldn't send for Dr Clarke just yet.

But, if Aunt Alice's recovery didn't proceed in the manner anticipated by Dr Austin, she reserved the right to summon him post-haste.

Throughout the night, in the blinks of an eye between sleep and consciousness, Jane forgot. Where she was, what she was doing, what she had witnessed. Then the dead hand of anxiety awoke and threatened to overwhelm her once more. Visions. Of a man on fire, a severed hand, a woman screaming for her baby. Of Mr Naylor. Smoke, soot, fire, dust, water. Children. Fred and Albert. Terrified. Aunt Alice. Prone.

And in between real images of the burning, sinking *Neapolitan* came imagined images of a distant, devastating battlefield. Magersfontein. Darkness, rain, gunfire. Young men felled by bullets, bodies mouldering in the sun. Bones picked dry by animals, brittle skeletons. RJ.

In the darkest moments of the night, it felt as if everyone Jane loved was leaving her, one by one.

When she next came to, she panicked. It was light. How could she have let herself fall asleep? What if …?

Aunt Alice's chest was still rising and falling. Thank God. Jane leaned across and held a beaker to her lips, carefully tipping it so that some of the tonic trickled in. Did her cheek feel less hot against Jane's fingertip? She readied her handkerchief to stop the drink spilling out of her mouth but for the first time there came a swallow. "Aunt Alice?" Jane stroked her hair then gently shook her arm. "Are you awake?"

"Hmm." Although it was the slightest of groans, it was the most responsive her aunt had been in hours.

"Can you hear me? It's Jane." There was a knock on the door. Mrs Cameron came in, followed by Dr Austin. "Aunt Alice took a drink!" Jane announced. "And she tried to say something."

She got up to let Dr Austin approach the bedside. He tested Aunt Alice's temperature and pulse again. "Yes, this is an improvement."

Jane put her hand to her mouth, not daring yet to hope that the worst might be over. Aunt Alice moaned again and half-opened an eye. Then she uttered something, which, although incomprehensible, was another attempt at speech. Jane took her hand. "Aunt Alice? How are you feeling?"

"Yes, these are good signs," Dr Austin said. "She's not as

hot as before and her heart rate's getting back to normal. But she needs to stay hydrated and—" Jane immediately lifted the beaker again. "—left alone to rest."

"Left alone?"

"Yes, Miss Knight. She needs to rest so her body can recover from fighting the fever. And, I would venture, you could do with a break too." He said it compassionately. "Your aunt's going to be all right. She's strong and—"

"One of us has to be." Jane spluttered a laugh, her eyes filling with tears of relief. "Is she really going to be all right, doctor?"

"I think so, yes. Now her fever's broken, if she gets some proper rest, and if things follow their normal course, we should see a marked improvement."

Jane released the breath she'd been holding. "Thank you, Dr Austin! Thank you."

"Well now, Miss Knight," Mrs Cameron said. "I don't expect you'll be wanting to sleep but how about you take some air? And when you get back, I'll have a nice breakfast waiting for you? You have to keep your strength up for your aunt. She'll need to rely on you for a bit until she's back to her usual self."

Jane gave a start at the realisation that it was now her responsibility to look after Aunt Alice rather than the other way around. Mrs Cameron was right; Jane owed it to Aunt Alice to be like her – strong – and to do what she would do.

"I'll rustle you up some pancakes and bacon. And I've just baked some bread."

"Thank you, Mrs Cameron. I'll take some air." That's what Aunt Alice would do. *Fresh air and exercise, dear, that'll cure most things.* "Breakfast when I get back sounds lovely. I can't thank you enough for everything you've done."

"Well, if you can't help your kinswomen, who can you help? On you go then. Your aunt will be just fine."

There came a soft voice from the bed. "Yes, Jane. Skedaddle."

∼

Outside, in the shade of the hotel's veranda, Jane looked across at Dr Austin's surgery. Adjacent to it was a grocer's-cum-general store, which looked a far cry from the sumptuous MacEwen Brothers of Stirling, whom Aunt Alice swore by for her provisions.

She meandered along the main street, pausing to study the fine brick building next to the hotel. It had a neat wooden fence along its boundary and the small area of ground to the front was divided by a path leading to white granite steps which rose to a high-arched doorway. Its central tower was constructed in geometric brick patterns and there were triangular dormer windows in its mansard roof. According to the plaque by the gate, it was a free public library and reading room, established as a memorial to a local man and his daughter. Aunt Alice would be impressed by that, given she was wont to agitate the bailies on Stirling Town Council's Public Library Committee to hasten the erection of the Carnegie Library, to which its benefactor had already donated £6000. "At the rate they're going, dear, it'll be the turn of next century, never mind this one, before the foundation stone's laid."

Drawn to the spire of the Methodist Church beyond, Jane continued past the mill buildings that backed onto the large pond, which Mrs Cameron had informed her, was actually neither pond nor lake but rather a dam. The church, lacking the austere gravitas of the stone kirks Jane was familiar with, offered instead a warmer welcome, with its bright red bricks and white window frames. She turned into the driveway and went to the foot of the wide staircase that led in three stages to

175

the entrance. She climbed the steps slowly, gazing up at the cross that glinted in the sun. Then she entered the vestibule.

Like its exterior, the church's interior was high and airy. Jane padded down the aisle, scanning the memorials carved into the walls. She stopped before the altar. Then she sat in the front pew, staring up at the figure of Christ in the stained-glass window high above.

"Might I be of service to you, miss?"

"Oh!" Jane put her hand to her chest at the sound of the voice from behind. A man wearing a black gown and white collar came towards her.

"I'm so sorry, I didn't mean to startle you. I'm Reverend Cunningham."

He was about fifty, with greying sandy hair and matching moustache. His accent betrayed that he wasn't from these parts but from somewhere much closer to home.

Jane shook the hand he was offering. "I hope you don't mind me coming in. I just needed—"

"May I?" he asked, gesturing at the pew.

"Oh, of course." Jane shuffled along to make space. "Yes, I hope you don't mind."

"Of course not." He slid in beside her. "God's house is always open to all."

"I just needed to ... somewhere to ..." She shrugged. "Well, to be honest, I don't really know."

"That's often the case. But God doesn't care why you're here. It's enough that you are here. Would you like to pray with me?"

She looked away. It was a logical enough question for a minister to ask someone who had just come into his church unannounced. Granted, Jane had prayed many times during the night. But had it helped Aunt Alice? Her aunt would probably have been right as rain anyway, like all the other travellers who seemed to have succumbed to a foreign fever. But her prayers hadn't brought RJ home and they hadn't helped those poor people on the steamer. "Thank you, no. To be honest, I don't really know what I'm doing here."

"And yet you're here."

Jane nodded. "Yet I'm here." When the lingering silence became too much for her, she added, "It's just that … my aunt is unwell."

"I'm very sorry to hear that."

"I mean, the doctor expects she'll be fine but I've just been worried that … you see, we experienced quite a lot on our journey here and, well, I recently … I recently lost someone …"

"Grief can make you anxious about others you love even when there's nothing to be anxious about. It's perfectly natural."

"Yes." Jane took a deep breath to settle herself. "But my aunt has faith so perhaps my coming here is for her, because she can't at the moment."

"Am I to take it then that, while your aunt has faith, you don't?"

Jane rubbed her hands together, a little ashamed. "Well … I don't *not* have it but …"

"It's been tested?"

"It has."

"And you're having doubts."

"I am."

"Asking questions."

She nodded.

The pew creaked when The Reverend Cunningham leaned back. "It's not wrong to ask questions, you know. Asking questions isn't the same as disbelief. Asking questions is about finding answers. But in the end … You know the story of Doubting Thomas, I'm sure? Jesus said to him: 'Blessed are they that have not seen and yet have believed.'"

Jane pursed her lips. She stared up at the shafts of coloured light streaming through the window. She truly wished she could have faith in something. Anything. For if she didn't have that, what did she have? And what was the purpose of anything that had happened? Had it all been for nothing? No purpose, no cause, no reason? Those were the questions she longed to ask The Reverend Cunningham. But if she did, she feared she might start to weep and never stop.

"Where are you from originally?" she instead asked. After all, Aunt Alice would want to know when Jane reported the encounter.

"Alloa. I came here seven years ago, met my wife and stayed. Do you know it? Where are you from?"

"Perth originally. But I've been staying with my aunt in Stirling, so yes, I know it. We came here with two boys who were going on to the County Distributing Home."

"Miss Frew's boys, by any chance?"

"Yes, indeed! You know of her?"

"Not only do I know of her, I know her. So you and your aunt are her emissaries?"

"Well, in a manner of speaking. It's not our normal occupation, but certain circumstances have led us here. How do you know Miss Frew?"

"I met her, oh, it must be twenty-five years ago now. She'd set up an Evangelistic Mission for young women and from time to time conducted services and house-to-house visits in Tullibody. Then she opened a home for destitute and homeless women which was so in demand that she moved to bigger premises and established a laundry to provide them with work, as well as a roof over their heads. That experience opened her eyes to the plight of neglected children and she opened Gowanlea in 1883, which was just before I came here. I haven't seen her since but, from what Miss Strachan tells me, it's gone from strength to strength. By all accounts, the children who come from there always seem to have successful placements."

"The two boys we escorted have already left to start new lives."

"I'm sure they'll do well."

"I hope so," Jane said. "And are you involved with the Distributing Home, Minister?" Perhaps he could shed some light on Hugh's situation.

"Goodness, yes! Miss Strachan worships here and I conduct services there, too. I also visit some of the children in their placements and advise on the suitability of applicants."

Jane sat forward. "Do you happen to know Mr MacLeod, a farmer, who's taken in boys over the years?"

"MacLeod, MacLeod," The Reverend Cunningham mused. "I don't believe so. He mustn't ever have been on my list. I only cover the area in the vicinity of town. Others more local to the farms cover the rural areas. Why do you ask?"

"We were hoping to see one of Miss Frew's boys who's placed with him but it turned out he was away on cattle-driving duties." It seemed The Reverend Cunningham wouldn't be of assistance after all. "Anyway, thank you for your words of wisdom. I must get back to my aunt now. She'll be delighted to hear about you and may even call on you herself. She's been a close friend of Miss Frew's for years."

"Well, tell her she's welcome any time. And if she would like – if she remains indisposed for a period – I'll happily call on her."

"I'm sure she'd appreciate that very much."

He stood to the side to let Jane out of the pew. "I trust, as well as offering wisdom, my words might also have offered you some hope."

"I think perhaps they might have."

When Jane arrived back at the hotel, one of the regular stagecoaches had drawn up to deposit and collect passengers. The horses were at the trough slurping thirstily, lapping water onto the dusty ground. At the sound of molten steel being dipped into a barrel, she glanced over to the blacksmith's. Through the steam, standing back from the entrance, was an unkempt young man of about fifteen or sixteen. His hair was fair, streaked by the sun, and his trousers and shirt were stained with mud and dust. When he spotted her looking his way, he took something out of his pocket and held it up discreetly. She peered for a few seconds before realising it was the postcard Aunt Alice had given Eileen for Hugh. When she recognised in his face a look of his sister, her heart gave an extra thump in her chest.

"Miss Knight?" someone called from behind.

Jane birled around just as Miss Strachan crossed from the other side of the main street.

"Miss Knight! I thought it was you."

Jane was terrified to look back at Hugh in case she gave away his presence. At best, Miss Strachan would insist on him returning to the Home; at worst she might take Mr MacLeod's side and have him punished.

"Oh, Miss Strachan." Jane tried to sound nonchalant. "Good day."

"First things first, how is your aunt?"

"Well, her condition worsened while I was visiting you."

"Oh dear."

"Yes. We had to call the doctor but he's hopeful she'll recover from her fever."

"That must be a relief."

"It is, yes." Jane shifted on the spot. "But I really must get back to her."

"In that case I won't delay you. All I wanted to tell you was that I've received word Fred and Albert have arrived safely at the Menzies' house. As I was in town, I thought you'd like to hear the good news."

"That is good news. Thank you. My aunt will be delighted too."

"Farewell again then, Miss Knight. I expect this will be the last time we'll be seeing each other. I assume you'll be returning home as soon as your aunt recovers?"

"That's certainly our intention." Jane willed Miss Strachan to turn and go.

"Safe journey then. Now where is my coachman?" Instead of heading back in the direction she'd come, however, Miss Strachan went towards the blacksmith's.

Horrified, Jane looked to where she'd last seen the boy; but Hugh McKellar was nowhere to be seen.

CHAPTER 21

WHEN, after two days, Hugh hadn't reappeared, it was Aunt Alice's idea that Jane should go to a discreet spot and simply wait.

"There are two scenarios – either he's been frightened off by seeing you with Miss Strachan and thinks we're in cahoots with her – in which case he'll be long gone. Or maybe he trusts, or is at least intrigued by, what you wrote in your note – in which case he'll be keeping out of sight very close by, watching for you and waiting for the right moment. If it's the latter, he'll come to you, but it needs to be somewhere discreet. And time is of the essence. For two reasons – firstly, he'll still be anxious about whether you're genuine or whether it's a trap, so he won't hang around too long. And, secondly ... we really have to start our journey home, dear."

Jane stared at her aunt. The fact she had been reluctant to face up to finally sank in. It made perfect sense, of course. Aunt Alice, though still fatigued, was over the worst of her fever. Fred and Albert had been safely delivered to the Distributing Home and Hugh had been contacted. It was up to him now. After all, they couldn't remain at Cameron's indefinitely on the off chance he'd return. What if he never returned? But – Jane took a deep breath – what if they left and, just a day later, he appeared, full of hope and expectation? How cruel that would be. "Yes, but, what if—"

"We've already been here longer than anticipated," Aunt Alice said. "We can't wait forever. We need to get home. *You* need to get home. You've done what you came for." She smiled sympathetically. "I'm proud of you, dear."

Jane squeezed the hand her aunt was holding out. "What will we tell Winnie if we don't ... if Hugh doesn't come back?"

"We'll tell her the truth – that he left the MacLeod's farm, that he had a friend who was helping him, and that he was heading to the city. That his prospects will be better there and that he'll no doubt write to her when he settles. But that he's safe now from MacLeod. Isn't that what he said he'd do in his last letter to her?"

"Yes. He said he was going to have to act soon because he thought something might happen."

"Well then. We can reassure her that he's out of that terrible situation."

"I suppose so, yes."

"She'll be relieved to know that, even if—"

"Should we tell her I saw him? That we were so close?"

"We still have today. He might still come."

"But if he doesn't?" Jane said. "Should I tell her I was so close to him, but that he didn't—?"

"Do you think it would be good for her to know how scared and dishevelled he looked? That he ran when he saw Miss Strachan?"

Jane stared at the floor. What was it Aunt Alice had told her at the County Distributing Home? *Sometimes the truth in spirit is better than the truth in fact.* "We could tell her you gave Eileen the postcard and that we're certain he'd receive it."

"I think she would appreciate hearing that."

"And that he had a very good friend in Eileen. Someone who loved him and who was taking care of him, giving him food and bringing him money so he could have a new start." Jane squeezed her aunt's hand. "Yes."

"All right. Let's get organised then." Aunt Alice went to the dressing table to put on her bonnet, though not moving quite as briskly as she normally did.

"Are you sure you're well enough to travel so soon?"

"I'm tired, granted. But the fever's passed and I need to get moving again. And if not now, when?"

"I suppose so."

"I'll have plenty of time to rest on the steamer. After all, there's nothing else to do! We won't have the boys to keep an eye on, nor ..."

"No," Jane said, thinking of Dr Clarke and how dull the return voyage was going to be without his company. "If you're sure."

Aunt Alice turned to her and raised an eyebrow. "Have you ever known me to have any doubts?"

Jane smiled. "No, Aunt Alice. Your faith never wavers."

"Why would it? I have the Queen, the Empire and the Lord. What else is there?"

Jane smiled. "Nothing, Aunt Alice. Nothing."

"Exactly. Now – you go out and see if he comes. I'll go to the draper's – or whatever abomination they call it here, the *clothing store*? – to get something decent for him to wear. We can't have the boy travelling if he looks the way you described. And if he doesn't come, I'll give them to Eliza. She'll find a home for them."

"What do you think Miss Frew would say if she knew what's been going on with Mr MacLeod and Hugh?"

Aunt Alice shook her head. "First things first, Jane. We'll have the voyage to consider what to tell her about all this. Come on now, chop-chop."

Aunt Alice went down the main street to the left, while Jane hung back by the stagecoach stop, periodically glancing over to the blacksmith's, idling to and fro, to be sure that, if Hugh was watching from nearby, he would see her. After lingering for the ten minutes suggested by Aunt Alice, she slowly strolled to the back of Cameron's, then set off for the dam where she was to wait.

The blue skies of previous days were gone. Instead, the water, the spire of the Methodist Church and the gentle hills in the distance were draped with grey. When she reached the wooden bench, Jane looked back along the path. There was no one in sight.

She sat down and scanned the water for fish jumping. But they seemed to have disappeared with the sun. It reminded her of when Aunt Alice had taken them to Loch Venachar, and RJ had spent an age staring at the water, calling for the trout to come to him. His efforts, of course, were to no avail, but his determination in the face of Aunt Alice's explanations about how to attract fish, was evident. Once he'd set his mind to something, there was little that would deflect him, short of the threat of a severe scolding and being sent to bed without tea. That was why he made a good officer, Father used to say, because, "whatever happens, he finishes the task he's been set." What had his tasks been at Magersfontein? Jane wondered. Had he finished them before he'd been cut down, the attack failed and the battle lost? According to Aunt Alice, the war was being won now, though. Bloemfontein had been annexed, British troops had entered Johannesburg, Pretoria had been taken, and the Transvaal looked as if it would be next. *Each battle, whether won or lost, leads to the end of the war and your brother is part of that victory.* Is that what Boer aunts told their nieces, too?

"Miss Knight?"

Jane gave a start. "Hugh!" How had he managed to reach her without being seen?

He took a step back, then looked around anxiously. His clothes were cleaner now and his hair was wet. Had he bathed in the dam?

She held up her palms to reassure him. "It's all right. I'm alone." She lowered her voice. "I don't have anything to do with Miss Strachan or the Distributing Home. I won't make you go back, I promise. My aunt and I were escorting two boys there, that's all, and Miss Strachan just happened to see me outside the hotel. She came to tell me about their progress. I came to Canada to find you. Winnie asked me to. She showed me your letter. I know what's been going on. My aunt and I went to see Mr MacLeod a few days ago and Eileen told us everything. We're here to take you home, Hugh, if that's what you want." She finally took a breath.

He came over to the bench. "How do you know my sister? How is she? Is she all right?"

"I've been helping Miss Frew at Gowanlea for a few months. Winnie's been helping me with nature classes. She shared her worries about you with me. I actually met her first when she was a little girl, not long after you'd left for Canada. My ..." Jane couldn't bring herself to say the word. "... and I met her in the garden at Gowanlea one day when my aunt called on Miss Frew. I was only fourteen then. She showed me a photograph of you, packed and ready to leave. You were sitting on your trunk and there were two other boys in the picture. And the wee dog, Rona. She was there too. She's still there, actually."

"Really?" Hugh smiled.

"Yes! And Jackie too."

"The collie?"

"Yes!"

He shook his head and stared at his feet.

"Winnie told me that day about how she was meant to go to Canada with you but she couldn't because of her chest. She told me you didn't want to go without her but you had no choice. She really missed you. Misses you. And then, a few months ago, I came to stay with my aunt in Stirling because ... and she got me involved with Gowanlea. I met Winnie again and she told me what happened to you. And when the two boys, Fred and Albert, needed an escort, that gave me an opportunity to come and look for you. So I asked Miss Frew if—"

"You told Miss Frew?" Hugh said, panicked.

"Not about your situation, no. Winnie was clear she didn't want her to know and that neither did you. So Miss Frew doesn't know anything about it."

"It's not her fault. Until I went to MacLeod's, everything was fine. I had a nice family, a nice house, I went to school, I worked, I earned money. Miss Frew gave me all that. But Mr MacLeod, well he was ..."

"You're safe from him now," Jane said when Hugh fell silent.

He sat down next to her and gazed over the water. "Can you really get me back to Scotland?"

Jane put her hand on his knee. "My aunt and I are taking the train to Montreal tomorrow then catching the first steamer to Glasgow. If you want to come with us, you can. Or, if you'd rather, you can stay here and go to the city as you planned. It's entirely up to you."

"I don't have any money for the train or the steamer."

"Don't worry about that. My aunt and I will take care of it. All you need to think about is whether you're coming or not. That's your only consideration. If you decide not to, at least I can tell Winnie that you're safe and you've got a plan. And who knows? Maybe one day you'll visit Scotland again or Winnie might come to visit you here. But if you're not coming, perhaps you could write a note for her. I know how much it would mean to her to have something that ... a letter from you that ... " Jane swallowed and opened her bag. "I've paper and a pencil in here somewhere."

Hugh clutched her arm to stop her. "I'll not be needing that, Miss Knight. I'm coming with you, if you'll have me."

"Of course we'll have you!" Jane put her arms around him

and held him tightly. "I'm so glad." She sprang up. "Come on then! There are things to arrange." But Hugh shook his head. "What is it?"

"I'll meet you at the railway station tomorrow."

"Why?"

"Someone might see me. I'm not going back to the Home. What if MacLeod found out and told Miss Strachan and she—"

"But where will you stay tonight?"

He laughed. "Where I've been staying every night since I ran away." He pointed to the forested area on the other side of the dam. "There's cover over there. It's dry. And warm enough at this time of year. I've made a roof with some branches."

"Outside?" Jane said, appalled.

"It's fine, miss, really. I don't want to risk anything. Not now. If they find me, they won't believe me. They'll believe him. But I didn't do anything wrong. I'm not going back to the Home. Or to prison."

"All right." Jane realised how misplaced her worry about Hugh sleeping outdoors was. The boy had been fending for himself for days without her help. "Be at the station in the morning so—"

Hugh laughed. "I'll be there long before you, miss. Don't worry. I'll be waiting for you."

"Of course you will."

Hugh looked around again, then got up.

"I'll wait here until you're out of sight," Jane said. "See you tomorrow."

She closed her eyes and let her head fall back. She could hardly believe he'd come. Was this God's work? Despite her doubts, she had prayed to Him for the boy to return. If it was His work, why had He listened to that prayer and not to her others? Perhaps it wasn't her prayer He'd answered, but Winnie's. What would The Reverend Cunningham have to say about that? Jane didn't know. But she did know what Aunt Alice would say if she saw her now – *Chop-chop, dear. The devil finds work for idle hands to do.* She opened her eyes and, as expected, Hugh was nowhere to be seen.

She scampered back along the path to the hotel, hoping Aunt Alice had been able to get clothes to fit him. He was tall for his age, a bit lanky like RJ had been, but his chest hadn't filled out yet. Jane stopped in her tracks, covered her face and started to weep. Her brother had been the inspiration for this astonishing journey and his memory had given her the strength to carry on each time things had seemed lost. Now that the journey was reaching its end, what would keep her going?

She went into her bag, dipped into the pocket sewn into the side, and took out his letter, her dearest possession. *Hold it to your heart*, he had written, *hold it to your heart*. She gazed at the envelope, at the line he had crossed the 't' of Knight with and the flourish he'd made under their Perth address. She pressed the envelope against her chest and looked up at the sky. *That way we will be together.* She kissed the air, then tenderly slotted the letter back into her bag. RJ would never be gone from her, she would always hold him in her heart. Aunt Alice was right – it really was time to go home.

When she reached the hotel, she crossed the main street and headed to the post office, which was just beyond the draper's, or the 'General Drapery'. So Aunt Alice was wrong about that – it wasn't called a 'clothes store'. Give thanks that the foundations of the Empire would remain unshaken. Jane glanced through the shop window but there was no sign of her aunt. Knowing her, she would have been in and out in hardly any time, having purchased exactly the right things for Hugh.

The post office, a few doors along, was a tiny building, with room for only a couple of people to stand in front of the postmaster's desk. When Jane opened her bag and took out some paper, he handed her a pen. She scrawled quickly, her breathing rapid.

*Leaving by train for Montreal tomorrow morning. Can you
be of service with transfer to, and tickets for, Glasgow
steamer? We are three passengers. My aunt and I would be
much obliged.*

Jane Knight

She read it back and scored out 'My aunt and'. Then she
gave the postmaster the piece of paper, along with Dr Clarke's
card. "I'd like to send a telegram please, sir. This message to
that address."

CHAPTER 22

ELIZA PAUSED at the bottom of John Street to allow a cart carrying grain to turn into the weekly market at the Corn Exchange. Then she crossed over onto King Street and looked up at the Steeple clock, which read ten.

She started down the sloping pavement towards the bank, instinctively clutching the carry bag containing the month's collections. Between the regular contributions and the additional ones garnished at the annual concert, it had been a very good month for offerings. What with Alice being away nothing had been received from District IX, but knowing her she would more than make up for it once she was back. Which, Eliza hoped and anticipated, wouldn't be too much longer – for not only were Gowanlea's coffers missing Alice's donations, Eliza was missing Alice's niece and her good influence on Winnie, who seemed to be getting more and more distracted of late. So it would be very welcome to have Jane Knight back in the fold, taking the Honour Bright Club and modelling polite behaviour.

More than that, Eliza hoped the trip to Canada had been a positive experience and would help the young woman come to terms with her loss. While admittedly she had initially thought it a ridiculous proposal, Eliza could think of no one better than Alice Knight to have been with Fred and Albert on the steamer. If anyone could cope with such a terrible situation, it was her. So however out of the question Eliza had first thought the proposal to escort the boys, time and again in the past days she'd realised it was one of the best decisions she'd made – for the boys, for Jane, and perhaps even for Alice, who judging from her letter, seemed to have discovered greater purpose in her faith. Eliza was certainly looking forward to discussing that particular matter with her dear friend.

As she approached the offices of Allan & Nicol Solicitors, two doors up from the bank, Eliza slowed, debating whether or not to pop in and ask Mr Rennie about the Court of Session's decision on custody of the Duncan girls. It seemed to be taking longer than usual, and Ann and Susan had been asking her about the outcome almost every day since Mr Lee had visited. She didn't want to be an inconvenience to Mr Rennie, and she was sure Mr Allan would have explained how she liked to be informed immediately of court decisions, but it would be helpful to know when she might learn of the judgement, if only so she could prepare the girls. Yes, she would pop in for the girls' sake, to quell their anxiety at the apparent delay.

When she entered the outer office, the clerk, old Mr Soutar, who had outlasted Mr Allan, got up from behind his desk and beckoned her. At least some things never changed.

If Mr Rennie had wanted to object to being disturbed by an uninvited visitor, Mr Soutar gave no such opportunity, waving for Eliza to follow him into the back office. The young solicitor peered over two precarious bundles of papers as they went in, then, realising Eliza was standing before him, jumped up.

"Ah, Miss Frew!" He rushed around to the front of the desk and moved a pile of papers from a chair. "Do sit down."

Eliza nodded in thanks to Mr Soutar; he slipped out, closing the door silently behind him.

"Please excuse the mess. It's an occupational hazard, I'm afraid."

"Indeed," Eliza agreed, scanning the disarray. The office had never been quite as haphazard as this when Mr Allan had occupied it.

"But you must have read my mind," he added.

"Oh?"

"Yes. I was just about to visit to tell you the good news about the Duncan girls."

"We have a judgement?" Eliza said, irked that she was only now to learn what it was.

"We do." Mr Rennie laid the papers he was working on to one side.

"And?" Eliza held her breath.

"The court has ruled in your favour, Miss Frew."

She sighed and leaned back in the chair. "Oh, thank goodness!"

"Yes, I found out yesterday, but by the time I got back from Edinburgh, it was too late to call on you."

Mr Allan would have called on her but Eliza let it pass. "That's excellent news, Mr Rennie. Thank you."

"Indeed. The court ruled unanimously – three judges – that it wasn't in the interests of the children to deliver them to the petitioner."

Eliza smiled and folded her arms. "Yes, I thought Mr Lee was minded to rule in our favour. He seemed impressed with what he saw at Gowanlea."

"Oh, it wasn't Mr Lee, Miss Frew." Mr Rennie shook his head. "No. He argued that the girls should go back to their mother, citing Macpherson v Leishman, 1887."

Eliza let her hands fall onto her lap. "He what?"

"Yes. He argued that, since there was no allegation of her unfitness to take charge of the children, she had an absolute right to them." Mr Rennie lifted some papers from his desk and started to flick through them.

Eliza grimaced, then sat forward. "What?"

"Ah, yes, here it is," Mr Rennie said, consulting the papers. "It says: 'He was impressed with the clean and tidy state of the house and was confident Mrs Duncan would to the full extent her means allowed prevent the children from being losers if they returned to her. He was satisfied she is respectable, sober and industrious and that—'"

"He was what?" Eliza said, aghast.

"'—no allegation against her present character could be supported.' Then he goes on to acknowledge that the girls regard you with 'affection and confidence' and that they fear a return to life with their mother. That they had told him they wanted to stay at Gowanlea as they were comfortable and happy there. But despite that, Mr Lee determined that Mrs Duncan's present character and conduct made her former abandonment of the children unimportant if she could ... Now what was it?" He ran a finger down the page. "Ah, yes. 'Show present willingness and ability to support her children'."

"'Present willingness and ability?' *Present willingness and ability*? Oh, my word." Eliza tutted. "What about the fact that Mrs Duncan won't be home during most of the day? What about the fact that her earnings would afford little promise of comfort to the children if they returned to her? And what about—"

"I know, I know." Mr Rennie was nodding.

"—the fact that they're only in their present healthy state due to the care and attention they've received at Gowanlea, which they couldn't hope to receive in their mother's home?"

Mr Rennie looked at the paperwork again. "Yes, Mr Lee recognised all that."

"But still he argued for Mrs Duncan?"

"Yes, he still argued for the petitioner." Mr Rennie put the paperwork back down on the desk. "However, as I said, thankfully the judges had more wisdom and all three of them put the interests of the children first and, thus, found in your favour. They said that while the proper place for children is with their mother, they had to take circumstances into account."

"Well, thank goodness for that," Eliza said, leaning back again. "Although it's hard to comprehend Mr Lee's mindset. You must remind me, should the need ever arise for an advocate for our cause, to reinforce to the Board that we must never, ever, employ him. The man doesn't have the sense he was born with. I mean, of course children ought to be with their parents, other things being equal. But other things are not always equal, Mr Rennie, are they? If they were, places like Gowanlea wouldn't exist." She shook her head. "Honest to goodness."

"Don't upset yourself, Miss Frew. The main thing is that you won and the girls can remain with you legally."

Eliza bristled. "The main thing is that Ann and Susan will now have a chance in life and will no longer have to worry about being taken back to a situation they fear. And all I can say is thank goodness for that, and for Lord Miller and his fellow judges."

"Yes, Mr Lee, along with Messrs. Macpherson and Leishman, will just have to put that in their pipes and smoke it. Their honours certainly agreed with you that a mother's right to the custody of her child is not absolute."

"I would have thought Mr Lee should have known better. But as they say, the road to hell is paved with good intentions," Eliza said, standing up.

"It surely is, Miss Frew, it surely is. Now I imagine the case will be reported tomorrow in the Court of Session round-up in the newspaper. But they'll only summarise the decision and not go into the details of the respective arguments."

"Well, it won't be the first time, Mr Rennie, there's a headline about Eliza Frew being in the Court of Session pleading for the bairns. But do you know what? The wee lambs always come out on top. In all my years of service, our Lord and King has never failed them."

"Indeed, Miss Frew. Indeed."

Mr Rennie got up and walked Eliza to the front door.

"Are you a Bible scholar, Mr Rennie?" she asked as they went.

"I'm familiar with the most common sections, I suspect."

"Well, nevertheless, I shall save you looking this one up. It is Luke chapter ten, verse nineteen: 'Behold I give unto you power to tread on serpents and scorpions, and over all the power of the enemy; and nothing shall by any means hurt you.'"

Outside, the rays of the rising sun were spreading across King Street, making the cobbles sparkle. Eliza closed her eyes, tilted her head upwards and inhaled the fresh air. How nice it would be to tell Ann and Susan their fates had finally been decided and that they wouldn't have to leave Gowanlea. Perhaps Mrs McCallum might bake some scones for the children to celebrate. And now that their futures had been settled, the girls could concentrate on their schoolwork and on securing decent positions when the time came. They needn't discover that Mr Lee had recommended that their comfort and happiness be risked by making them go and live with their mother. Who, apparently, was *respectable, sober and industrious.* If that were true, it would be the first time in years.

Eliza opened her eyes and shook her head. She mustn't express her irritation about Mr Lee to the girls; she must tell them that three judges put their interests first and respected their wishes. That was the main thing, and the only thing that mattered in law. She nodded to herself and started down the street towards the bank.

"I do hope you're not having legal problems, Miss Frew."

At the sound of Thomas Keith's voice, she spun on her heels. He was standing just a few paces behind her, grinning.

"Have you been following me?"

"And a very good day to you too," he said, tipping his hat.

Eliza, feeling immediate guilt in his presence, glanced up and down the street. "Have you?"

"Well, if you won't let Winnie act as intermediary and you won't welcome me to Gowanlea, how else are we to conduct business?"

She clutched the bag against her chest. "How dare you? We have no legitimate business together. This is beyond the pale."

Mr Keith smiled. "But Miss Frew, all you need do is provide me with another of your envelopes and I'll let you go about your business. It's really quite simple."

There was smugness in his raised eyebrows and conceit in the curl of his upper lip. If Eliza had ever thought he might stop his persecution of her, one look at his self-satisfied face told her that he would not. The only one who could stop it was her. She looked at her feet to compose herself, then raised her head slowly. "Mr Keith, there will be no more envelopes."

His eyes widened momentarily before he managed to control his surprise. "Now, Miss Frew, that really isn't wise. I've tried to do this the easy way, but make no mistake – if you don't give me what I want, I will expose you for what you are."

Eliza nodded, believing that he would. And if he did, she would deny whatever claim he made. Whose word did he think people would believe, if it came to it? As for the letter she'd written to William all those years ago, she would say it related solely to her not telling Catherine about her fiancé's reprehensible conduct and behaviour. And that it was William, and William alone, who had taken Nellie's baby and left it to die.

"Do your worst, Mr Keith."

As Eliza turned away from him, a woman came running towards her, arms flailing and eyes burning. Eliza stepped back, fearing she was about to be knocked over. The woman stopped so close to her that their bodies were almost touching.

"Here she is – here she is! The blessed Miss Frew, who'll no' give a mother back her bairns. Who thinks she's better than anyone else and that she kens best what's good for other folk's weans, and for Ann and Susan Duncan."

"Mrs Duncan, please! Step back," Eliza said.

There was saliva in the corners of the woman's mouth and on her chin, and strands of blonde hair were stuck to her cheek. Was this what Mr Lee considered 'respectable, sober and industrious'? Mrs Duncan thrust her face in Eliza's and started wagging her finger. "Aye, well, you're no saint. You're a holier-than-thou, hoity-toity besom who's turned my lassies against me and filled their heids wi' lies. Well I'm telling you, you'll get your comeuppance, you and all the high heid yins you go about wi' and who live off other folks' misery. You don't deserve the credit you get from all those high-falutin folk you hobnob wi'. You'll no' get your reward in heaven, I'm telling you that, 'cause you're going straight to hell. And before you do, I'll make it too hot for you to live here."

"Madam, stop," Mr Keith shouted, grabbing Mrs Duncan as she raised a fist to strike Eliza. "Stop at once!" He pulled her away, holding her firmly by the shoulders. "If you know what's good for you, you'll leave quietly and without causing any more of a scene than you already have. You're lucky I don't have you arrested."

Mrs Duncan shook him off but remained on the pavement, still staring and snarling at Eliza.

"Did you hear what I said?" Mr Keith took a step towards Mrs Duncan. For a moment, Eliza thought she was going to rush her again, but instead she spat in her direction, then stomped off. "Away to hell wi' you. Away to hell."

Eliza's knees were shaking. She'd been threatened before, of course, and had had harsh words thrown at her, but no one had ever tried to assault her.

"Well, that was most unpleasant," he said, watching Mrs Duncan go down King Street then skulk onto Port Street.

Eliza stepped away from the wall against which she was leaning and brushed herself down. "Thank you, Mr Keith. I'm most obliged to you for your intervention." And much though it pained her to say it, she was.

"Not at all, Miss Frew. We can't have women behaving in such a loutish way in the street. Really, what is the world coming to? No, disagreements should be settled in a mannerly fashion." He turned and stared at Eliza. "Which is how I hope you and I will conduct our business in future. For the alternative, as I told you, will be most unpleasant."

Thomas Keith looked at her with a contempt she had never seen before, even in those who professed to hate her. Even in Mrs Duncan. She held his gaze determinedly. She would not be cowed any longer. She thrust her shoulders back and went towards him. "Jesus said: 'Do not fear any of those things which you are about to suffer. Be faithful until death, and I will give you the crown of life.'"

He stepped back. "Well, Miss Frew, you can't say you haven't been warned. Good day to you." He started to walk on, then paused and turned back. "Do take care going home. You never know what sort of louts are hanging about the streets, waiting in the shadows these days."

CHAPTER 23

Hugh had materialised, from where Jane didn't know, as soon as they'd arrived on the platform. Then, just as quickly, he disappeared into the gentlemen's waiting room to change into his new clothes, purchased courtesy of Aunt Alice, who was already on the train. As Jane waited for him to come back out, she glanced up at the station clock. There wasn't long to go. They'd have to hurry. She turned to open the door, to chivvy Hugh along, then froze at the sight of Miss Strachan fast approaching her.

"What are you doing here?" Jane spluttered, backing into the door.

"Good morning, Miss Knight. Isn't that your train about to depart?"

"Em ..." The guard set off from the end of the platform, slamming the doors of each wagon.

"Miss Knight, I'll spare your blushes. I know Hugh McKellar's in there." Miss Strachan stepped forward. Jane gripped the door frame. "What are you doing? Are you preventing me from going in?"

Jane dropped her hands by her side again. "Well, it is the

gentlemen's waiting room, so I hardly think it's appropriate you enter. You never know what you might see."

"Oh, I know exactly what I'll see. I'll see Hugh McKellar, about whom Mr MacLeod has made some serious allegations."

Jane was dumbfounded. "What?"

"Yes, and if half of what he says is true, then that boy has some very difficult questions to answer. So it's in his interests to come with me right now. Mr MacLeod says that if I handle matters personally, then he'll not involve others."

"Others? What others? In what matters? This is outrageous." Fury rose in Jane. "Hugh McKellar's done nothing wrong. If MacLeod's made serious allegations about him, then he's getting his defence in before he's attacked." She thrust her hands on her hips. "Do you know what MacLeod's been doing to him?"

"Giving him a job and a home!" Miss Strachan retorted vehemently. "Mr MacLeod is one of our most loyal patrons. He's taken in countless boys over the years and—"

"He may well have done. And, for all I know, he's been good to them. But I also know that he hasn't been good to Hugh McKellar. So if you really want to talk about involving others, let's start there."

"Pah! Nonsense."

"And not only have I Hugh's word for it ..." If they'd been men, Jane and Miss Strachan would have been squaring up to each other. "... I have MacLeod's niece's word for it."

Miss Strachan looked puzzled. "His niece's? But Mr MacLeod said that she—"

"Said what?" Jane demanded.

"Well, it's rather indelicate ... but ... he said that Hugh had ... well ..."

"Taken liberties with his niece, Eileen?" Jane's voice was getting higher.

"That was the gist of it."

"Well, let me tell you that Eileen MacLeod told me – *and* my aunt, so I have a witness, if it comes to it – all about how cruel her uncle was to Hugh and about how, far from taking liberties, Hugh was nothing but a gentleman to her. She was in love with him, for heaven's sake!"

"In love?" Miss Strachan said, as if she'd never heard anything so preposterous.

"Yes! Why else would she have passed our message to him when he'd run away? Why else would she have given him food and money? Why else would she have told us everything her uncle did to him? It's because of Eileen MacLeod that Hugh McKellar is, yes, you're correct, standing behind that door, about to board the train with me."

"So that's what you're at. I wondered why he was hanging around Cameron's Hotel."

"You saw him?"

Miss Strachan laughed. "Of course I saw him, looking shifty and signalling to you. And then when Mr MacLeod got in touch I realised—"

"Oh, I wouldn't back MacLeod, Miss Strachan," Jane said, shaking her head, her dander up. "He's hardly a good reflection of the Distributing Home's claim to have oversight of all its placements. And I'm sure you wouldn't want it to be known that one of your stalwarts is suspected of mistreating at least one boy. How many others might there have been over the years?"

"Our procedures are very sound. Every child who ..."

Miss Strachan hesitated.

Sensing an opportunity, Jane softened her tone. "I'm also sure, of course, that if you'd been aware of any issue with Hugh, you would have acted immediately."

"Of course I would." Anxiety was starting to creep over Miss Strachan's face.

"And I truly believe you have the best interests of all the children at heart and that your intentions are good. So if that is the case ..." Jane paused to offer Miss Strachan an in.

"It is."

"If that is the case, you'll walk away and not look back when I open that door and Hugh McKellar accompanies me onto the train. If it's not the case ..." Jane gripped Miss Strachan's arm and said coldly, "... then know that my aunt and I will do everything in our power to expose Mr MacLeod and, by association, the County Distributing Home."

Miss Strachan pulled away. "You wouldn't!"

Jane's legs were trembling but she had to press on. "Bringing Hugh McKellar home was the only reason I came to Canada. So believe me, I very much would." She folded her arms and waited, praying she could sustain the bravado for a few moments longer.

Miss Strachan ruminated for what seemed like an eternity. "I suppose in this instance ..." She gave an imperious sniff. "... discretion may be the better part of valour."

Jane looked up at the clock. There was a minute until the train departed.

"But don't think, Miss Knight, that because you have—"

"Just go!" Jane shrieked. "Now!"

The ferocity in her voice seemed to shock Miss Strachan into scuttling away. Jane threw open the waiting room door. "Come ..."

Hugh was standing right behind it. "Was bringing me home really the only reason you came to Canada?" he said, before she could speak.

"What? Yes, I told you it was. Now come on!" He didn't move. "We need to hurry!"

"But I thought you were escorting the two boys from Gowanlea and that's why you came?"

"So we were. But I only did it to come to get you. I wouldn't have done it otherwise."

"You wouldn't?"

"No. Miss Frew would've been able to find another escort, I'm sure. Or she could have had Fred and Albert join one of the larger groups from Glasgow. In fact, she might have preferred that. But it was only because of what Winnie told me that I decided to come. Without her, I wouldn't be here and you wouldn't be coming home. And if you don't come with me now, neither of us will get home."

She pulled Hugh out and they dashed across the platform, reaching the train just as the guard raised his flag and the whistle blew. Hugh hauled open the wagon door, jumped in then pulled Jane up. She fell against him and they steadied each other, before he slammed the door.

They hurried along the corridor and bundled into their compartment. Aunt Alice looked at her watch. "For goodness sake! Where have you been? Were you trying to give me a heart attack?"

"I'll tell you about it later," Jane said, in a tone she hoped Aunt Alice understood. "But everything's fine now. Hugh?" He looked suddenly haunted, as if it was just dawning on him what he'd been through and what was still to come. "You sit by the window opposite Aunt Alice. You'll see the scenery better from there." He immediately did as she suggested, angling himself toward the glass.

"My, don't you look smart," Aunt Alice said to him. "I'm glad it fits. I wasn't sure of your size."

Jane took a moment to regard him; Aunt Alice was right, he did look smart in the dark suit, quite a different person from the grimy boy she'd seen at the blacksmith's. He would easily pass now for her younger cousin, which is how they'd decided to describe him should anyone enquire. Master Hugh Knight. Poor boy. He probably wouldn't feel safe until the steamer was on its way to Glasgow.

Jane took off her bonnet, loosened her shawl and settled in, her heart gradually slowing after the unanticipated contretemps with Miss Strachan. Pray to God Dr Clarke had received the telegram and would be on hand at Montreal to assist with their transfer. Not just for the sake of convenience, or because she wanted to see him again, but because having a man guide them might help put Hugh's mind at ease. She really should confess that she'd requested Dr Clarke's services. She glanced over at Aunt Alice, whose eyes looked heavy. Perhaps she would let her nap a while first.

The movement of the train was certainly lulling and it wasn't long until both her aunt and Hugh were dozing. Poor Aunt Alice – she couldn't have imagined when she first suggested accompanying Jane to Canada that the journey would turn out to be quite so eventful. And poor Hugh – how his life was going to change. Again. At the thought of Winnie's reaction to seeing him after so many years, Jane swallowed a tear, glad that her two travelling companions had their eyes firmly closed. And what of Jane herself? What was she to do, assuming the return journey was negotiated without incident? Would she stay on at Aunt Alice's, or was it time to go back to Perth? She better understood now her mother's decision to travel to London with her father; after all, had Jane too not fled in her grief? But she had come to understand that no matter how far she fled, she would never escape her feelings. And as to feelings, much though she had enjoyed volunteering at Gowanlea, she wasn't sure she was temperamentally suited to any long-term commitment in the field of child rescue. It had been harrowing enough saying goodbye to Fred and Albert, harrowing enough trying to help Winnie. Jane wasn't so naive as to think every ending would be a happy one, and she was honest enough to know that she didn't have the heart for it.

"Are you all right, dear? You're looking thoughtful."

"I thought you were sleeping," Jane said.

"Just resting my eyes, dear, just resting my eyes." Aunt Alice sat up from the slightly slumped position she had adopted in her slumber. "Well? Are you?"

"I'm fine, yes. I was just thinking about when we get home."

"Ah. Yes. There are some things to decide."

"There are." Jane looked out at the passing greenery for a moment. "Aunt Alice?"

"Yes, dear ..."

There was at least one thing she had already decided upon. She took a deep breath. "Harold and I aren't getting married. We agreed months ago to call off the engagement but we didn't want to announce it, with RJ and everything. But when I get back, we're going to let everyone know."

"I thought as much," Aunt Alice said calmly.

"You did?"

"Of course!" Aunt Alice laughed. "You've not mentioned his name once in all the time we've been away. And not once have you said you're missing him. Hardly the behaviour of someone who's looking forward to getting married now, is it?"

"I suppose not, no. But you see, after RJ, we both realised that perhaps we were doing it for the wrong reasons, that we had just sort of ended up engaged without really having thought about whether or not it was what we both wanted."

"And you realised it wasn't, I take it?"

"We realised it wasn't."

"So your heart isn't broken then?"

Jane smiled. "No, Aunt Alice, it's not."

"Very good. Then it's probably the right decision. Though your mother will likely faint with the shock of it. But never mind her!"

"I think perhaps she's stronger than either of us think."

"You may be right about that, dear. Anyway, you'll have enough time over the coming days to think about how you break it to her." Aunt Alice stretched her arms above her head, then moved her neck from side to side. "Now, when we get to Montreal, we need to go to the ticket office and I need to send a telegram to Eliza to tell her she can expect us back."

"But you're not going to mention Hugh, not yet," Jane said.

"Of course not. Not in a telegram."

"Good. But about the tickets and the like ..."

"Yes?"

"Well, I took the liberty – since he'd stressed how much he wanted to be of assistance if ever we needed his help while in Canada – I took the liberty of sending a telegram to, em, Dr Clarke ... to ask whether he might meet us off the train and accompany us to the steamer. I thought it would be much easier and more efficient for him to arrange things. After all, he knows the area and the arrangements that have to be made and ... anyway, I told him there'd be three of us, so he'll probably be wondering who our companion is."

Aunt Alice folded her arms. "Well, well, well."

"Are you angry? Have I done the wrong thing?"

"Oh no, dear! I think you've done exactly the right thing. I only wish I'd thought of it myself. Although you've probably been thinking about Dr Clarke a good deal more than I have since we parted company from him."

Jane felt her face redden. She stared into the corridor just as the guard was passing by. And when she glanced back, Aunt Alice's eyes were closed again.

CHAPTER 24

JANE MUST HAVE BEEN RESTING her eyes too, for the next thing she knew, she was being prodded on the leg. Slightly befuddled, she peered at Aunt Alice, who was gathering her things together in her carpet bag, and then at Hugh, who was reading a book.

"It's just some Kipling I brought with me," Aunt Alice explained. "To help pass the time."

"Oh." Jane rubbed her eyes.

"Anyway, get yourself ready. We've arrived in Montreal."

"What?" Jane jumped up and went to the window. She pressed her cheek against the glass and squinted ahead. It was true – a station was coming into view. "Goodness!" She smoothed down her dress and reached up to the rack to retrieve her bag. "That didn't take long."

"Well, you were asleep for most of it, dear."

As the train slowed to a halt, Jane glimpsed the faces of the people waiting on the platform, but recognised none of them.

"I'll hail a porter to get the trunks," Aunt Alice said, sliding the compartment door across. "Come on, Hugh. You can lend me your arm."

Hugh tucked the book into his jacket pocket, put on his cap

and got to his feet. "Of course, Miss Knight." The arrival at a new place, far from Brome County, seemed to have melted the tension from his face. For the first time, Jane saw him genuinely smile.

The platform heaved with new arrivals and travellers waiting to depart for Quebec. As Jane stepped down, she scanned left and right but couldn't make out anyone in the melee. She trotted behind Aunt Alice and Hugh, whose head above the crowd helped her navigate the route to the main concourse and exit, where a huddle of people were commissioning carriages. When Aunt Alice and Hugh came to an abrupt halt, Jane paused. She felt her heart leap to her mouth and her throat go dry when Dr Stephen Clarke appeared in the gap between them.

"Miss Knight, how lovely to see you again," he said, coming forward, his hand out.

"Dr Clarke!" Jane had no hesitation in giving him hers, which he kissed delicately. She tried to compose herself. "Thank you so much for meeting us. I wasn't sure if you'd get the telegram, or if you did, that you'd be free to attend to us." Her entire body was shaking.

"Miss Knight, there's nothing that would've stopped me answering your call." He bowed slightly, his brown eyes twinkling. Jane looked down to try and conceal the flush she felt spreading up from her chest.

"Yes, it really is most kind of you," Aunt Alice said, stepping in to save her niece's blushes. "We really are most appreciative."

"Not at all, Miss Knight. I'm only too pleased to help. As I told you, I'm always at your service. And, as such," he said, raising his hand and waving forward two porters, "I've arranged for your luggage to be taken directly to the port. I've reserved three tickets for your party and taken the liberty of reserving first class, should you wish to avail yourself of it. I understand why you didn't on the way over, but perhaps after your travails it might be more comfortable for you and ..." He glanced at Hugh. "... your young companion. The steamer doesn't leave until tonight, so in the meantime, I've arranged quarters for you at the Windsor Hotel so you can have something to eat and somewhere to rest before heading to the port later on. It—"

"The Windsor?" Aunt Alice said.

"Yes. And if you feel up to it, you can dine in the Grand Dining Room. I've made a provisional booking for our party."

Jane glanced up at him. *Our party?* Was this what it felt like to be swept off one's feet?

"Goodness. Jane, Hugh – The Windsor," Aunt Alice explained, "is the most magnificent hotel in the Dominion of Canada. If I'm not mistaken, it hosts The St Andrews Society's annual ball. Is that correct, Dr Clarke?"

"It is, Miss Knight."

"And if I recall correctly, Princess Louise attended its inauguration."

"That is also correct," Dr Clarke said.

"Yes, it's one of the prides of the Empire. I can't wait to see it. What a treat!"

"I'm sure you won't be disappointed. Let's not keep you waiting any longer, Miss Knight," Dr Clarke said. "Two carriages are waiting out front to take us there."

"Dr Clarke, you've thought of everything! Thank you," Aunt Alice gushed. Then she turned to Jane and grinned. "Aren't we lucky to have someone like Dr Clarke looking after us?"

"Indeed we are, Aunt Alice."

"So, two carriages you say, Dr Clarke?"

"Yes, Miss Knight. Do come this way. If you ladies would like to take the front one, this young man and I will take the one at the rear."

Aunt Alice paused when they reached the street. "I've been thinking, Dr Clarke – why don't you and my niece take the frcnt one and Hugh and I take the other? I have one or two things to discuss with him before we reach the hotel. You wouldn't mind, would you?"

Dr Clarke looked as surprised as Jane at Aunt Alice's suggestion. "Certainly not! Whatever you prefer, Miss Knight. Your wish is my command."

"Excellent. Right, come, Hugh. This gentleman will show us to the carriage," Aunt Alice said, pointing at the porter and ushering him on his way.

Jane and Dr Clarke glanced at each other, then smiled simultaneously.

"Your aunt seems none the worse for her adventures," he said eventually. "I take it her shoulder isn't giving her trouble since she's no longer wearing a sling?"

"Yes, it's much better. But that was the least of her worries."

"Oh?"

"Yes, she came down with fever from an infection. But I'm pleased to say that she seems to have recovered and is none the worse for the ordeal. But it was worrying for a time."

"And did she receive treatment for it?"

"She did. A Dr Austin."

"I assume he met with your approval?"

"Well, I ..."

"Yes, these small-town doctors do an excellent job with hardly any of the facilities we enjoy here in the city. And of course they see so many more ailments than I ever do. Everything under the sun! I admire them very much."

"Yes, indeed. And Dr Austin was very ... yes ... I believe he was very highly regarded by the whole town."

"Very good. But perhaps I can also give you a tonic for your aunt to take on the voyage, if she feels the need."

"I'm sure she'd appreciate that," Jane said, grateful that Aunt Alice was now providing a topic for conversation that covered their mutual embarrassment.

Further diversion and relief were offered when the carriage

pulled up. But after Dr Clarke had helped Jane inside and the door was closed, there was no avoiding the subject that was hanging in the air between them. As the coachman set off, Dr Clarke made the first move.

"Miss Knight. Since we may not get another chance to be alone, I wanted to ask if you'd received my letter and considered my request to correspond with you?"

"I did. I have."

"Good. Now I most certainly wouldn't want to do anything improper," he said, raising his hand, "but, as I said, I feel that we have all – you, your aunt and I – been through something so unique that—"

"My aunt *and* I?"

"Of course. Yes. I would never dream of, since you're to be married, putting you in a position where—"

"But I'm not to be married!" Jane blurted.

"You're not? I thought you were engaged to a childhood friend of your brother's?"

"I was. I still am." When his face fell, Jane rushed to reassure him. "But only technically! I'm not marrying him, because we agreed many months ago that we weren't suited and the wedding wouldn't go ahead. We've just been waiting for the right time to announce it. And the right time will be as soon as I get back home to Scotland."

Dr Clarke stroked his chin. "I see." He looked out the window. Unsure of herself, Jane did the same.

They passed a large square punctuated by areas of close-cut grass and neatly trimmed trees. Horse buggies were parked along its length, and on its opposite side was the biggest church Jane had ever seen, its huge copper dome dominating the skyline.

"It's intended as a replica of St Peter's in Rome," Dr Clarke said.

Jane had seen pictures of the original in one of her father's books. "Of course, I see that now."

"And that monument in the square is to Mr Macdonald, the first prime minister. He came from Glasgow, you know"

"Really?"

"Yes."

The awkward pair made to look outside again, then Dr Clarke slid forward in his seat and reached for Jane's hand. "Miss Knight, in light of what you've just told me, let me be more forthright." When her hand started to tremble, he held it firmly. "Since we parted, I've thought about you constantly. And not because of the bond we have, given events off Moville. It's more than that. I have, Miss Knight, strong feelings for you." Jane closed her eyes as she listened, his speech getting quicker. "I know, of course, that circumstances don't favour the development of our acquaintance, with me here and you there, but I hope to return to Glasgow next year again for the conference, and well, if you agree to a correspondence, I'll make sure I return. There are opportunities there for young doctors so I'm sure I'd be able to obtain a position if ..."

Jane opened her eyes as the carriage slowed. "Yes?"

"... if you felt there would be any merit in my making such a move." He raised his eyebrows in question, then let go of her hand and sat back.

Jane held his gaze. He was so handsome – she had thought so from the moment she'd first seen him. Not handsome in the way Harold was handsome; Dr Clarke's features weren't even, his jaw wasn't square and his hair wasn't thick. But there was something ineffable about his attractiveness, which was more than simple appearance, and even though she had only known him for a couple of weeks, her response to him was truer than anything she'd ever felt for Harold.

Dearest Harold. Were the feelings she'd had for him ever really love, the sort of love she expected to have for her future husband? One that was different from the love for a brother or a friend? Having met Dr Clarke, it felt as if she had really only ever loved Harold as she would a friend. The only way, of course, he could love her.

Poor Harold. What would become of him? Would he live his life in fear of being exposed? Would he quickly find another woman to marry in order to live up to expectations? What was his alternative? A long, lonely life? She hoped that somehow he could find a way to live that would bring him happiness. For he had done her a favour; his confession, far from the disaster she had first thought it, looked now to be a blessing in disguise. He hadn't just freed himself from the prospect of a loveless marriage, he had saved her from one too. So when she returned to Stirling, she must write to him to progress the cancellation of their engagement. Enough time had passed and her extended stay in Stirling, not to mention her trip across the ocean, would offer ample reason for their having grown apart. There would be no need for further explanation.

Jane looked out the carriage window at the blur of trees lining the boulevard, hoping the beating of her racing heart wasn't showing through her bodice.

"So may I write to you?" Dr Clarke asked hesitantly.

She smiled. "You don't have my address."

"True."

"But I have yours."

"Yes, you do!" Dr Clarke reached into his jacket. "But let me give you my card again in case you lose the first one."

"I also have your letter."

"Well, in case you lose that too. It would be terrible if you decided to write to me but then couldn't find the address. That would be a tragedy from which I don't think I'd recover!"

"Don't worry. Your address is etched in my mind."

"So you'll consider writing to me?"

"Yes, I'll most certainly consider it, Dr Clarke."

"Well then, Miss Knight." He beamed. "I can ask nothing more of you than that."

CHAPTER 25

E̶LIZA TURNED her head slowly from right to left. The view from Gowanlea's garden was one she never tired of. In the clean light of an early June morning, with the town bathed in the gold of the rising sun, the River Forth sparkling and the Abbey Craig glinting, was there any greater vista than this? Eliza hadn't yet seen one, although it was true, she was not well-travelled. She had visited the surrounding towns for evangelistic talks in her youth and, when she was a child, their father had taken her and Catherine to Edinburgh to visit the castle, which she still thought second best to Stirling's. And, once or twice, during their engagement, she had gone on trips with her sister and William; there was a train trip to Glasgow she remembered and a boat trip up the Forth. But that was about it. Nothing as adventurous as Alice, who had travelled to India and back, and now Canada, too.

Eliza was so looking forward to seeing her again in a couple of days. Her latest telegram had been short but clear, typical of Alice Knight: *Departing on next steamer. All well. Will call on our return.*

It would be good to hear her opinion of the Brome County Distributing Home and of Miss Strachan. For although Eliza had been in correspondence with the Home's superintendent for years and had heard excellent reports of her establishment from others, she had never met her, and had never seen for herself the place to which she had sent numerous youngsters. Learning about the set-up directly from a trusted friend would be invaluable.

However, the question that was bothering Eliza, that had her up as the sun was rising, was whether Alice Knight would remain a trusted friend once Thomas Keith exposed her actions to anyone who wanted to listen. Eliza didn't doubt there would be plenty who would, for Mrs Duncan wasn't the only desperate mother in the last twenty-five years who had threatened to bring her down. No, there had been plenty like Mrs Duncan over the years. But with the courts, the council and the church behind her, not to mention righteousness on her side, there was nothing Eliza had feared from their harsh words. Thomas Keith's harsh words, on the other hand, could well be her undoing. *There's no smoke without fire.* How often had Eliza herself said that of others? What was it the good book said? *Where no wood is, there the fire goeth out; so where there is no talebearer, the strife ceaseth. The words of a talebearer are as wounds, and they go down into the innermost parts of the belly.*

If Alice had ever suspected anything, not once had she raised it. Not when Eliza had publicly set out her stall at the prayer meeting presided over by Mr Moody and Mr Sankey, nor when Catherine and William's engagement was called off. Indeed, if Eliza recalled correctly, the only thing Alice had said about that was she was sure Catherine would realise that losing a fiancé such as William would turn out to be no loss at all, since his opinion of his qualities far exceeded any objective assessment of them. Not that she was ever anything less than sympathetic in Catherine's presence, who, although maintaining the decision to end the relationship had been a mutual one, was clearly at best disappointed, and at worst broken-hearted.

Eliza had comforted her sister as best she could; after all, it was the least she could do. And when Catherine died just a couple of years later from tuberculosis, Eliza, holding her hand as she slipped away, couldn't help but wonder whether the blow of losing William had hastened her demise. So many times that day, by her bedside, Eliza wondered how things might have been had she never got into the carriage with William that dreadful night. Catherine and he would surely have married. Perhaps they would have had a child; maybe a boy who'd have inherited William's uncle's watch. Catherine would probably still have passed away, leaving William a young widower; after a suitable time, he would have remarried and gone on to have more children. Nellie would still be dead, the baby would still be dead, but Eliza would be blameless. Thomas Keith would never have been born and Eliza wouldn't now be facing her demise.

She closed her eyes, clasped her hands together and prayed. The Lord acknowledged that bad things happened and Jesus said that those things were not to be feared. "Be faithful until death, and I will give you the crown of life," she whispered.

She breathed slowly out, then turned and leaned against the wall, looking up at Gowanlea, her home for so many years. Her *life*. Was she soon to be banished from it in disgrace, with everything she had worked for diminished? Where would she go and what would she do? The money she had inherited from her parents had been poured into her rescue work, invested in bricks and mortar for the waifs and strays, not for her. She glanced over to the Gowan Hills and shuddered; plenty of dissolute women had slept there – was that to be her fate, too?

Eliza shook her head in an attempt to dispel her doom-laden thoughts. This simply wouldn't do, she had to get a grip on herself. She stamped one foot on the ground, then the other. The wicked may have drawn out their swords but their swords would enter their own hearts and their arms would be broken.

She curled her fingers into fists and punched the air to gee herself on. She would fight Thomas Keith and the Lord would uphold the righteous. The tightness drained from her neck and shoulders and Eliza sighed with relief that He had provided her with strength to begin another day working in His service.

As she started back to the house, there was a movement at one of the windows of the girls' dormitory on the top floor. She paused and peered up at the small gap in the curtains, where first one child appeared at the glass, then another.

"What on earth?" Eliza said, recognising Ann and Susan Duncan. When they caught her eye, she gave a little wave, making them disappear behind the curtain again. Eliza looked at her pocket watch – it was still only four forty-five, long before six-thirty, when the children were due downstairs for worship then breakfast. And usually the Duncan girls had to be cajoled out of bed of a morning. Eliza couldn't remember them ever being up at this time before. She hurried from the garden back into the house and quickly made her way up the stairs to the top floor.

The door to the girls' dormitory was ajar, so she stuck her head around it and peered into the room. Ann and Susan were sitting serenely on their beds, still in their nightgowns. Eliza slipped into the dormitory and tiptoed along to them, anxious not to wake any of the other children. When they spotted her, the girls got up and padded over to greet her.

Eliza kneeled down and spoke quietly. "Good morning. What are you two doing up so early? Are you all right?"

"Aye, we're all right," Susan said, not bothering to lower her voice.

Eliza put her finger to her lips. "Shush. Come on. Let's go into the hall to talk." She took each girl by the hand and led them out onto the landing, then gently pulled the dormitory door closed. Ann and Susan looked at her, bleary-eyed. "So what are you doing up so early and looking out the window?"

Ann was first to begin the explanation. "We were seeing if the man's still there or if he's away."

"Aye, but he must be away because we can't see him," Susan added.

Eliza screwed up her face. "What? What man?"

"The one who came to see us last night," Ann said, as if it were a perfectly routine occurrence.

"But there aren't any men here," Eliza said. "It must have been a dream. Or are you sure it wasn't one of the bigger boys? You know that sometimes Dick sleepwalks."

"Naw, it wasn't Dick. It was a man. He came when it was dark and he said he'd come to tell us our mother loved us and to give us a present from her."

Eliza shivered. "He what?"

Ann reached into the pocket of her nightdress and pulled out a yo-yo. "Aye, he brought us one each and said they were from our mother. He asked if we wanted to go with him to see her. But we didn't want to."

"Naw. He said it would be all right though, that we'd no' get into any trouble or anything, but we didn't want to."

Eliza's legs buckled and she grabbed the newel post.

"Aye, and we told him what you said, Miss Frew, that whatever the judges decided was what was to happen and that we had to do what they said."

"Aye, then Winnie came over and told us to get back into bed and go to sleep. Then she spoke to the man and—"

"What? Winnie?" Eliza got her bearings again. "Winnie spoke to him?"

"Aye."

"What did she say to him?"

"I'm no' sure. I couldn't really hear them. Something about letting us sleep and she'd go wi' him instead."

"Aye, and then he came back over and said we were to stay in bed until morning 'cause he'd ken if we got up 'cause he'd be outside in the garden watching and that we'd be in trouble wi' you if we got up, Miss Frew."

"Are we in trouble, Miss Frew?"

"Of course not, no. What did he look like, the man?" Eliza said. She was sure that, had it been any man other than Thomas Keith, Winnie would have sounded the alarm.

The girls shrugged. "It was dark."

Eliza pushed open the dormitory door and glanced up at Winnie's bed at the far end of the room. It was unoccupied. She pulled the door back again. "And Winnie, she went with him?"

"Aye."

"And then the man went away with her and didn't come back? Is that what you're saying?" Eliza asked, trying to keep the panic out of her voice.

"Aye."

"He didn't hurt you or anything?"

"Naw, he was all right."

Eliza's head fell forward and she put a hand to her brow. The thought of Thomas Keith inside Gowanlea at night while she and the children slept was chilling.

"Aye, he was all right. So has he gone from outside, Miss Frew?"

"What?" Eliza looked up. "Oh, yes. He's gone. Yes. And, em – everything's all right. So why don't you two go back to bed for a wee while? Yes. It's a bit too early to get up. But when you do, I'll get Mrs McCallum to make something special for breakfast."

Ann and Susan beamed.

"Right then," Eliza said, opening the dormitory door. "Quietly now."

She took the girls back to bed and settled them in. Then she tiptoed to the end of the dormitory to check on Winnie's space – her bed was indeed empty and her clothes gone from the basket by the bedside.

It took Eliza all her strength not to sprint downstairs,

screaming at the top of her voice. She stopped in the hall to catch her breath, then ran into the kitchen in case Winnie was making herself some hot milk before Mrs McCallum arrived for work. But there was no one there.

She returned to the hall and looked along the corridor. Maybe Winnie was in the classroom or the dining room. Eliza rushed along and flung open the doors. Both rooms were empty.

She hurried back. When she passed her study, she noticed the door wasn't firmly closed. *Thank goodness, the girl must be in there.* "Winnie?"

Eliza went in. Her desk drawer was splayed open. She put her hand over her mouth; after the incident in the street with Mrs Duncan, she had come back to Gowanlea rather than carrying on to the bank and depositing the money. She took a step forward and stared into the drawer – the canvas sack with the month's donations was gone. Eliza felt sick. If she'd only given Thomas Keith some money, then that was all she would have lost; as it was, now she'd lost every sense of security she'd ever had.

She pulled out the desk chair, where the small key to the drawer had been left, then slumped down. He couldn't have known where to find it. The only explanation was that Winnie had told him. How could she do such a thing after everything Eliza had done for her? How could she betray Gowanlea like this? Had she known Thomas Keith was coming? Had she let him in? How else would he have been able to get into the house without the dogs barking?

Eliza leaned her elbows on the desk and put her head in her hands. She had no savings of her own left to replace the collection money. Receipts had been issued for all the donations, so how was she going to explain to the Board that the money was gone?

The study door thudded. Rona and Jackie came in, tails wagging. Jackie nuzzled Eliza's thigh in greeting, then licked her arm, while Rona weaved in and out of her legs under the desk. Soon after the dogs came Mrs McCallum.

"Good morning, Miss Frew."

Eliza didn't move.

"Miss Frew? Are you all right?" Mrs McCallum stepped forward and put her hand on Eliza's shoulder. "Whatever's the matter? Are you unwell?"

Eliza lifted her head slowly and blinked. "No, Mrs McCallum, I'm not all right."

"What's wrong?"

Eliza began to weep, then nodded at the open drawer. "The monthly takings are gone."

Mrs McCallum stared down. "What? How?"

"Winnie's gone too. Disappeared."

"No!" Mrs McCallum gasped.

Eliza nodded.

"Miss Frew, you're not saying that—"

"I really don't know what I'm saying, Mrs McCallum. But Ann and Susan Duncan said they saw her get up and leave during the night and that—"

"No, Winnie wouldn't do that, surely not. You can't think she would do something like that, after everything you've—"

"I don't know what to think, Mrs McCallum," Eliza said. "All I know is that the money's gone and Winnie's gone."

CHAPTER 26

JANE PUT the two letters she'd just written side by side on the table in Aunt Alice's drawing room, then re-read them to make sure their contents dovetailed.

Dearest Mother – Aunt Alice and I have returned from our trip and what a trip it's been! I can tell you now that we crossed the ocean and visited Canada on a very special mission, the details of which I can't wait to share with you and Father. I'm so pleased you'll both be returning to Perth soon. I think it's time. Not just for you, but for me as well. I'm looking forward to our reunion.

There is one thing, though, that can't wait until then, which is that Harold and I have agreed to call off our engagement. It's a mutual decision that we both believe to be correct for our future happiness. We will of course remain close friends. We have known each other too long, and shared too much, to lose the friendship we've built over the years, and which I trust will continue for many more years to come. I hope you and Father will understand that this is what we want, and that your affection for Harold, and the high regard in which you hold him, will remain undiminished. I'll explain more when we're all back in Perth.

Aunt Alice sends you and father her best wishes and says she's looking forward to regaling you with tales of our trip.

Your loving daughter, Jane

Dear Harold – I trust you are well. Aunt Alice and I have now returned from a most eventful trip, which I'll tell you all about when we next meet – which I hope will be in the not-too-distant future. I wanted to let you know immediately, however, that I've told Mother we've called off our engagement, that we are both content it's the right thing to do and that we intend to remain the closest of friends. I would have no objections now to you informing your parents and acquaintances of our decision.

I truly wish you every happiness, Harold, and will write again when I return to Perth.

Your dearest friend, Jane

She nodded to herself. Yes, these letters would do.

As for the one to Dr Clarke, she would compose that later, in the privacy of her room, taking time to make sure that every word she committed to print was exactly the right one.

She folded the letters and put them into the envelopes she had already addressed. "That's them done," she said, tapping them on the table.

Aunt Alice looked up from her book, Hugh from his feet. He didn't seem at all comfortable sitting there on the couch. Hardly surprising, for he'd wanted to go straight to Gowanlea when they'd arrived back from Glasgow the previous evening. It was only with difficulty that Aunt Alice had persuaded him to wait until morning. "After all, young man, it's going to be quite a shock for Miss Frew, and especially your sister. Jane and I have to prepare the ground. So let's get a good night's sleep and we'll call first thing in the morning."

By the look of the dark rings under his eyes, though, Jane doubted Hugh had slept for a single hour. In truth, she was anxious with anticipation too, praying that Miss Frew wouldn't react badly to what she was soon to discover and that Winnie wouldn't be overcome at seeing her brother. Although, how could she not be after fearing she might never see him again? Jane knew only too well the agony of that.

"All right, let's go," Aunt Alice said, getting up and looking out the window. "Our carriage awaits."

As they left the house, Jane handed the envelopes to Hugh. "So after you post them, come up to Gowanlea and wait at the bottom of the drive. I'll come and get you once Aunt Alice has explained everything. All right?"

Hugh accepted the letters with trembling hands, then nodded repeatedly.

They dropped him off in Murray Place and, as the carriage proceeded along Barnton Street, Jane drummed her fingertips on the window ledge.

"Don't worry, dear, once everything's out in the open, you'll feel much better," Aunt Alice said.

"I just hope Miss Frew isn't angry."

"If I know Eliza Frew, it's not angry she'll be, at least not after it's sunk in. It's guilty."

"But it's not her fault Mr MacLeod was the way he was."

"No. But she'll still feel responsible. That's how she's always been – she feels responsible for every child at Gowanlea. But I'm sure once she's spoken to Hugh and realises he doesn't blame her, she'll be glad he's home."

"Do you think so?"

"Well, I certainly hope so."

Before they were halfway up the drive, Rona and Jackie

bounded down from the house, jumping up in greeting and barking with excitement.

"Well, at least someone missed us," Aunt Alice said.

When Jane glanced at the house, a lump formed in her throat. Any second now Miss Frew would appear on the step to ascertain the cause of the commotion.

When the front door opened, Miss Frew put her hands to her mouth in surprise. Then she gave a huge smile and trotted down to meet them, arms open. "Alice! Miss Knight! How wonderful to see you back!" She embraced Aunt Alice, who responded in kind, with what looked like relief and real affection. Then the women separated, reverting to the business-as-usual manner that Jane was more accustomed to.

"Come on, come away in," Miss Frew said, sweeping them into Gowanlea. "I'll get Mrs McCallum to bring some tea." She shouted towards the kitchen and the cook stuck her head around the door. "Look who's back? Tea for three, please." Before Mrs McCallum had the chance to say anything, Miss Frew bustled Jane and Aunt Alice along the corridor and into her study. "Sit down, sit down." She cleared the chairs of paper. "Tell me all about it!"

Jane glanced at Aunt Alice; perhaps she wasn't the only one whose anxiety was making her excitable. Aunt Alice gave a nod of confirmation, which was the sign for Jane to tell the tale of Fred and Albert.

"Well, I know you'll be anxious to hear about the boys, so I'll begin with them. They were chosen by a nice couple, the Menzies, and left with them to their new home on a farm just a day after arriving. The Menzies were so impressed with them and thought them so smart and well-mannered. A credit to you, Miss Frew. And the Menzies took them both, so they'll be together. I was worried they might be separated but in the end it all worked out and—"

"And the boys? Were they happy to go with the Menzies?"

"Oh, yes. Very much so. They were delighted. Couldn't

wait, in fact." Jane laughed. "When I went to say goodbye to them, I was more upset than they were! They were such lovely boys and on the steamer, after the explosion, they ..." Jane tailed off as she felt the emotions rise.

"We'll tell you about that bit of the adventure at a later time," Aunt Alice chipped in. "It's perhaps too fresh in our minds to discuss today."

"Of course," Miss Frew said. "But I must say, Alice, that I couldn't have been more relieved to receive your telegram and then your letter. We were all so fearful." She shifted in her chair. "But, as you say, that's for another day. So back to Fred and Albert, Miss Knight – you were content that the arrangements made by Miss Strachan were appropriate for them?"

"Very much so. But I must say, Miss Frew, I don't know how you do it. If I were to work in your field, I think my heart would be broken every time I had to say goodbye to one of the children. I don't know how you've done it for so many years. Your heart must be very robust!"

"Or some people might say I was just heartless," Miss Frew said, serious at first but then giving a little smile. "And Miss Strachan, Alice? Were your impressions of her favourable? We've been in correspondence for many years and she seems a respectable and upstanding woman who is highly regarded. But there's no substitute for looking someone in the eye to truly see their character."

"Indeed. I can honestly say, Eliza, that you'd be impressed with the establishment she runs. It's large and comfortable, and the children are very well provided for. She, and those who work with her, seem kind, and I have no doubt they've the best interests of their charges at heart. Miss Strachan is organised and efficient, and she outlined to us all the procedures they have in place to make sure the placements are a success."

Jane's heart started to beat faster in anticipation of Aunt Alice mentioning Hugh.

"That's good to hear, Alice. It's what I thought, and hoped, but to hear it from someone so astute a judge of character as you fills me with relief and confidence."

"Indeed. But Eliza, there's something else that we really must tell you."

Mrs McCallum bumped the door with her hip, then looked around for a place to put the tea tray. Miss Frew pushed aside the paperwork on her desk. "Just there's fine, Mrs McCallum, thank you. And you're spoiling us with some baking, I see."

Jane studied Miss Frew. There was something in her jolliness that didn't seem quite in character. Although who was Jane to judge? She had only known the woman a few months. Given the explosion, Miss Frew would have been concerned about the Gowanlea party and have prayed for their safe return. It would hardly be surprising if she wasn't her usual placid self.

Aunt Alice waited until the tea was poured and Mrs McCallum had left the study before continuing. "Yes, as I was saying, Eliza. Despite Miss Strachan's best endeavours and her establishment's rigorous approach to placements and the selection of guardians for the children, she couldn't be criticised if, on occasion, things didn't go to plan."

"If everything I've heard about the lady is true," Miss Frew said, "I would be very surprised if anything ever goes wrong." She bit into her scone and Aunt Alice did likewise. Jane followed suit, savouring the delicious mixture of butter and strawberry jam. They might have had the best apple juice in the world in Canada but their jam wasn't a patch on Mrs McCallum's.

"Yes, sometimes despite every effort, and due to no fault on anyone's part, things can go awry," Aunt Alice said.

"Well, just as they don't go awry at Gowanlea, I'm sure

they don't at Brome County Distributing Home," Miss Frew said, pushing some stray crumbs back into her mouth.

Aunt Alice put her cup and saucer back on the tray. "Eliza, there's something you need to know. It's about—"

"Mmm." Miss Frew drained her cup as if she had the thirst of a navvy. "I needed that. I feel like I've already done a day's work and it's not even noon." She went to pour herself more tea but Aunt Alice leaned across to stop her.

"Eliza, put that down for a minute and listen. There's something I need to tell you."

"But—"

"It's about Hugh McKellar."

Miss Frew let go of the handle of the teapot. "Hugh McKellar?" She glanced at Jane then stared at Aunt Alice. "What about Hugh McKellar?"

"While we were in Canada, Eliza, it came to our attention that Hugh was having a rather difficult time at his new placement. In fact, things were really rather bad for him. We were able to contact him, however, and well, to cut a long story short – and it is a long story, Eliza, which I promise we'll tell you fully in due course – but for the moment, the main thing I must tell you is that Hugh ..." Aunt Alice paused. This time, Jane gave her a nod of encouragement "... Hugh has come back to Scotland with us and is currently residing at home with me." Aunt Alice leaned back in her chair and clasped her hands together. "So there you have it."

Jane tried to interpret the resulting silence. It was as if Aunt Alice couldn't believe what she'd said and Miss Frew couldn't believe what she'd heard. If Jane was inclined to intervene with further explanation, an exchange of looks with her aunt left her in no doubt that she should make no contribution to the discussion. She turned to the window, then looked away quickly when she spotted the photograph of Hugh and his travelling companions on the wall. There was nowhere to look, nowhere to turn, nowhere to go.

Miss Frew suddenly swung round in her chair and started sifting through the papers on her desk. She unearthed a folder and leafed through it. "Yes, yes, I thought so!" She held it up to Aunt Alice and tapped a letter with her index finger. "That's Hugh's last letter. He sent it at Christmas. He doesn't mention anything amiss. In fact, he says ..." She turned the folder back and read speedily from the letter. "'*Dear Miss Frew ... I am in good health and enjoying life ... I've grown a lot in the last while and can do a lot of things on the farm now ... We have eleven horses and two foals*' et cetera et cetera ... ah, now, here we are – '*I have a splendid home ...*'" Miss Frew said, emphasising each word individually. She paused and peered over her spectacles at Aunt Alice. "... '*and live with exceedingly nice people*'." Then she closed the folder, put it back on the desk and turned her palms upwards.

Aunt Alice sat forward, calmly. "Eliza, I don't deny that's what he wrote to you. He didn't want you to know what had happened. He holds you in the highest esteem and is very grateful for everything you've done for him and his sister ..."

Miss Frew shifted in her seat at the mention of Winnie.

"... but he didn't want to worry you. And he feared he'd get into trouble if he made allegations against Mr MacLeod. Miss Strachan didn't know of it either. I'm sure if she had, she would have taken action. But the fact is that Hugh ran away and we offered him the chance to come back here or the means to go to the city and make his way in Canada. He chose to come home." Aunt Alice leaned across and took Miss Frew's hand. "The details don't matter just now. There will be time enough for them. But now all Hugh wants to do is see you and, more importantly, see his sister. He's waiting at the foot of the drive for us to call him in."

Miss Frew pulled away from Aunt Alice. "He's here? But—"

"Of course he's here! Where else would he be?" Aunt Alice said. "Do you think I'd leave him at the house? He's desperate to see Winnie. It was all we could do to persuade him not to march up here as soon as we arrived at Stirling station last night. Should Jane go and bring him up then? And you can call for Winnie?"

Miss Frew stood up and started to pace the study, shaking her head. "No. No."

"What do you mean 'no'? Why ever not, Eliza?"

"Because he, because she—"

"But the boy's almost exploding waiting to see her!" Aunt Alice said, impatient now.

"He can't see her, Alice!" Miss Frew snarled.

"Why ever not?"

Miss Frew stopped in the middle of the room. "Because she's not here. Winnie's gone."

CHAPTER 27

"WHAT DO you mean 'Winnie's gone'?" Miss Knight said abruptly. She'd been so quiet while Alice had been talking that Eliza had almost forgotten she was there.

"Jane! Leave this to me. What do you mean *she's gone*, Eliza?" Alice said.

Eliza went over to the window and looked outside. There was no sign of Hugh McKellar at the front of the house and she couldn't see to the bottom of the drive from the study. But if what Alice said was true, he was standing there now, barely a hundred yards from her door. She took a step back and looked at the photograph of him taken on the day he'd left for Canada – a glum little boy staring into the distance, reluctant to leave his sister behind, grimly accepting the fate Eliza had decided for him. The fate that was meant to be the making of him and provide him with opportunities he could never have hoped for in Stirling. The fate that was to confer upon him unspeakable blessings.

Emigration had been shown to be the best thing, not just for the children, but also for the nation's economy. There had been some exceptional instances, Eliza had heard, when it hadn't been as successful as initially anticipated. But every child who'd gone abroad from Gowanlea had made something of themselves. Hadn't she told Hugh's father about the children who had left her and become farmers, tradesmen and even doctors? And no child from Gowanlea had ever reported experiencing anything other than kindness and support. All their letters were filled with stories of lives with promise and security. It wasn't as if Hugh McKellar was a troublesome boy; in the few months he'd been with her, he had been polite, well-behaved and industrious. He didn't belong to degraded parents, his father was respectable and hard-working, so of the many boys she'd seen off to Canada, Hugh was not one she would have imagined encountering difficulties.

"Eliza?" Alice was tugging her arm. "Come and sit down. Tell me where Winnie's gone."

Eliza lingered in the space between the window and her chair, trying to organise her thoughts and choose her words. Of all the scenarios she had anticipated and feared, this one, so outlandish, hadn't for a moment crossed her mind. How could it have?

Eventually, she sat down. "You say Hugh's waiting at the bottom of the drive?"

"He is. And Jane will go and get him whenever you're ready." Eliza glanced at Miss Knight, who smiled sympathetically. "But perhaps before we call him in, you should tell us what's happened to Winnie, so we can decide how best to explain it to him. He's going to be so disappointed after everything that's happened."

Eliza looked at the floor.

"I just don't understand it," Miss Knight started to say. "Winnie was—"

"Jane!" Alice said sharply. "Let Miss Frew tell us what's going on."

Miss Knight closed her mouth and rubbed her hands together impatiently.

"Well, Eliza?"

Before she spoke, she asked silently for His forgiveness. "There's no other way to say it so I'll just come out with it – she's run away. Eloped."

"What?" Miss Knight stood up. "She can't have!"

"Jane, sit down!" Alice said. "Let Miss Frew speak. Eloped with whom, Eliza?"

She looked up at the ceiling. *Lying lips are an abomination to the Lord.* "Thomas Keith."

"What?" Alice and her niece said at the same time and in the same tone of disbelief.

"He came for her the other night," Eliza said. "Two of the girls saw them leave together and—"

"No, no," Jane Knight was saying.

"... in the morning, after they'd gone ..."

"No, no ..."

Eliza opened the small desk drawer. "... the monthly takings were gone too."

Miss Knight stood up again. "That's impossible!"

"Well," Eliza said, "I can only tell you what I—"

"And it's impossible because—"

"Jane!"

"... she knew we were going to look for Hugh. She would never have willingly left before she'd heard from us. I know she wouldn't. Never! Never, ever, would she have left without knowing what had happened to her ..." Miss Knight began to sob, then took her seat again. "... brother."

If a galloping horse had knocked her down, Eliza wouldn't have felt more winded. She stared at Alice's niece in utter shock. "Winnie knew about all this? But how did she, if you—"

"It was Winnie who asked me to go," Miss Knight managed to splutter. "Hugh wrote telling her how awful things were at his new placement and how he feared if he didn't get away that he'd ... that something terrible might happen. I saw the letter. And then, when I knew you were looking for an escort for Fred and

Albert, I thought I could try and do something to help Winnie. She was demented with worry about Hugh. And utterly helpless to do anything for him. I know what that feels like so ..." Miss Knight started to weep, then covered her face with her hands.

"What Jane says is true, Eliza. I spoke to the girl myself. She gave me a postcard to give to Hugh."

"You knew as well, Alice?" Eliza gasped, in growing astonishment. "Before you went?"

"I did."

"But why didn't you tell me?"

"Because I wasn't sure it was true and I didn't want to accuse anyone without knowing the truth. And if it wasn't true, I thought the journey, in any case, would be good for Jane to help with her ... well, her own sadness about ..." Alice leaned over and rubbed her niece's shoulder to console her. "It's all right, dear. You've been through a lot." She turned back to Eliza. "What Jane said is right, though. Winnie wouldn't have run away without finding out if we'd seen Hugh. And if she hasn't run off, what's happened to her?"

Eliza shuddered as it dawned on her. "He's taken her." She would never forgive herself if Winnie came to any harm at Thomas Keith's hands.

"What?" Alice said. "Thomas Keith's *taken her*? Why would he have taken her?"

Miss Knight dabbed her red eyes. "That day I saw him with you in the garden, he was threatening you, wasn't he?"

"What?" Alice said. "Is that true, Eliza?"

She nodded.

"But why?"

She looked at her friend, then closed her eyes and breathed deeply.

"Miss Frew, we need to know so we can find Winnie," she heard Miss Knight say.

Eliza clasped her hands together and said aloud: "'Peace I

leave with you, my peace I give unto you. Let not your heart be troubled, neither let it be afraid.'"

When she opened her eyes, Alice and her niece were staring at her with a mixture of anticipation and apprehension. "He's taken her because ... Alice, you must forgive me for what I'm about to tell you. If I'd known what he would do, I would never have acted the way I have."

"Eliza, what has Thomas Keith done?"

"He's taken Winnie because ... because he was blackmailing me and I refused to give him any more money."

"Blackmailing you?" Alice laughed in confusion. "He doesn't even know you. What could he possibly be blackmailing you over?"

Eliza hung her head; this wasn't how she had imagined the truth coming out.

"Jane?" Alice said. "Perhaps you could leave Miss Frew and me for a moment."

"No. Your niece has a right to hear this too, given everything she's done for Winnie."

Miss Knight glanced at Alice then sat down again.

"You remember, I'm sure, Alice, the day we went to hear Mr Moody and Mr Sankey and I committed myself to the life I now have?"

"Of course."

"And you remember Catherine told us of the death of Nellie, the Keiths' former maid?"

"Yes. But—"

"And do you recall the week before a newborn was found dead, abandoned at the poorhouse?"

"Yes."

"That was the child of William Keith and Nellie."

Alice put her hand over her mouth.

"William came to see me. Nellie had just left the child with him. He wanted my help to find it a good home. I refused, and at first wanted nothing to do with him. I was going to tell

Catherine. But then he said I would ruin her life if I did, and that not only would his family lose their reputation, but we would lose ours too. He suggested we take the child to the poorhouse and they would take it in. It was alive at the time, I swear, Alice. I thought if they took it in, then at least it would have some chance and that Catherine would be spared any heartache. So I waited while he left it on the doorstep, and we thought that was that. But then it died, Alice. It died! And when I discovered that, I couldn't live with what we'd done and so—"

"But you didn't do anything, Eliza!" Alice kneeled beside her. "It was William, all William."

"But I helped him! I should have—"

"What choice did you have? What else was he going to do? He wasn't going to claim the child as his own, was he? And he wasn't going to marry Nellie either. And if he couldn't find a family to take it in, and he didn't take it to the poorhouse, what else would have happened to it? Gowanlea didn't exist then. He would have left it to die. You wouldn't have let him do that, would you?"

"Of course not!"

"Well then!" Alice squeezed Eliza's knee. "And you didn't intend for it to die, did you?"

"No!"

"Exactly."

"But Thomas Keith knows. Thomas Keith told me William revealed it to him on his deathbed and he said that, if I didn't give him money, he'd expose what I'd done. At the time, I wrote to tell William he had to break it off with Catherine, that I wouldn't be able to live with myself if he became a member of the family. I told him if he didn't let her down gently, I'd reveal everything I knew and confess all I'd done."

"But you didn't do anything!"

"But Thomas Keith has the letter, Alice," Eliza protested. "He has the letter!"

"No, Eliza. It was only because William came to you. It was he who put you in that position and it was he who was wrong. *He*, Eliza. William. Not you. And even if you did make a mistake, what real choice did you have? My goodness, you've made up for it over the years! Hasn't she, Jane?"

Miss Knight slipped from her chair. "Of course you have, Miss Frew."

Eliza put one arm around Alice and the other around Miss Knight. "I was so afraid of what he might say that I gave him all my savings. But then—"

"You haven't, Eliza!"

"... once they were gone, I told him I wasn't going to give him a single penny of Gowanlea's donations and that he should do his worst. I was preparing for him to expose me. He warned me he would when I was in the street and Mrs Duncan was ..."

She paused; Ann and Susan Duncan had said that the man had come to tell them their mother loved them, to give them a present from their mother, to ask if they wanted to go and live with their mother. How did Thomas Keith know any of that unless he'd been in contact with Mrs Duncan?

"What is it, Eliza?"

Maybe he'd come to snatch away Ann and Susan but Winnie had disturbed them; maybe in exchange for leaving them be, he'd taken her. And either – pray to God – she had gone with him voluntarily, albeit reluctantly, or she'd been taken by him unwillingly.

"Oh dear Lord." If he'd hurt a single hair on Winnie's head, Eliza wouldn't be responsible for her actions. *If thou do that which is evil, be afraid; for he beareth not the sword in vain: for he is the minister of God, a revenger to execute wrath upon him that doeth evil.* "He's taken her so that I'll give him more money."

Alice stood up. "We have to go to the police. This has gone too far."

Eliza rose too. "No, no! I don't know where he's taken her

but I suspect I know who might. Let's try that first. Alice, please! Otherwise I'll have to explain everything and everyone will find out about William and Nellie and the baby, and what good would that do after all these years?"

"Well, I ..."

Miss Knight got to her feet. "What about Hugh? What are we going to tell him? We can't leave him standing out there forever."

Alice hesitated.

"She's right," Eliza said.

The seconds before Alice replied felt like hours to Eliza. Then her friend gave a determined nod.

"All right. This is what we'll do – Jane and I will go and get Hugh and give you a few minutes to compose yourself, Eliza. We'll tell him Winnie's not here but that we've a plan to get her home. Then we'll bring him in to see you. You have to see him, Eliza, you know that."

"Of course! While I'm talking to him, can you secure a cab? There's somewhere we need to go."

"Very well. Come on, Jane. Leave Miss Frew to sort herself out and we'll go and get Hugh."

Eliza remained for a moment in the quiet safety of her study, devastated by regret that she was about to shatter Hugh's hopes. That poor, poor boy, who was standing at the foot of the drive, excited and anxious, just waiting to be called, believing it only minutes before he'd be reunited with his sister. His spirit was about to be crushed. Again. It was just as well people didn't know what lay ahead.

At the sound of crunching outside on the gravel, Eliza gave a start. She rushed from her study and went to the front door, which Alice had left wide open. A lump came to her throat when she watched Jackie and Rona race to greet the tall young man who was already bending down to pet them. The dogs might not have changed much, but Hugh McKellar surely had. He was a head taller than the ladies he was accompanying and his light brown hair was thicker than Eliza remembered. And how smart he looked in that dark suit, collar and tie – that would be Alice's doing.

When Eliza went to the front step, Hugh raised his head. On seeing her, he slowly got to his feet and went forward, Jackie and Rona padding behind him, tails wagging.

"Miss Frew," he said, tears in his eyes.

Eliza swallowed. She embraced him, holding him tightly. "Hugh, son. I am so, so sorry."

Hᴜɢʜ'ѕ ꜰᴀᴄᴇ froze in horror before contorting in anger. Then it melted in fear.

Eliza put her hand on his shoulder. "This is what we're going to do – Miss Jane and I are going find out where Winnie is and you and Miss Knight will stay here. I'll ask Mrs McCallum to make you something to eat. And once we—"

"No! I'm coming too! I need to find her."

"No, listen – you need to stay here and calm yourself. I promise you, when we find out where she is, we'll come back and get you. And we'll all go together."

She watched Hugh mull over her plan, and hoped he had more faith in it than she did herself. But it was the best Eliza could come up with. Mrs Duncan was the only link she could think of. And of course she had no idea where Thomas Keith lived, where he stayed when he visited Stirling, or who he fraternised with. He had talked about relocating his business and she'd assumed it was based in Glasgow, but she didn't actually know. In fact, she didn't know anything about him at all, other than that he was a man of exceedingly poor character. Worse than his father, who, while he might have been stupid and vain, and a deceitful and manipulative fornicator, behaved the way he did because he thought he had no other choice. Thomas Keith had plenty of choice and he had chosen blackmail and kidnapping.

"You promise you'll come for me as soon as you find out where she is?" Hugh said.

Eliza squeezed his arm. "Of course I will!"

"All right then. I'll stay with Miss Knight, if that's what you think's best, Miss Frew."

"Excellent. Well, there's no time to waste."

When Eliza went to open the study door, Hugh tugged her arm. "But there's one thing I'm telling you now, Miss Frew." His face contorted again. "If that man's laid one finger on my sister, I'll kill him."

"Hugh McKellar! What does the good book say in Exodus and Deuteronomy?"

He looked at his feet, the way he used to as a little boy when he'd been caught doing something he shouldn't. "Thou shalt not kill."

"Precisely. Thou shalt not kill. So we'll have no more of that talk, thank you very much. In any case, I've told you, he won't harm Winnie. He's only interested in getting money from me and this is how he thinks he'll get it. It won't benefit him to hurt her, and that's all he cares about – how he can benefit from a situation."

Hugh gave a long sigh. "All right." He nodded. "But I just hope you're right, Miss Frew."

Right? Of course she was right. Hugh would have no cause to kill Thomas Keith, because if he'd laid a finger on Winnie McKellar, Eliza would kill him herself. *If a man have a stubborn and rebellious son, which will not obey the voice of his father, and that, when they have chastened him will not hearken unto them; then shall his father lay hold on him and bring him; and all the men of his city shall stone him with stones, that he die.* It said that in Deuteronomy, too.

"Good. Right. Now, come on – let's go and see if that cab's there."

～

As the carriage trundled out of town through Newhouse and St Ninians towards Bannockburn Road, Eliza watched the stone villas disappear and the rows of cottages rise up. Labourers, quarrymen and mill workers lived in them, and Eliza had made many a trip over the years to their cramped, sometimes squalid, homes.

"Miss Frew?" Miss Knight shifted on the bench opposite. "I hope you don't mind me saying this but ..." Eliza cast a glance in her direction that she hoped conveyed the message that she did, in fact, mind. "... I've been thinking about what you told us about your sister and—"

"Miss Knight, I—" Eliza said, holding her hand up.

"Please, Miss Frew, let me say this. You were put in a terrible situation by Thomas Keith's father and you did what you thought was best for your sister and your family. If I'd been in that situation, I believe I would've done the same." Miss Knight tapped the bench with her fingers. "There, I've said it. I'm sorry if I've offended you but I just wanted you to know."

Miss Knight turned away from her and stared out the window. Despite herself, Eliza was touched. Miss Knight's heart might still be wounded from grief, but it was a good heart and a brave heart. She leaned forward and patted the girl's knee. "Thank you." Miss Knight reciprocated with a sad smile. "You know ..." Eliza sat back again. "... I still remember very clearly the day your aunt brought you and your brother to Gowanlea and you waited in the garden while we talked. I thought you were twins at first."

Miss Knight faced Eliza. "Yes, I recall."

"You were the same height, had the same colour hair and

eyes. The same dimples. And when I asked if you were twins, you looked very pleased with yourself and your brother looked distinctly dissatisfied!"

"Ha! Yes, it used to annoy him because he always wanted people to know he was older. It happened quite a lot when we were children."

"My sister and I were never taken for twins. There was only a year between us but we didn't look alike and our characters couldn't have been more different."

"She was so young when she died. It must have been very difficult for you – especially given what had happened," Miss Knight ventured.

Eliza sighed. "It was, dear. But you know, when it happened, it strengthened my resolve to serve the Lord and to give myself completely to His service. What happened with William Keith and that poor girl and her baby was terrible, and what happened to Catherine was terrible, but from these terrible things so much good flowed. Of course, I wish none of it had happened, that William and Catherine had married, had had children of their own, and that Nellie had lived and made a life for herself. But I wonder then – would I have done what I have? Would there have been a Gowanlea? Would so many little lambs have been saved? How different might the lives of so many have been?" She took Miss Knight's hands in hers. "You must feel that, too, about your brother's death."

"Well, I ..." Miss Knight looked away.

"It doesn't mean you loved him any less, dear. If anything, it shows how much you loved him. It was because of that love you were prepared and able to do what you've done for Winnie and Hugh."

Miss Knight opened her handbag, took out a handkerchief and blew her nose. "Thank you, Miss Frew. Thank you."

The carriage slowed, then drew up at the last row of single-storey, slate-roofed brick cottages. The end one was Mrs Duncan's, who had moved there from Cambusbarron after

Hayford Mill closed and she lost her job. From what Eliza had heard, she worked at Rockvale Mill in town now.

When they got down from the carriage, Eliza went to the threshold of the open door and peered into the house. There was one large room with a bed on the right, a table and chairs in the middle, and a small stove on the left. Mrs Duncan was standing by the stove, her back to the door. When Eliza knocked twice, she turned around with a start.

"In the name o' the wee man!" Much to Eliza's relief, Mrs Duncan set down the knife she had been holding before approaching. "Miss Frew! What are *you* doing here? Have you come to have me lifted for the other day? I never touched you!"

Eliza stepped back when Mrs Duncan got to the door. "No, it's nothing like that. I can understand you must have been upset about the outcome of the custody hearing."

"Aye, I was that." She folded her arms and pushed out her chest. "But you ken I didn't touch you."

"No, you didn't," Eliza said, "although perhaps not for want of trying." She hinted at a smile and Mrs Duncan reeled back slightly. "However, that's not why I'm here, I can assure you."

"Well, what are you doing here then?"

"I wanted to ask you about Thomas Keith."

"About who?"

"Thomas Keith."

"Who's he?" Mrs Duncan stepped outside and glanced up and down the street.

"He's the man I was talking to on King Street the day you accosted me."

"Aw, him? He told me his name was Kennedy. William Kennedy."

"You spoke to him then?"

"Aye, he came running after me and was wanting to ken all about what my problem wi' you was."

"And you told him, I presume?"

"As I said, I was upset, and well, he offered me a few pennies so I told him my story then he said he might be able to help me out 'cause he could speak to Ann and Susan and give them a message for me and maybe get them out o' Gowanlea."

"And do you know where he is now, Mrs Duncan?"

"I wish I did. He said he was going to come back and tell me what the girls said but I've no' seen hide nor hair o' him since. Another feckless man, if you ask me."

"Did he happen to say where he was living at the moment? Or where he might be going?"

Mrs Duncan raised her eyebrows. "Why do you want to ken? What's he done that you're looking for him? It must be something important for you to come all this way." She looked Eliza's companion up and down. "The pair o' you."

"It is something important," Miss Knight was prompted to say. "And we'd be most grateful if you have any information about Mr Keith's – Mr Kennedy's – whereabouts."

"And who might you be?" Mrs Duncan said.

"Miss Jane Knight. I take the nature club at Gowanlea that Ann and Susan attend. I know them very well."

"Oh you do, do you?"

"Yes. And they're lovely, intelligent girls who were protected from Mr Keith – Kennedy – by another lovely girl who we have reason to believe may be being kept against her will by him."

"What? He took her?"

"We think it's possible," Miss Knight said. "So, Mrs Duncan, for the sake of that girl, who has been so good to your girls, if you know anything about this man's whereabouts, I beg you, tell us."

"I see." Mrs Duncan stroked her chin, then turned back and addressed Eliza. "Did you ken that one o' the judges at the hearing said I should have 'reasonable access' to my girls?"

"No, but I haven't seen the full written ruling yet."

"Aye well, he did. So how's about – you make sure I have *reasonable access* and I tell you what I ken about where your Mr Keith might be at?"

"Do you know where he is?" Eliza said.

"I'm no' sure exactly but he mentioned an address."

"What address?"

"*Reasonable access*?"

Eliza glowered at Mrs Duncan.

"I could be there to supervise any meeting," Miss Knight said quickly.

"Well?" Mrs Duncan said.

Eliza tutted. What had it come to when she was haggling on the doorstep of a millworker's cottage? God forgive her, but needs must when the devil drives. "All right. But only at Gowanlea. And only if the girls want to, and only if it's made clear to them they can stay there as long as they want to."

Mrs Duncan thrust her hand out. "Deal."

Eliza rolled her tongue in her mouth, then as lightly and as briefly as she could, brushed her hand against Mrs Duncan's. "Deal," she muttered.

Miss Knight played mediator again. "Thank you, Mrs Duncan. So, what was the address Mr Kennedy mentioned to you?"

"He said he'd rented a room from ex-Provost Brown at the Top o' the Town somewhere and that he was going to set up a business or something or other. To be honest, I wasn't really listening. He's too fond of his own voice, that one."

"What?" Had Eliza heard that right? "Ex-Provost Brown owns property at the Top of the Town?"

"Aye, according to your Mr Kennedy, or Mr Keith, or whoever he says he is."

Eliza was flabbergasted. The medical officer had been telling the burgh's Public Health Committee for years that some of the houses at the Top of the Town were unfit for human habitation and should either be improved or condemned. But, it was said, the landlords wouldn't fund the work. Ex-Provost Brown had sat on that Committee, and might even have chaired it at one point. Had he pontificated for years about the terrible conditions the children who came to Gowanlea lived in, while benefitting from their misery as a slum landlord himself?

"Surely not?"

"Aye, so he said."

Eliza shook her head. Ex-Provost Brown should be ashamed of himself. Something would have to be done. But first things first.

"And I mean, who actually is he, this Kennedy Keith? And what was he doing talking to you in the street, Miss Frew?"

"He's someone you really don't want to know, Mrs Duncan, believe you me," Eliza said.

"Aye well, if he shows his face round here again, he'll get short shrift, I'll tell you that for nothing."

"As he most certainly should. Anyway, thank you, Mrs Duncan, for the information. I know you didn't have to tell me what you know, or even speak to me. So, for that, I thank you."

"Well, Miss Frew, I don't suppose we'll ever be friends, but we can at least be civil to one another. Especially since I'll be coming to Gowanlea to see the lassies. Now, would next Saturday afternoon suit you?"

Eliza smiled somewhat ungraciously. "Of course, Mrs Duncan. I'll see you then."

She knew exactly where to find ex-Provost Brown – the public house on Port Street that he was known to frequent at certain times on certain days. She despatched the coachman into the insalubrious premises with a warning: "If he's not keen to come out, or if he tells you to say he's not there, tell him that if he doesn't come out, Miss Frew will have no hesitation in coming in and that he shouldn't risk calling her bluff!"

Although Eliza had been inside slums and had worked with women and children who lived the most demeaning lives, she had never set foot in a public house and had no intention of ever doing so. She pulled the window blind half-down so she was less conspicuous to those passing by, then tapped her fingers impatiently on the sill. "Avert your eyes, Miss Knight."

After a few moments, there was a knock on the carriage door.

"Oh, it's yourself, Miss Frew!" ex-Provost Brown said, reeling slightly as he pulled it open. "I wouldn't have believed it."

Eliza could smell the ale on him from where she sat. "Get in and shut the door behind you!" she snapped. "I don't want people seeing me hanging about here."

With some difficulty, he climbed into the carriage and fell heavily onto the seat beside her. Eliza pulled the window down for some fresh air and instructed the coachman to take them to Gowanlea.

"What's going on, Miss Frew?" ex-Provost Brown said, swaying with the motion of the wheels on the cobbles.

"I believe you've rented a room to Thomas Keith at the Top of the Town?"

"What?" he said, looking bemused. "Why are you—?"

"I don't have time for explanations, although we'll certainly return to the subject another day. Now where is the room you've rented to Mr Keith?"

"And who is this young lady?" ex-Provost Brown asked, seeming to notice Miss Knight for the first time.

"I think it would be better all round if we just pretend that the young lady isn't here. What is the address?"

"Thomas Keith, you say, Thomas Keith? Oh, you mean Mr Keith from Glasgow? Yes, yes, he's an ambitious young man. He's going to be relocating his business here and he wants a place to store merchandise until he gets more suitable premises. He—"

"Address!" Eliza shouted.

As the carriage rounded a corner, ex-Provost Brown tipped over and banged his head against the side.

"Well?"

He sat up, rubbing his temple. "Now was it 23 or 25 ...? Or 45 Broad Street?"

"How many rooms do you own there?" Eliza said, astounded.

"I think it's No. 25. Yes, 25. He took the room vacated by Mr Campbell. Well, I say *vacated*, but he's actually in prison now. Although I suppose he did vacate it, even if it wasn't by his own choice."

When ex-Provost Brown chuckled at his own remark, Eliza leaned across and knocked on the cabin to attract the driver's attention. "Drunken oaf," she muttered.

The carriage pulled up and the coachman came down and opened the door. "Yes, Miss Frew?"

She pulled ex-Provost Brown's arm and levered him towards the door. "He'll walk home from here. The fresh air will do him good." Then she shoved him out of the carriage.

"Now, quickly, back to Gowanlea."

CHAPTER 29

THE DESIRE TO find Winnie overcame Jane's breathlessness and the stitch that was getting stronger in her side. Ahead of her, Miss Frew and Hugh stomped up Bridge Street like clockwork soldiers, arms swishing high through the air and legs strong and straight. For every one of Hugh's strides, Miss Frew took two abrupt steps. Jane linked arms with Aunt Alice and powered on.

As they got to the top of Bridge Street, it levelled off and narrowed into St Mary's Wynd. The high, looming buildings on either side blocked the sun and, in the shade of the lane, two pipe-smoking, grimy-faced men stepped out of the way of the approaching group. Miss Frew and Hugh parted to skirt around a pile of rubble, then came together again with perfect synchronicity as they marched on. Jane stumbled over some uneven cobbles outside the tavern at the junction of the Wynd and Broad Street; Aunt Alice pushed her on quickly. "This isn't the spot to pause, dear."

Hugh and Miss Frew stopped in the middle of the street, scouring the blackened walls of the street's three- and four-storey sub-divided buildings, which had once been the mansion houses of earls and merchants. They went up to the Mercat Cross, on the steps of which bare-footed, squealing children were running up and down. If Jane recalled correctly from Aunt Alice's many local history lessons during childhood walks, this was the place where wrongdoers had once been exhibited in the stocks and criminals marched from the adjacent Tolbooth to be hanged. In former times, Thomas Keith wouldn't have had far to go to meet his fate. But the scaffold hadn't been erected in the town in more than fifty years so fate was on Mr Keith's side. Not that Jane rated his chances much if Hugh or Miss Frew were to get their hands on him; she had never before seen such quiet fury.

"That's it there," Miss Frew said, pointing at the three-storey house to the left of the Tolbooth. "This way. Come on."

Jane stopped to peer down the dank close that Miss Frew and Hugh were already heading along.

Aunt Alice gave her a little nudge. "You heard her."

Jane stepped over some malodorous effluence that was trickling down the street, following the course of the spaces between the cobbles. She paused a few paces into the pend. Some empty barrels were stacked along one wall and two mangy dogs were stretched across the passageway. Miss Frew and Hugh turned into the back court and started to shout Winnie's name. Then the banging started.

"Go on! Get moving, Jane!" Aunt Alice hissed.

Jane hoicked her skirts up and hastened on tiptoe to the end of the close where Hugh was pounding on a wooden door. Strips of its peeling green paint cracked to the ground.

"There's a key up there, missus."

They all turned to the street urchin who had materialised and was pointing to the top of the door. Hugh reached up, ran his fingers along the lintel and snatched a key.

The child held out his hand for a reward. "Ah," Aunt Alice said. "You have initiative. Eliza, shut your ears. Young man, is it worth a farthing for you to stand here and come and alert us if anyone comes?"

"Alice!"

The boy's eyes lit up. "Aye, missus."

Aunt Alice delved into her pocket and plucked out a coin. "Right, here's one farthing now. You'll get another one when we come back. All right?"

"Aye! All right."

"Alice," Miss Frew scolded.

Hugh turned the key in the external door and it opened into a shared corridor, off of which were several more doors. He started along – Miss Frew not far behind him – pounding on each door and shouting for Winnie. Suddenly, amid the ruckus, Jane thought she heard something from the second door they passed.

"Miss Frew! Hugh! Shush!" Everyone froze. "Listen." She was right – there was tapping in short bursts of three coming from somewhere. Hugh ran back along, putting his ear to each door and calling his sister's name. Jane cocked her head, screwed up her face and concentrated on the sound. It wasn't coming from the other side of any of these doors, it was coming from above. "Up there!" she shouted, pointing to the ceiling.

They hared to the end of the corridor, where a spiral staircase led upstairs. Hugh bounded ahead and was already hammering on the doors on the first floor when the ladies caught up.

"Winnie! Winnie!"

The tapping seemed louder. *And* – Jane looked to the ceiling – was that a shout? "The next one up!"

Hugh rushed back to the staircase, Jane belting behind him, leaving Miss Frew and Aunt Alice puffing in the corridor. When Jane reached the second-floor landing, Hugh was hammering the end door with his fist. He stepped back and kicked the door with all his might, then rammed it with his shoulder. The door shook but remained closed. The state of the tenements might worry the burgh medical officer but their front doors certainly seemed robust enough.

There was a call from inside the room: "Hugh? Hugh? Is that you, Hugh?"

"Winnie! I'm coming! It's me! I'm coming!"

As he started kicking the door again, Jane looked around for something that might act as a battering ram. Then it struck her. "Try above the door!" she shouted.

He reached up to the lintel. There it was.

"Is she here?" Miss Frew and Aunt Alice had made it to the second floor.

Hugh's hands were shaking so much it seemed to take him forever to unlock the door. But when the key finally turned, he burst in, closely followed by Miss Frew.

Jane and Aunt Alice collided in their effort to get into the room. Jane elbowed her aunt out of the way, then put a foot over the threshold, rearing at the smell of mould, damp and human waste that wafted out. She covered her mouth and nose with her hand. Aunt Alice was behind her, peeking over her shoulder. "Oh, thank God."

Winnie was in the middle of the room, weeping in Hugh's arms. Miss Frew was embracing them both. When Jane began to sob, Aunt Alice hugged her; Jane could feel Aunt Alice sobbing too.

Once she acclimatised to the dimness, Jane saw that, except for a bed, a stool and a bucket in the corner, the room was bare, its single window boarded up. She stood aside to let Aunt Alice see, then gripped her hand and went in.

Winnie, startled by their footsteps, jerked her head around. Her hair was tangled and her face smeared. "Miss Knight! Miss Knight! I don't know how to thank you. Thank you so much for bringing him home." She fell into Hugh's arms again, wailing.

"Winnie, we need to leave," Miss Frew said, "urgently. I

know you want to be with Hugh but we need to get out of here before Thomas Keith comes back and finds us."

Winnie separated from her brother and wiped her nose with the back of her hand. "He said earlier on he was going to Glasgow and that he'd be back this evening. I'm so sorry, Miss Frew, I didn't mean to, but he made me. I didn't want Ann and Susan to come to any harm, so I went with him. He threatened me and said that if I didn't go with him he would ruin you."

"Never mind that just now. There's plenty of time for that," Miss Frew said. "We just need to get you back home to Gowanlea."

Hugh took Winnie's hands in his. "Did he hurt you? Did he ... touch you?"

She shook her head. "He didn't do anything to me."

"Thank God."

"He just said I had to stay here until he'd sorted things out with Miss Frew. But he locked me in and I had no way of getting out and—"

Miss Frew squeezed her arm. "Shush. It's all right, Winnie. But you need to come with us now."

Hugh held her tightly again. "Come on, Win. Let's go. Everything's going to be all right. I'm here now. I'm here."

"Haw! Missus! The landlord's coming!" The urchin was standing on the threshold.

"What?" Aunt Alice reached into her pocket again. "Where is he?"

"He was coming along the close so I ran to tell you. Just like you said, missus."

"Yes, thank you." She gave him another coin. "Here. Now go back down again and let us know if anyone else is coming."

"Right, missus!"

As the urchin sprinted away, ex-Provost Brown appeared in the corridor, flushed and panting. "What on earth is going on here?"

Aunt Alice stepped towards him but Miss Frew pulled her back. "I'll deal with this, Alice."

"Be my guest, Eliza."

"Miss Frew!" Already reeling from having seen her in the vicinity of a public house, ex-Provost Brown seemed hardly able to believe his eyes that she was now standing in one of his rooms.

Miss Frew stepped forward. "*What on earth is going on here?* That's exactly the question I'll be asking the council, the Public Health Committee and the burgh medical officer. How dare you keep dwellings like this? They're worse than pigsties. In fact, I've seen cleaner pigsties. Pigs would turn their noses up at this. How dare you sit round that council table for years saying that dwellings like this should be condemned when you're one of the very landlords who won't put their hands in their pockets to bring them up to scratch." Ex-Provost Brown went to say something, then seemed to think better of it as Miss Frew continued her diatribe.

"What's more, you've had the cheek to lecture anyone who'll listen about the awful situations my children have come from, when you've been complicit in creating these conditions yourself. And worse, you're now doing business with the likes of Thomas Keith, who kidnapped this young girl and was going to do who knows what with her in a property rented to him by you. Never in all my days have I—"

Ex-Provost Brown was jolted into speaking. "Kidnapped?" he said, horrified. "Miss Frew, I can assure you, I—"

"I should march you right now straight to the Chief Constable myself."

"... I had no idea about any of this! As I told you earlier, Mr Keith told me he needed somewhere to store some merchandise for a business venture. If I'd known he—"

"Oh, so you remember our conversation earlier today. I thought perhaps you might have been too drunk." Miss Frew began to rant again. "How a man in your position can behave in such depraved ways, I cannot fathom. But no more, I tell you. No more. I won't allow it. As soon as I've got this poor girl back to Gowanlea, and settled, I'll be paying a visit to people who will put a stop to this once and for all."

"But Miss Frew! Please! You can't," ex-Provost Brown pleaded.

"Oh I assure you, I can."

"I had no idea about the girl. I wouldn't have given Mr Keith a room had I even suspected what his intentions were. You must believe me. And of course, now that I do know, I will be severing all ties with him, I can assure you of that."

"That won't help the poor people who have to live in your slums," Miss Frew continued masterfully. "This cannot be allowed to continue. I will have to report the matter to—"

"Miss Frew, please! I promise you, I'll undertake improvements to all my tenements. Everything the Public Health Committee recommends. Everything. And more! If only you'll give me time."

"Oh, I don't think—"

"I'll get the work commissioned straight away. Today. There's no need to alert anyone to the matter. Surely?"

Jane held her breath as Miss Frew tapped her toe on the floor in contemplation. She had never seemed so impressive.

"By the time I sort out this business with Mr Keith, I expect to see this place riddled with tradesmen. If it's not—"

"It will be, Miss Frew, it will be." Ex-Provost Brown looked as if he might weep.

"Well, if it's not, I don't need to tell you what the consequences will be."

"Yes, thank you, Miss Frew," he grovelled, "thank you."

"Now get out of our way," she said, shoving the wretched man aside. "There are more worthy things than you that need my attention."

The march back down to Gowanlea wasn't quite as brisk and fervent as the one up. Miss Frew led the way, while Hugh cradled and protected Winnie. Jane and Aunt Alice brought up the rear, glancing around constantly, on the alert for Thomas Keith. If what Winnie said about him not returning until evening was true, they had a few hours yet until he made his appearance. But they couldn't be too careful.

As they were heading up the driveway of Gowanlea, Jane's legs started to tremble. She held on to the wall to steady herself, then reached for Aunt Alice's hand and pulled her back. "We'll go into the garden and give you some time alone," she called, as Winnie, Hugh and Miss Frew reached the front door. Then she scuttled down the path and rushed through the garden gate to the swing. She collapsed on the seat and clung to the chain with both hands, fearing that, if she let go, her body would be forced to the ground by every emotion she had been trying to control for the past six months.

"What is it, dear?"

Jane put her arms around her aunt, and hung onto her as if her life depended on it.

She wasn't sure how long Aunt Alice held her, but when Jane's head eventually cleared, the sun had dipped behind the castle. What a day it had been, and how drained she felt. She had loitered outside two public houses and been inside a Broad Street slum. She wouldn't be telling her mother about that bit of the amazing adventure. She opened her mouth to speak but could only manage a croak.

"What's that, dear? Are you feeling better now?"

Jane coughed then cleared her throat. "I was just thinking about Mother and what she'd say if she knew the places I'd been today."

"Oh heavens! Don't even think about it. Canada will pale into insignificance at the mention of the Top of the Town!"

Jane gave a little splutter and wiped her eyes. "Thank you." She hugged Aunt Alice. "For everything."

Aunt Alice sighed. "You're going to be all right, dear, you really are. And I couldn't be prouder." Aunt Alice took a step back. "And you'll need to start thinking about your future soon. Where you see yourself, what you want to do. After all, you weren't planning on staying here forever when you wrote to me, were you?"

Jane shook her head, thinking back to the day in her father's study after seeing Harold when in desperation she'd put pen to paper. Never could she have imagined what would come to pass.

"And you know, there are opportunities open to you that I could never have dreamed of. That your mother could never have dreamed of. That Miss Frew could never have dreamed of," Aunt Alice said. "You have choices, Jane dear. Lots of choices. You must see that now, after everything that's happened. You're strong. You can do whatever you put your mind to."

Jane looked over to the Ochils, their mix of mauves, browns, yellows and greens standing out crisp and clear in the late afternoon light. "I suppose you're right."

"And whatever you choose, you'll have my complete support. Only do choose well, dear. I don't want to be listening to your mother complaining about it for the next thirty years."

The gate squeaked. Winnie and Hugh, hand in hand, came across the garden, Miss Frew by their side. Winnie looked much better now, face washed, hair brushed and in fresh clothes.

Jane started towards her. "Are you all right?"

"Miss Knight, I don't know how I can ever thank you – and you, too, Miss Knight ..." Winnie said to Aunt Alice, "... for everything you've done for me and Hugh." She gazed at her brother. "I can't believe he's here. I thought ... well, you know what I thought. But that's all in the past. He's home and it's the future that matters now."

"That's exactly what I was telling Jane," Aunt Alice said. "Onwards and upwards."

Winnie nodded. "We'll be forever in your debt. You saved our lives."

"And you saved mine. I mean it, both of you," Jane said.

"Oh, Miss Knight." Winnie hugged her, then her brother did the same.

"Miss Knight?" Hugh looked up at the castle. "Winnie and I are going to Ballengeich to visit our mother and father's grave. Would you come with us?"

"I'd be honoured to."

"Don't be long," Miss Frew said. "I'm anticipating a visit from Mr Keith and we must prepare for it."

Jane skipped a breath. Yes, what a day it had been. And it wasn't over yet.

CHAPTER 30

Eliza paused in the hallway and ran through her mental checklist: Winnie and Hugh were on lookout duty at the windows of the girls' and boys' dormitories; Alice and her niece were in the kitchen, in case Thomas Keith thought of sneaking in the back way; the front door was open to welcome him; the light in her study was on and the door ajar. Yes, everyone was all present and correct. What they needed now was the leading man to make his entrance. Which surely he would. Eliza didn't know him well, but she knew him well enough, and had seen his type a hundred times before: *Proud and haughty scorner is his name who dealeth in proud wrath.*

The kitchen door opened and Alice came out, holding out a glass of water.

"What are you doing?" Eliza said. "I told you to stay there so you can hear everything."

"Here, take this. Sip it, it'll keep you calm. You're looking a bit peaky."

Eliza accepted the offering. "Thank you. I suppose I am feeling a bit ... well, *beleaguered*. These past few days have been a tad testing, I admit."

"Haven't they just? But it's nearly over."

"I sincerely hope so."

Alice touched Eliza's arm. "Are you absolutely sure this is the way you want to do it?"

She shuffled on the spot and glanced over to the front door. "Yes I am."

"I mean, he really deserves to be in prison for what he's done to you and Winnie."

"I know he does. But if we have him arrested, he's going to bring up the past. And what good would that do? It'll only ruin me. But it's not going to bring back Nellie, or her baby. It's not going to bring Catherine back."

"But no one would believe him, Eliza! Not a man like that, not after everything he's done."

"Probably not. But wouldn't they wonder why I allowed him to behave the way he did for so long? And if none of it was true, wouldn't they wonder why I gave him money? He'd make sure all that came out."

"You could deny it."

"I could. But you know what they say, Alice."

She nodded. "There's no smoke without fire."

"Exactly. No, I know he deserves to go to prison. But, taking everything into account, and thinking of Winnie, too, I think it's best this way. I mean, she doesn't want to be getting involved with the police and the courts and the like. She just wants to forget about it all. So if we can banish him, it's the best thing to do." Eliza swallowed. Perhaps not the right thing, but the best thing. For her and for her family's reputations. *For the good that I would I do not: but the evil which I would not, that I do.* "Anyway, thank you for this," she said, toasting Alice. "Now, go back in and make sure you hear everything that wastrel says."

She waited until Alice returned to the kitchen then went to her study. The day's mail was sitting, unopened, in a neat pile on her desk. She put the glass of water down and flicked through the letters, stopping at one postmarked 'Canada' and addressed to her in the hand of a child. She sat down, slit the envelope open and pulled out the single sheet of paper.

Dear Miss Frew – We are in good health and enjoying life and we hope you are the same. We live with Mr and Mrs Menzies now and they are very nice. They helped us write this letter. They say it's important that we can speak and write properly. The house is very nice too. There are 4 horses, 8 milk cows, 8 young cattle, 4 calves, 3 pigs, 50 hens and 20 sheep on the farm. We like working on it more than going to school but Mr Menzies says we have to go to school for a few years yet. Please say hello to Miss Jane and Miss Knight and tell Miss Jane that we have no problems and are growing big and strong.

Your boys, Fred and Albert

Eliza closed her eyes and put her hand to her forehead. Those dear, dear children. Pray to the good Lord that Mr and Mrs Menzies turned out to be loving and caring guardians, and that those charged with protecting Fred and Albert didn't end up being those who would do them harm. That was something that was waiting for Eliza once she had dealt with Thomas Keith – her day of reckoning about what had happened to Hugh.

"Miss Frew! Miss Frew!" The sound of shoes sliding along the polished floor came from the corridor. Hugh appeared in the doorway. "He's coming up the drive."

"Right! Shush now!" Eliza said, springing up. "You and Winnie wait in the kitchen with Miss Jane and Miss Knight and I'll get him to admit what he's done. Listen to every word he says. All right?"

"Yes, Miss Frew!" Then as quickly as he had appeared, Hugh withdrew. After a few seconds, the house was quiet again.

Hands trembling, Eliza lifted the glass and took some gulps of water. She had to muster the strength to get Thomas Keith out of her life and to make sure he never came back. She closed her eyes and looked upwards; God could deal with her other trespasses in due course, but just now, strength was all she asked of Him.

Rona, lying underneath the desk, raised her head and cocked her ears. Eliza heard the click of footsteps in the hall and held her breath. There was a momentary silence, Mr Keith, no doubt, wondering why Gowanlea was open yet seemingly so quiet.

"Hello?"

Eliza gave a start. Now he was coming along the corridor. She took a deep breath.

When he arrived at the door, she made her best effort at a smile. "Ah. Good evening, Mr Keith. And pray, what might I do for you?"

He stepped into the study, not returning her smile. "Where is she?"

"Where's who, Mr Keith?"

He came closer. "You know perfectly well *who*. You were seen."

Eliza stood her ground. "*Seen*, Mr Keith? By whom? Where?"

"I'm warning you." He jabbed his index finger at her. "Now where is the girl? Winnie."

"Why? Do you have some business with her?"

"Where is she?" he spat.

Eliza swayed but remained on her spot. "Is that why you kidnapped her? Because you had business with her? Well, I'm sure the Chief Constable would be most interested to hear about that. I happen to know him very well."

"Don't you threaten me," Thomas Keith snarled. "Remember, I still have this." He pulled the envelope containing her letter from his jacket pocket and waved it in her face.

Before she could think, Eliza panicked and abandoned her ruse. She snatched the letter from him.

"Oi!" He yanked her hand. "Give me that!"

When Eliza tried to pull away, he raised his arm and struck her face with the back of his hand. She fell, hitting her chair on her way to the floor. Rona rushed out from under the desk, teeth bared and growling. When Thomas Keith bent over to retrieve the envelope, Eliza's loyal little dog snapped. He backed off.

Both man and dog jumped back when the door was hit with such force that it slammed against the wall. In a flash, Hugh leapt on Thomas Keith and wrestled him to the ground. As Hugh started to pummel him, Eliza scrambled away from the scrum. She struggled to her feet and attempted to pull the boy off, trying to make herself heard above Rona's barking. "Hugh! Stop!" She was pushed out of the way by Miss Knight and Winnie, who, also having deserted their posts, took a shoulder each and tried to haul Hugh back.

"He's not worth it!" Miss Knight shouted.

"Hugh, please! Stop!"

At the sound of his sister's voice, Hugh's fist froze in the air. He let it fall by his side. He slid off Thomas Keith, who was bleeding from the mouth and nose.

"Oh, my goodness." Alice said, coming in. "Are you all right, Eliza?"

Unable to think of a single thing to say or do, Eliza merely managed a nod.

"Well, this wasn't in the plan."

Winnie began to sniffle. "Is he dead?"

Alice lifted the glass from Eliza's desk and got down on the floor beside Thomas Keith. She threw the water in his face. After a few seconds, he came to, with a moan. "No, he's not dead."

Hugh was panting. He rubbed his knuckles and glared at his victim. "More's the pity."

"Prop him up," Alice said.

Miss Knight put her arm out to stop Hugh as he stepped forward. "We'll do it." Then she and Winnie manoeuvred Thomas Keith so that he was slumped against the wall.

He groaned again and Alice leaned over him. "Can you hear me, Mr Keith?"

"Hmm."

"Good. Well, listen to me and listen well." She grabbed his jaw and shook it. "Are you listening?" He opened his eyes. "Right. This is what's going to happen. You're going to leave this house and never come back to it. You'll go to the railway station, you'll leave here, never to return. Between us, Miss Frew and I know every powerful man in this town: the Chief Constable, the Sheriff, the Lord-Lieutenant, solicitors, doctors, businessmen, bankers, teachers, councillors, justices of the peace, ministers of every faith, colonels, lords, Provosts, Lord Provosts, MPs, the presidents of every political association, publicans, pawnbrokers, undertakers. You name them, we know them. In fact, between us, you might say we have the whole town sewn up. So if you don't leave, we'll alert them to what you've done, which, I'm led to understand, is blackmail and kidnapping. We'll alert them and you'll go to prison for a very long time. And when you eventually get out of prison, your face and name will be so well-known that you'll not be welcome anywhere. Not only that, if you were so unwise as to return, then Miss Frew and I also know our fair share of men from, shall we say, the lower echelons of society. Men who are much harder than you, who would be only too happy to help a lady out, and who would take a very dim view of your behaviour. So, if you ever were so reckless or arrogant as to think about showing your face again, it wouldn't be for long. Do you understand what I'm saying, Mr Keith?" He nodded. "Good. They say people always have a choice so let me make yours explicit: your choice is to go somewhere else if you want to continue your immoral life, or stay here and make preparations for the end of it. Do I make myself clear?"

Eliza glanced at Miss Knight and Winnie, who were staring, open-mouthed at Alice. Eliza knew her friend was formidable but had never seen her quite as formidable as in that moment. The generals in South Africa might do well to consult Alice Knight on their strategy. The war might have been over by now.

Mr Keith drew his hand across his mouth then wiped the blood off on his trousers. "Yes, clear," he said feebly.

"Excellent." Aunt Alice patted Rona's head then went to get up. "Oh, before I forget." She turned back to Thomas Keith, who flinched. "I believe that as well as blackmail and kidnapping, we can add theft to your list of crimes. Where's the money you stole from Miss Frew?"

The merest of glances at his jacket was enough to set Alice raking through his pockets until she found the canvas sack. She pulled it out and shook it. "Is it all here?"

"Almost. I had to pay Provost Brown for the room," Thomas Keith said.

"Pah! Well, we'll easily get that back from him." Alice got up and handed the sack to Eliza. "With interest."

Eliza put it on her desk next to the pile of unopened letters.

Then Alice picked the incriminating envelope up off the floor and handed it to her. "I think this is yours. We'll escort Mr Keith off the premises while you gather yourself. Get him up," she instructed her squaddies. "And no more fisticuffs, Hugh – I think Mr Keith's got the message loud and clear."

Eliza stood in the corridor while the youngsters, supervised by Alice, got Thomas Keith to his feet and shuffled him out of the study. As they reached the entrance hall, she opened the envelope and took out the letter. Her heart thumped when she saw that it was nothing more than a blank sheet of paper. She looked inside the envelope again. It was empty.

She bolted to the front door and rushed down the driveway to catch up with the group. "Wait! Stop!" She stood in front of Thomas Keith and waved the envelope at him. "Where's the letter?" He looked at the ground. "Where is it? You heard what Miss Knight said about the people we know. If you don't tell me where it is I'll—"

"There is no letter!"

"What do you mean?"

Thomas Keith smiled. "There is no letter."

Eliza looked at her handwriting on the envelope and took a step back. "What? Well, how do you—"

"There was only ever the envelope. My father kept it in a drawer by his bedside."

"So you never had the letter?" Thomas Keith shook his head. "But you said your father revealed to you that—"

"I said he revealed certain matters to me."

"What matters, exactly?" Eliza said, barely controlling her agitation. "What matters?" she shrieked. Thomas Keith was silent. A chill ran through Eliza. "He didn't tell you anything at all, did he?" she said flatly. She prodded Mr Keith on his chest. "Did he?"

"He told me he'd done something when he was younger that had terrible consequences and that he'd got you involved, though you were blameless, and that because of what he'd done he couldn't marry your sister, who he loved very much. He said he'd destroyed your letter, but he kept the envelope so he'd never forget what he'd done. He was very remorseful at the end."

Eliza crumpled the envelope and threw it to the ground. "Well, bully for him." She started back to the house. "Get out of my sight."

Jackie was waiting for her on the doorstep, the red ball from the garden between her front paws. Eliza picked it up, then leaned in and nuzzled the dog. "You don't judge, do you?"

Rona came trotting over to join them and Eliza and her two companions returned to her study. Eliza sank into her chair as Rona went under the desk and Jackie lay on the floor. It could have been a scene from any of the thousands of evenings they'd spent together over the years.

She glanced again at the day's post; she'd better go through it so a backlog didn't build up. And what with everything that had happened, she'd been neglecting the children; she would have to catch up with their teachers to find out if there were any issues. And then there was Mrs Duncan's visit to prepare Ann and Susan for, heaven help them. Although, their mother had been a shrewd enough judge of character when it came to Mr Keith, which was more than could be said of Eliza. How could she have been so foolish? How could she have given him her life savings and risked the future of Gowanlea? And how, God forgive her, could she have put Winnie in such danger? For all her faults, Mrs Duncan would never have allowed that to happen to her daughters. Eliza had failed Winnie and she'd failed Hugh. She put her head in her hands and wept. How many others had she failed?

She hadn't moved when Alice came back in and put a hand on her shoulder. "Are you all right?"

She sat up and wiped her cheeks. "Yes, yes, I'm fine. I was just—"

"He's gone now and he's not coming back. It's over."

Eliza rested her head on her dear friend's hand. Thomas Keith might be gone, but it wasn't over. Nor would it be until Eliza's day of judgement.

CHAPTER 31

Jᴀɴᴜᴀʀʏ 1907

Aѕ ᴛʜᴇ ᴅɪɢɴɪᴛᴀʀɪᴇѕ approached the small platform on the grassy area of the esplanade, the regimental bands put down their instruments and a silence descended among the onlookers crowded on the vantage point atop the outer defences of Stirling Castle.

Jane leaned forward for a closer view, and Aunt Alice, at her side, cleared her throat; not in a sign of emotion but of disappointment, since the memorial was no longer to be unveiled by Princess Louise, who, for reasons unknown, was unable to attend as expected.

"I missed Queen Victoria here in 1849 and then the King ... well he was Prince of Wales then, in 1859. And now I'm not to see Princess Louise either."

"You hardly missed Queen Victoria – you weren't born then! That's like saying you missed seeing Mary Queen of Scots when she was here," Jane replied.

"Be that as it may, I was looking forward to seeing Princess Louise nonetheless."

"And you saw the King in Edinburgh at the castle a few years ago. And then in Glasgow the day after."

"That's not the point. The point is, I want to see them here. I want them to come to us."

Jane glanced along the row of family members, sensing her mother's disapproving eyes on them. "Shush!" she said, elbowing Aunt Alice. "It's starting."

The official party stepped onto the platform, first the Duke of Montrose, attired as a regimental colonel, then the Duchess, solemn and all in black. The hush deepened as Padre Robertson, chaplain to the Highland Brigade in South Africa, opened the proceedings with a prayer.

As he spoke, Jane half-closed her eyes, trying to imagine what was under the Empire flag draped over the new memorial. A few of the long line of soldiers, in full dress, who were providing the cordon around the proceedings seemed to be doing the same. How smart they looked in their kilts, scarlet jackets, white boots, ceremonial head dress and sporrans, their weapons at ease by their sides. If RJ had lived, he would have been standing proudly among them.

With the prayer over, the Duchess approached the covered memorial. The crowd seemed to take a collective deep breath. She spoke clearly and loudly: "This memorial is dedicated to the lasting memory of those brave men of the 1st Battalion of the Argyll and Sutherland Highlanders who lost their lives in South Africa in the service of their country." She pulled the cord so that the flag dropped to the ground. Jane, and everyone around her, gasped.

The eight-foot-tall bronze statue of a soldier at engage was truly magnificent. Set on a red granite pedestal of similar proportions, his eyes were fixed firmly on the sculpture of another warrior, King Robert the Bruce, at the opposite side of the esplanade. The detail, from the pleats of his kilt and the laces of his boots, to the creases on the back of his jacket, was exquisite. As applause broke out, Jane looked at her parents, who seemed both wistful and proud.

The pipers began to play 'Flowers of the Forest'. Jane welled up but didn't cry. Seven years on, this was as near to a proper funeral for RJ as they were going to get, and she was going to be as dignified as she could for him. She might never be able to visit his grave, wherever that might be, but at least now he and his fallen comrades would be remembered.

"It's all right, my love, you can do it," Stephen whispered to her. Jane took her husband's hand, then closed her eyes tightly until the end of the lament and the dedicatory prayer.

The Duchess returned to her seat on the platform and the Duke stood. Aunt Alice took Jane's other hand. "It's very fitting, dear, isn't it?"

"Very."

"... every man went into action," the Duke was saying, "with the determination that whatever he found with his hand to do, he would do it with all his might. That that determination was nobly carried out was proved by the heavy loss the regiment sustained in the Modder River and Magersfontein actions. They lost their colonel and eight officers, and two hundred and fifty non-commissioned officers and men were killed and wounded."

Jane and Aunt Alice squeezed each other's hand.

"Their names are inscribed on these glorious, but melancholy, tablets that surround the memorial. The battalion could not have a higher tribute to their loyalty and courage."

While Lieutenant General Leach and Provost Thomson spoke, then Colonel Urmston offered the vote of thanks, Jane gazed over at the brass plates on the sides of the pedestal, speculating where RJ's name might be. She was in danger of allowing tears to come again as the bugler played 'The Last Post' but she willed herself to retain her composure – RJ would have expected no less.

Aunt Alice straightened up as the national anthem was

played and the official party made its way into the castle for luncheon. "Shall we go down now and get a better look, dear?"

Up close, the statue was even more impressive. Jane wondered if the moustachioed soldier it portrayed was modelled on someone real. She read the dedication on the plaque on the front of the pedestal, then went to the one on the right-hand side. Heading the list of officers killed in action was Lieutenant-Colonel Goff, who had led RJ and his colleagues from Richmond barracks to the King's Bridge terminus. She scanned the list of names and caught her breath when she finally saw it. She stepped up to the plaque and ran her fingers lightly over the raised letters: *Lce Corpl R.J. Knight.*

'Lieut-Colonel G.L.J. Goff' and 'Lce Corpl R.J. Knight', their names now together in perpetuity.

She stepped back and stood next to Stephen, while her parents and Aunt Alice studied the plaque in silence. Her father walked slowly around the pedestal, taking time to review the roll. He would probably save the newspaper clippings of the occasion and copy out the name of each soldier in his scrapbook.

Jane looked across again to the statue of King Robert the Bruce. Winnie had said she would meet her there after the ceremony so they could go and pay their respects to Miss Frew. Hugh wasn't coming because he had to work, but Jane knew that he would have sent his warmest regards for Winnie to pass on.

Aunt Alice appeared at Jane's side, then suddenly ducked down behind her.

"What on earth are you doing?"

"Shush! I'm hiding from – oh, Lord." Aunt Alice pretended she was removing a thread from the back of Jane's dress.

"Miss Knight? I thought it was you. How lovely to see you. It was a splendid occasion, I think you'll agree?" ex-Provost Brown said.

"Oh, Mr Brown ... yes, hello to you. Yes, a very fitting

occasion, I think," Aunt Alice said. "This is my niece, Mrs Jane Clarke. You may remember her from ..." Ex-Provost Brown squirmed. "Yes well, anyway, she's an artist now. Exhibited in Glasgow. And this is her husband, Dr Stephen Clarke. He's a surgeon."

"My! You must be very proud, Miss Knight. A pleasure to meet you, Dr Clarke, and, em, Mrs Clarke."

Jane couldn't bring herself to say 'likewise'. As Aunt Alice was fond of saying, the man 'wasn't fit to hold the title of the fine office of Provost'. Although he had, at least, arranged excellent positions for Winnie and Hugh when the time had come. Mind, what choice had he had? What was it Aunt Alice had told her Miss Frew had said to him? "Repent ye therefore, and be converted that your sins may be blotted out." It hadn't been difficult for him to call in a few favours. Just as Miss Frew held something over him, he held something over others. *And that's how politics works, Jane dear.*

"Anyway, Miss Knight," he said, "when I spotted you, I just wanted to come over and say that you'll have my complete support if, as a little bird tells me, you decide to go forward for election to the town council later in the year. And not only my support, but that of my many colleagues, both current and former."

"Oh, well, thank you. I'll take that into consideration when coming to my decision."

"Good! That's excellent, Miss Knight." Jane didn't think ex-Provost Brown had picked up the sarcasm in her aunt's voice. "Anyway, I must be on my way. Things to do and people to see."

"Goodbye then, Mr Brown!" Aunt Alice called after him. Then, as he moved out of earshot, she muttered, "Awful man."

"Never mind that," Jane said, "what's this about you running for town council? When did you decide that?"

"I haven't decided anything as yet. Others have just suggested I should consider it a possibility."

"And are you going to?" Stephen said.

"Oh, I don't know. An old woman like me? Although, men of my age seem to be considered in their prime."

"Oh, just try stopping her!" Jane laughed.

"Well, for what it's worth, Alice," Stephen said, "I think you'd be splendid. It's about time there were some ... lady councillors."

"*Women*, Stephen dear, not ladies. "

Jane stifled a giggle. Stephen and her aunt got on so well. He was very, very fond of her, and not just because she had encouraged his long-distance romance with Jane, smoothed out things with her parents at the prospect of an engagement, made introductions for him when he arrived in Scotland, and acted as not-too-diligent chaperone when they began courting in earnest.

"What?" he said, noticing Jane's amusement.

"Nothing, darling."

"I couldn't agree with you more, Stephen," Aunt Alice said. "And someone's got to take on Mr Bannerman."

Jane spluttered. "Mr Bannerman? It's the town council you're standing for, not parliament!"

"Yes, but now that Mrs Pankhurst's on the march, dear, I need to do my bit for the cause so that when the time comes ... you know! Onwards and upwards, Jane, onwards and upwards."

Jane glanced at Stephen, then smiled and shook her head. Dear Aunt Alice was incorrigible.

"Ah, look," Aunt Alice said, pointing across the esplanade. "There's Winnie now. I take it you and she are going to visit Eliza?"

"We are."

"Then Stephen can escort me and your parents to the tea room and we'll see you there in, what, twenty minutes, shall we say?"

"Yes, twenty minutes," Jane said, waving as Winnie came towards her.

"Mrs Clarke!"

"Miss McKellar!"

They embraced, then stood back and nodded at each other in approval.

"Thank you so much for coming," Jane said.

"I wouldn't have missed it. It was a very fitting ceremony. Hugh sends you his regards. He's very sorry he couldn't make it."

"I completely understand. Of course, he has to work. That must come first. And when I last saw him, he was certainly thriving in it. If he keeps it up, I've no doubt he'll attain a higher position. And then, when he's in charge, he can take time off whenever he feels like it! Now, shall we?"

"We shall."

They went arm-in-arm down the steps at the top of the esplanade and walked in silence along the paths that bordered the neatly manicured lawns of the Drummond Pleasure Ground. When they reached the Star Pyramid, they turned into the Valley Cemetery and headed towards Ladies' Rock.

Miss Frew's headstone was on a corner, at the junction of two paths. Every time she visited, Jane thought how fitting its location was, surrounded by statues of martyrs and reformers. And, of course, according to Aunt Alice, Henry Drummond's final resting place was nearby in the church cemetery. "So no doubt they'll be having theological discussions as they step out together in heaven. He never married either, you know, dear," Aunt Alice even now still liked to quip.

Jane and Winnie stood in silence, heads bowed, before the headstone. Miss Frew was never quite the same after all that business, almost as if she was willing her time to be up. Jane slowly read down the names of the others who were buried there. Miss Frew's parents and her sister, Catherine. Below theirs, the letters of Miss Frew's more recently carved name were clearer and darker. "At least they're together now again."

"They were always together, even when they were apart. Like me and Hugh," Winnie said.

"Yes."

"And you and RJ."

Jane looked up at the sky. The early morning rain had cleared, leaving an azure sky and bright sun. She put her palms together: Winnie was right – whether in this life, or the next, the love that she and RJ had was forever, outside the touch of time.

She looked at the ground then gathered herself, cleared her throat. "Shall we join the others now?"

"Let's."

"After you then, Miss McKellar," Jane said, making a sweeping gesture with her hand.

"Why thank you, Mrs Clarke," Winnie said, turning in the direction of the tea room in Castle Wynd.

Jane glanced over her shoulder towards the castle esplanade, then took a final look at the words at the base of Miss Frew's headstone: 'From this day will I bless thee.'

"No, thank *you*, Winnie McKellar. Thank *you*."

HISTORICAL NOTE

The spark for this novel was my discovery that Whinwell Children's Home, established in Stirling in the late 1800s by Miss Annie Croall, sent destitute children abroad over several decades. For the character of Eliza, I drew on the beliefs, convictions and sayings of Annie, who in the 1920s wrote about her experiences of 'child rescue'. Eliza, Jane, Aunt Alice and the other main characters, however, are fictional.

The storylines are fictional too. They are based, though, on real life contexts, so actual historical settings, events, publications and individuals are referenced. Accordingly, some of the opinions held and the language used by some characters, which may be abhorrent to us now, were acceptable at the time.

Between the 1860s and 1960s, child migration was UK government policy and was implemented by major charities and local institutions. The policy was believed to offer a solution to destitution by offering children prospects they might not otherwise have had and by reducing the fiscal burden.

The Scottish Child Abuse Enquiry (which began in 2015 and was ongoing at the time of writing) concluded that notwithstanding the 'good intentions' of the agencies involved in sending children abroad, the whole system of child migration was abusive. It also found that successive UK governments failed to stop it. In 2010 UK Prime Minister Gordon Brown apologised to former child migrants and their families for allowing vulnerable children to be sent away.

Readers might be interested in the following works and sources I consulted when researching some of the topics relevant to the novel:

- The Scottish Child Abuse Inquiry, https://www.childabuseinquiry.scot/
- Child Abuse and Scottish Children Sent Overseas through Child Migration Schemes Report - Executive Summary, Constantine, S., Harper, M. and Lynch, G., 2020
- British Home Child Group International, http://britishhomechild.com/history/
- 50 Years on a Scottish Battlefield, Annie Croall, 1923
- Public Lives, Women, Family And Society In Victorian Britain, Eleanor Gordon & Gwyneth Nair, 2003
- Evangelicals in Action, Katherine Heasman, 1962
- The Children's Home-Finder, Lillian Birt, 1913
- Adventurers & Exiles, The Great Scottish Exodus, Marjory Harper, 2004

Elaine Whiteford, July 2024

ACKNOWLEDGEMENTS

I would like to thank everyone who helped me get to this stage in my writing journey. Particular thanks to Lesley, Susan and Fran for being loyal beta readers. And most of all, to my husband, Hamish, for reading umpteen versions of the manuscript, for correcting the same mistakes time and again and for supplying tea and sympathy always.

Elaine Whiteford is a writer of fiction and non-fiction. *The Rescue Sisters* is the first of her historical novels to be published. In non-fiction, she is the author of *The Story of Stirling Golf Club* and a contributor to *Wild & Temperate Seas*. Find out more at: https://www.elainewhiteford.com

www.ingramcontent.com/pod-product-compliance
Lightning Source LLC
Chambersburg PA
CBHW051136190726
48290CB00006B/1866